Praise for *The Last Forever*

★ "Wholly absorbing."
—*Horn Book*, starred review

★ "Featuring sharp-witted first-person narration, some fascinating facts about plants and seeds, relatable characters, and evocative settings, Caletti's (*The Story of Us*) inspiring novel eloquently depicts the nature of mutability. As with her previous books, this love story reverberates with honesty and emotion."
—*Publishers Weekly*, starred review

★ "Caletti writes movingly here, particularly as Tess reflects on her mother's final days, and offers up a surprising story about love, loss, and putting down roots in a world that's constantly changing."
—*Booklist*, starred review

★ "Caletti's writing is seamless and fluid, rich with descriptions of Tessa's physical world as well as her inner ruminations."
—*Kirkus Reviews*, starred review

"Caletti creates a wonderfully unique voice in Tessa, filled with wit, confusion, and mature reflection."
—*School Library Journal*

Also by Deb Caletti

The Queen of Everything
Honey, Baby, Sweetheart
Wild Roses
The Nature of Jade
The Fortunes of Indigo Skye
The Secret Life of Prince Charming
The Six Rules of Maybe
Stay
The Story of Us
Essential Maps for the Lost

And don't miss
He's Gone
The Secrets She Keeps

the last forever

DEB CALETTI

Simon Pulse

NEW YORK LONDON TORONTO SYDNEY NEW DELHI

SIMON PULSE

An imprint of Simon & Schuster Children's Publishing Division

1230 Avenue of the Americas, New York, New York 10020

First Simon Pulse paperback edition March 2016

Text copyright © 2014 by Deb Caletti

Cover photograph copyright © 2014 by Diane Kerpan/Arcangel Images

Also available in a Simon Pulse hardcover edition.

All rights reserved, including the right of reproduction in whole or in part in any form.

SIMON PULSE and colophon are registered trademarks of Simon & Schuster, Inc.

For information about special discounts for bulk purchases, please contact

Simon & Schuster Special Sales at 1-866-506-1949 or business@simonandschuster.com.

The Simon & Schuster Speakers Bureau can bring authors to your live event. For more information or to book an event contact the Simon & Schuster Speakers Bureau at 1-866-248-3049 or visit our website at www.simonspeakers.com.

Book design by Regina Flath

The text of this book was set in Adobe Caslon Pro.

Manufactured in the United States of America

2 4 6 8 10 9 7 5 3

The Library of Congress has cataloged the hardcover edition as follows:

Caletti, Deb.

The last forever / Deb Caletti. — First Simon Pulse hardcover edition.

p. cm.

Summary: After her mother's death, it's all Tessa can do to keep her friends, her boyfriend, her happiness from slipping away. Even the rare plant her mother entrusted to her care starts to wilt. Then she meets Henry. Though secrets stand between them, each has a chance at healing . . . if first, Tessa can find the courage to believe in forever.

[1. Grief—Fiction. 2. Death—Fiction. 3. Friendship—Fiction.

4. Love—Fiction.] I. Title.

PZ7.C127437Las 2014   [Fic]—dc23   2013031010

ISBN 978-1-4424-5000-4 (hc)

ISBN 978-1-4424-5002-8 (pbk)

ISBN 978-1-4424-5001-1 (eBook)

For John, always

acknowledgments

Pages upon pages of appreciation to my longtime agent and cherished sidekick, Ben Camardi, and to Annette Pollert, for her kindness, care, and thoughtful editing of this book. Big hugs as well to Jen Klonsky and Shauna Summers, my treasured editors and dear friends. So lucky to have you all.

My most heartfelt thanks as well go to my S&S team: Jon Anderson, Bethany Buck, Mara Anastas, Paul Crichton, Lydia Finn, Lucille Rettino, Michelle Fadlalla, Venessa Carson, Anthony Parisi (and Ginger), Ebony Ladelle, Jessica Handelman, Regina Flath, Katherine Devendorf, Julie Doebler, Carolyn Swerdloff, Emma Sector, Matt Pantoliano (and sons), and my sales force, most especially my dear Leah Hays and Victor Iannone. Your years of support and hard work on behalf of our books means more than I can say.

Oh, family—thank you, as always. Mom and Dad, Jan, Sue, Mitch, Ty, and Hunter, smooches of appreciation. Renata, here's to another thirty-eight years. And to my daughter, Sam, and my son, Nick—you two sweeties have my last-forever love.

chapter one

Silene steophylla: narrow-leafed campion. Seeds from this delicate, white-flowered plant were found in a prehistoric rodent burrow in the Siberian permafrost. Scientists were able to successfully grow them, making these twenty-three-thousand-year-old seeds the oldest living ones ever discovered.

In those early months, when the beautiful and mysterious Henry Lark and I began to do all that reading, I often skimmed over the name. *Svalbard*. I'd see all those consonants shoved together and my brain would shut off. I thought it sounded like a Tolkien bad guy, or a word that might cast a spell. Here's what I suggest—don't even try to pronounce it. Just imagine it. I love to imagine it: a hidden building, a narrow wedge of black steel jutting from the ice. When I close my eyes, I see its long, rectangular windows—one on the roof, one at the entrance—a beacon of prisms glowing green in the deep twilight of the polar night. Fenced in and guarded, with steel airlock doors and motion detectors, it is the most protected place on earth. Outside, polar bears stomp and huff in the frigid air.

Or imagine this: that first monumental day of excavation, when the mayor of Longyearbyen, Kjell Mork, stood on the chosen spot with a fuse in his hand, ready to blast open the side of a frozen mountain. *Longyearbyen, Kjell Mork*—more Tolkien words, and Kjell Mork himself looks like a Tolkien king, with his snowy white hair and full blizzard of beard, the ceremonial chain of silver discs around his neck, representing his people and his place. Okay, he's also wearing a blue hard hat and an orange construction vest, which would never work in the film version. But that fuse burning down, it would. He looks grim but determined in the pictures.

It all sounds like a fantasy novel, but it's real. As I write this right now, as you read this, that place is there, tucked inside that mountain. As I pour my cereal or shove my books into my backpack, as you pay the cashier at the drive-through window or stare at the moon, it's there. And it's all—the guards, the buried chambers, the subzero temperatures—in service of the most simple, regular thing: a seed. Actually, a lot of seeds. Three million seeds. That's what it's for. To protect seeds in the event of a global catastrophe. To make sure that, even if there's a nuclear war or an epidemic or a natural disaster, even if the cooling systems within Svalbard itself are destroyed, the seeds will survive for thousands upon thousands of years.

What should never be forgotten is this: Even when times are dark, the darkest, even when you are sure that life as you know it is over, there are still things that last. I learned that. Henry Lark and I both did. You may not be able to see those things. They may be hidden deep under the ground, or they may be tucked even deeper into your heart, but they are there.

And how did I, a regular person, as regular as those seeds themselves, become connected to a frozen vault 3,585.1 miles from home? (5,769.7 kilometers and seven hours and twenty-seven minutes away by plane, to be exact.) You never know what life will bring; you never do. It's something my mother always said. In good times and in the worst times she said that, and she was right. We—that vault and me—we're an unlikely pair. There is that land of wintry wildness and midnight sun and the eerie blue of polar nights and then there's me, a person who chops her bangs and reads too much. But I am now forever connected to this most brave and defiant place.

How and *why* is what this story is about. *Here* to *there*. *Here* to *there* is where all the stories are. *Here* to *there* is the sometimes barren land you must cross to find the way to begin again.

chapter two

Mucuna pruriens: velvet bean. One of the most irritating, confusing, multifaceted, and helpful seeds ever. The velvet bean can be deadly if eaten, but it's often used as a food source for animals and a coffee substitute for humans. It causes terrible itching upon contact, but it's also medicinal—supposedly curing sexual dysfunction, snakebites, Parkinson's disease, and depression. Sometimes it's smoked for its psychedelic effects. As a whole, if this seed were a person, it'd feed you, cure you, kill you, or drive you crazy.

Let's start here. The papers my father uses. They come in an orange envelope, and they're called Zig-Zag. There's a picture of a man on the package—he looks like Jesus if Jesus got a good haircut and trimmed his beard. Step one: Take out a paper and lay it on the table, sticky side up. Step two: Curl a tiny piece of cardboard into a cylinder. Step three: Lay the "weed" onto the paper in a line. ("Weed," which is what he calls it, makes it sound unplanned. Like it just happened to appear in his yard, so what's a person to do?) Step four: Pinch, roll, and then lick the end down.

Dad pats his jeans, then the chest of his T-shirt, where the pockets would be if it had pockets. "Okay, where'd you go?" he says, as if his lighter is prone to practical jokes. Dad hunts around in the Folgers can by the telephone, which has a bunch of spare change in it, and then he fishes through the junk drawer—out comes masking tape and loose batteries. Now out comes a screwdriver, a key chain that says I SHOWER NAKED, a mini Magic 8 Ball, and farther back, the manual to an Osterizer blender we don't have anymore. You get the picture of Mom and Dad right there in that drawer. Mom, the fixer of things, the saver of instructions, part-time office manager for Dr. Ned Kelly, DDS, and Dad, the guy who'll take a glowy green triangle at its word. *It is certain.* Shake again. *My sources say no.*

Dad's black-gray hair is in a ponytail, and, hey, that's one of my elastic bands. He's been wearing that same shirt for days. My father would say he's been adrift since my mother died, but she and I would both argue that point. He's always been adrift. I think my mom blamed Dad's own mother, Grandma Jenny. Something about how Grandma Jenny used to do his homework for him, which saved him from "the consequences of his actions."

"O-kay," Dad says. He's found another lighter. It's a fast-food yellow, the shade of one of those plastic lemons with the juice inside. He holds it in the air in triumph, then flick-flick-flicks the metal wheel with his thumb a few times before a flame appears. "Man make fire," he says in a caveman voice. "Man make fire, hunt bear, smoke joint."

I know what he'll do next, and sure enough, he goes into the living room and the rocking chair begins to creak. Sometimes he just sits there, and sometimes he puts Bob Marley on the stereo (a cliché, dear Dad), and sometimes he just stares at the news or old reruns of *I Dream of Jeannie*, which he says he loved as a kid, with Major Healey and the jeweled bottle with the pink smoke, from the time when people knew the names of astronauts.

I think he's depressed. Depressed and trying to hide it. He doesn't hide it well. He watches entirely too much television, for one thing. I hear him flip through channels—*A fifty-dollar value for . . . After severe weather pounded these parts . . . The island is a stop along an ocean-wide migra . . . Difficult or painful swallowing, headaches, stomachaches . . .* I put everything he's left on the counter back in the drawer; then I start dinner. Mac and cheese, hot dogs. Fill both pans with two-thirds of a cup of water, and when the noodles are done, it's one-quarter cup of margarine and one-quarter cup of milk and the package of cheese dust.

I hate it when he's hazy; I hate the unfocused eyes. It makes me get that middle-of-the-night feeling, when you wake up and lie there in bed, sure you hear a sound when you probably don't hear a sound.

"Ah, excellent! Thanks, babe," he says, when I bring him dinner.

"Catch," I say, and toss him his lost lighter, his favorite, the one with the picture of the two dolphins leaping from the sea, which I found in the silverware drawer.

"There it is!" He tucks it into the pocket of his jeans. "Hey, I just remembered. I heard something about dolphins today. Some scientist discovered that they give each other *names*."

"Wow." That is so cool. I love that idea. "How did they figure that out?"

He shrugs. "Didn't hear the whole thing. What do you think they call each other?"

"Bart?" I suggest. I chuckle. Sometimes I crack myself up.

"Gino the Nose. Jimmy 'Big Fin' Balducci."

We laugh. I should also say how much I love this guy, my father. I love him to bursting. My mom did too. "And Flipper is the common name, like John," I say.

"You gonna eat with me?" He's already shoveling it in.

"I've got homework. All the stuff they pile on at the end of the year."

"You work too hard; you know that? Life is short."

He realizes what he says. We catch eyes for a second, and there's this awkwardness in the room. I wade through it to get to the doorway. I feel guilty leaving. My whole back, now turned to him, is crawling with guilt. You'd think that someone dying would draw people closer, but it doesn't work like that. Or else, it didn't work that way for us. What happened over the last six months is too intimate and important, and now neither of us knows what to do with it all. What is unspoken between people—it has a life of its own, I'll tell you that much. It's like some wild animal cub you find orphaned in the woods. The mistake is bringing it home at all, because of course it's going to grow. Of course it's going to get bigger and fiercer than you first think, looking at its harmless little face.

My bowl of mac and cheese is on my desk, and so is my laptop, and of course, the last pixiebell, with its delicate, clover-shaped leaves and its sturdy stalk rising from its terra-cotta pot glazed blue. Right away, I think of doing what I would have always done in the past (something I was excellent at: procrastination), calling Meg, my oldest best friend, talking for twenty minutes about nothing, her new shoes, what she heard Jessie say in the bathroom. *Next year when we're seniors we're gonna* . . . Or I could call Caitlin, who recently went on one of those trips to Costa Rica, the tree-planting/shelter-building-type trip everyone goes on now, to some country with bad water and patchy Wi-Fi that makes all of them, including Caitlin, come home changed and with a new worldview. At least, they stop dyeing their hair and getting pedicures for a couple of months before everything goes back to being exactly as it was before. Sorry. I'm so negative sometimes. Planting trees is a good thing.

I also think of calling Dillon Moore, who I am sort of seeing. We kiss a lot, anyway, which is interesting, but truthfully, a kiss needs something more important than curiosity. A kiss needs desire. A kiss should rocket past the excitement level of eating lettuce. I'm terrible. I am. I care about Dillon.

I don't call anyone, though, because a loved person dying can make you feel distant from everyone, not just the person who's gone. There's grief and then there's the loneliness of grief. The way it's just yours and yours alone. After six months, the excitement of it is over for everyone else. They're ready to move on from being the supportive, understanding friends, which is fine—God, more-more-more than fine—but nothing about it is over for you. It's just getting started. You have gone on a long trip, the longest, and the water is very, very bad, but when you come back, the change is permanent.

I can hear Dad in the living room. It's not old *I Dream of Jeannie* reruns, but *Gilligan's Island*. There's the disgusted voice of Skipper: *Gilligan, you idiot!* and the capable tones of the professor, who after all these years is still trying to make a phone from a coconut. "Fuck, man," Dad says, and laughs. In this story—well, pardon my father's bad mouth. I sincerely apologize. I'm not responsible for him. He's not responsible for him either, but I believe we've covered this already.

In the end, I don't call anyone. Instead, I get right to work, finishing up the semester's final project in state history. Fort San Bernardino, 1851, where early settlers protected themselves against desert Indians, a to-scale model. Three feet equals one and a quarter inches. Honestly, it's a step above those dioramas we made for book reports in elementary school, but I like doing it anyway. Cardboard, X-Acto knife, glue. Tiny rooms with thumbnail doorways. It's a fort, and I sort of even like to imagine I'm inside it. A tiny me in the tiny rooms. After a long while, Dad pops his head in the doorway.

"Tessa Jane?"

"Thomas Quincy?" Imagine having a middle name like Quincy.

"Want to make that road trip to the Grand Canyon? Want to just fucking *do* it?"

San Bernardino to Barstow, Route 66, 70.6 miles. Interstate 40 east to Williams, Arizona, 319.5 miles. From Williams, Arizona Route 64 north, fifty miles to the south rim of the Grand Canyon. Seven hours and we'd be there. We'd planned this trip the night our neighbor, Peggy Chadwick, Brianna Chadwick's mother, brought us over a casserole dish of baked ziti. You want to be bold when people feed you, or else pity makes you restless, or maybe Italian sausage is more energizing than you'd think.

"When?"

"Tomorrow."

I laugh. He's got to be kidding. "Um, your *job*? And school's not out until next week."

I'm sure that's the end of it. But here's the tricky part. Endings and beginnings sit so close to each other that it's sometimes impossible to tell which is which.

I bring the fort to school the next day. It's bigger than I realize, and for a minute I think I'm going to have to strap the thing to the top of my (Mom's) old Taurus. After much sweating and maneuvering and hoping no one's watching, I finally wrestle it into the backseat. Thank God state history is first period, but I'm also sort of sad to see the fort go. It's one of those projects you really want to get back, but once you do, it sits in your room taking up way too much space until you end up dumping it anyway. I'm not good at throwing stuff out. Well, Henry Lark would be the first to say so, but he'd make it sound like a compliment.

It's a dusty hot day, and you can feel the school year ending. It's all flip-flops and skipped classes and the slam of lockers and laughter. Jessa Winters and lots of other girls are wearing their skin-snug shirts that show a stripe of tanned stomach, and everyone's stressing about AP tests, especially the people who never need to stress. Walter Nguyen, valedictorian, for example, who hunches over a stack of three-by-five cards like he's trying to solve the global health crisis instead of memorizing orchestra vocab. It's the end of junior year, the year of acronyms: AP, SAT, ACT, GPA. Everyone wants to be done at this point, to just get out of here, except for maybe little Ben Dunne, who does every sport and after-school activity because his parents are both alcoholics.

I eat lunch with Meg and Caitlin and C.J. and Adam and Hannah. Someone throws a tortilla. Adam is bragging that he came in early to lift weights, but you can tell he didn't shower after. He starts every sentence with "Being as awesome as I am" until C.J. socks him.

"Being as awesome as I am, I won't even seriously hurt you for that," Adam says.

Jacob Newly comes by, bends down, says, "Feel my hair." He's just gotten a buzz cut, and everyone takes a turn.

"Ooh," Caitlin says. "Nice."

"Very grassy," Adam says.

"I thought you said 'very gassy.'" C.J. rubs Jacob's head. Jacob is loving this way too much, in my opinion. "Dude, you look like ROTC."

"Don't you think that's just *wrong*? You don't hang up on someone. You just don't," Meg says to me. "You're not even listening."

"You don't just hang up on someone, you said." I eat a container of yogurt. Everything feels silly to me. Haircuts and arguments, lockers and flip-flops and yogurt, even. Forts in miniature and the amount of time it takes to memorize *larghetto* versus *allegretto*. Every *etto* in the world feels silly, and so does Mr. White's striped necktie, as Mr. White paces the cafeteria trolling for bad behavior, and so do plastic, elastic cafeteria-lady hats and Caitlin's tube of lip gloss, which she is now winding upward.

"You okay?" Meg asks. She knows me so well. She rubs my back. I love her like a sister even though I never had a sister, but right then her touch makes me cringe. Nothing seems right, not concern, not distance, not sandwich bags with zippers. Meg and me—we've been friends since the first grade. Our mothers took us trick-or-treating together when we were both tiny princesses. We know everything about each other. But she can't know *this*, this grief-land I'm in; she thinks she's here beside me, but that's not possible.

I get up. I need to get out of there. I smile. I rub her head. "Very ROTC," I say.

"Next time, listen when I talk to you," she says.

Between fourth and fifth period, I meet Dillon at his locker. We kiss, and Señora Oliver sees us. It makes me feel bad. It's just a kiss. I can feel so guilty for every little thing.

"We haven't hung out in so long," he says.

"You always have track," I say.

"Since before track."

"This weekend," I say.

"Tomorrow. Friday night."

I kiss him again before we go to class. I wonder—if I knew that was the last time, would I have tried to make it more meaningful? It's one of those things you think about later.

Dad's truck is in the driveway. It's the middle of the day, so this is strange. He's often at Plum Studio until seven or even later if there are a lot of orders for the handcrafted furniture he makes. But he's never home after school. Inside, there's a case of Manny's Pale Ale and a six-pack of Diet Coke on the kitchen counter. Then the door to the garage flings wide and bangs hard against the doorstop because Dad has kicked it open with one foot. He stands there, hefting the large red cooler in both hands. The sight of him makes my heart leap, and I can't tell if it's a good leap or a bad one.

Dad's got a map held in his teeth. His hair has those side-tracked wisps around his face, but his grin is huge and he's wearing his lucky Grateful Dead shirt, the one he had on when he'd bought a lottery ticket that won him twelve hundred bucks. He sets the cooler on the kitchen table and takes the map from his mouth.

"Get a move on, girlie. Fifteen minutes, we're outta here."

The awareness of an ending beginning or of a beginning starting—it comes from the same place inside that senses when a thunderstorm is imminent, or a snowfall. I drop my backpack and stare at him.

"Dad, we can't."

"Sure we can."

"School's not even out."

He just looks at me like I'm crazy. I think about distance and loneliness and what my life feels like right now and then I think, why not? Why the hell not?

I throw on some shorts and a tank top. I stuff a bunch of clothes into my duffel; they're light summer clothes, so I can jam a lot in there. Books to read, mandatory. I have a film version moment and pack my photo album, too, but let's not linger over that. What am I going to do, leave her behind? I can't bear that, even for a few days. My mother had never even been to the Grand Canyon. Of course she's going now.

And then, wait. The last pixiebell. I don't know how long we'll be gone. If I leave it, it might die. I can never, ever let that happen. Never. Grandpa Leopold Sullivan, Mom's dad, stole the seed of this extinct plant some sixty years ago, pinching it from the home of a professor he knew, an expert on the flora and fauna of the ancient Amazonian rainforest. The theft occurred during a Christmas party, after Grandpa Leopold excused himself to "use the facilities." Apparently, Sully was a bit of a klepto. What are you going to do? When he died, they found spoons from the Ambassador Hotel and saltshakers from the RMS *Queen Elizabeth*, and several herringbone overcoats that weren't even his size.

After he stole that last, one-of-a-kind seed, he put it in a pot and grew it. It was a kind of miracle. And after Grandpa Leopold was felled by a heart attack one cold New Year's morning, my mother took care of that plant. She kept it alive all these years, taking it with her every place she moved, from her college dorm room forward. My mother vowed that the last pixiebell would never die on her watch, and now that I have it, it isn't going to die on mine, either.

I find a shoe box under my bed, dump out the old boy-band CDs that I loved when I was twelve. But no—it'll slide around too much in there. I fling open the closet in Mom and Dad's room and grab one of my mother's running shoes. I set it in the box, and then wedge the pot of the last pixiebell into the shoe. I tie it up snugly.

In a few moments, I'm in the passenger side of Dad's truck,

and just like that, we're heading out of the driveway, away from our house and everything around it: our scratchy tan lawn, the row of mailboxes, the neighbor's dog, Bob, who always stands at the corner and watches traffic.

"Adios, Bob," I say out the open window.

"For fuck's sake, Bob, get a life," Dad says.

chapter three

Merremia discoidesperma: Mary's bean. This tropical seed has long been considered to be good luck. In Central America, the seeds were handed down from mother to daughter as treasured keepsakes. The Mary's bean is elusive, though. Its thick, woody coat and internal air cavities enable it to drift for thousands and thousands of miles. Sometimes, it can spend years upon aimless years at sea.

I know you are just waiting to hear about Henry Lark, and you are right to want to get to that part, even if only for the way Henry's black hair falls over his eyes when he is thinking hard. But we are not at that part of the story yet. No, we are at the part where my father and I are on Route 66, which is a two-lane road Dad says we have to take because that's what you do on a road trip. The two-lane road is slow and traffic is all jammed up, but Dad isn't bothered in the least. He drives with one elbow out the window, his T-shirt sleeve flapping when the semis rattle past. The afternoon is hot, and by the time we stop, the backs of my legs are slick with sweat against the vinyl seats and my hair's a big mess from the wind whipping through the open windows. We get into Barstow about an hour and a half later, a half hour behind schedule. Dad says there shouldn't be a schedule, but let's just say we're different that way.

We fill up with gas at the Rip Griffin truck stop and stop for a cheeseburger at Art's El Rancho Coffee Shop, a place with plastic menus and a ketchup bottle next to the sugar packets and a stickiness from the last people at the table who had pancakes. We drink root beer floats and Dad raises his. He says, "Here's to . . ." But, I don't know, there's something dangerous about finishing that sentence. All this newness and celebration feels sort of disloyal. He stops there. We just clink glasses, nothing more. We slurp to the brown-white swirly liquid bottom. Dad pays the check at the cash register and snags two rectangular mints wrapped in green foil.

"'We were somewhere in Barstow on the edge of the desert when the drugs began to take hold,'" Dad says, and hands me a mint.

I scrunch my eyebrows together to form a question.

"Hunter Thompson," he says.

Suicidal stoner and gonzo journalist, our road-trip role model. God help us.

It's still light out, barely. We drive beside a train on I-40, the rail cars coursing over the flat, yellow ground. "Wanna race?" Dad shouts to the train. He steps on the accelerator, and his old truck roars and rattles and the compass that Dad has on his dashboard shimmies in its plastic ball.

I grip the armrest. "Dad!"

He slows, but not much. "We could have beat that bastard," Dad says.

He thinks he's hilarious, but it's not funny. Death-defying acts are stupid and insulting when you think about all the people in those waiting rooms, reading magazines or knitting or sitting silently before it's time for their treatment. Praying, maybe. Talk about a whole other world going on while you just eat your TacoTime and text your little heart out and gossip about Simona's Spray Tan Incident. It's like Armageddon down there, except for the knitting. *Down there*, because that's where you go. You ride the elevator into the basement, another kind of vault, where the doors all have big yellow radiation signs, three triangles set around a circle. That place isn't hidden inside an icy mountain, but it may as well be.

It's dark by the time we get to the Shady Dell Motel in Williams, Arizona. It's darker here than the dark in San Bernardino. It's desert dark, the sky wide and the stars so bright and close you can almost breathe them in. We get out, slam the truck doors. I expect the night to be more silent out here, but there's the rush of cars whipping past on the freeway and crickets chirping and the sound of canned sitcom laughter from a television in the motel office.

"You coming in?" Dad asks.

"I'll wait here."

I lean against the truck and gather my hair into a ponytail, let the night air cool my neck. VA NCY, the sign reads. ROOMS WITH ZENITH CHROMACOLOR TV. I count thirteen rooms, eleven with little yellow lights glowing outside, moths circling. Someone, somewhere, lights a cigarette—I smell the nicotine as it wanders over. I hold my nose, just in case. I know what they say about secondhand smoke.

Dad comes back with the key and a credit card slip, which he crumples up and tosses in the back of the truck.

"You made sixteen miles to the gallon," I tell him as we walk to our room.

"I'll remember that next time I'm on *Jeopardy!*" he says.

We hurry out of there in the morning, which is fine by me. The Shady Dell is a place where you want to wear your shoes in the bathroom. Even the dresser tells too many stories— cigarette burns, permanent three-quarter rings of coffee, mysterious gouges that make you think someone got hurt.

It's bright on the other side of those heavy plastic motel curtains. I squint. The air smells like bacon cooking. I love that smell so much. Right there—the hope of bacon is a reason to love life. But Dad edges coins into the vending machine outside the motel office and down clunks a Reese's and a Butterfinger and a Baby Ruth and M&M's and a package of those orange crackers with something resembling peanut butter between them. He tosses them to me one at a time and I catch. "Breakfast," he says. "Just call me the B&B Gourmet." *The B&B Gourmet* is a cooking show my mother loved to watch, hosted by Willa Hapstead, plump proprietress of Red Gate Inn.

The wrappers litter the floor of the truck. It's a fifty-mile drive to the south rim, but the way Dad's driving, we'll be there in thirty-five minutes. "'The length of the Grand Canyon is two hundred seventy-seven miles,'" I read from a pamphlet I found in the motel's dresser drawer. "'The average rim-to-rim distance is ten miles. The average depth is one mile.'"

Dad isn't listening. "I wonder how many people have fallen in."

Neither of us cares about the visitors center. Who wants to see an IMAX movie of the Grand Canyon when you're at the Grand Canyon? The walk to the rim lookout is surprisingly cool. It's dusty, though—my feet already feel gritty in my sandals. When we finally stand on the overhang of Mather Point—our first good view—I forget about the dust. All I can think is how it looks just like the pictures you see of the Grand Canyon. Then I try to remember to be awestruck. Dinosaurs walked there once. Once, the rock formed the bottom of a shallow sea.

"That is some big hole," Dad says. He has his camera around his neck, same as everyone else, and he leans far over the top of the fence. Looking down makes my stomach flop. It's crowded at the lookout. There are little kids and strollers and tourists.

"Tessie? Let's get out of here, okay?"

"Yeah."

"Let's drive over to the trail. I can't get the I'm-so-small-in-the-grand-scheme-of-things feeling when someone's elbow is in my back."

It's fine at first, the trail along the rim. The beginning is paved, and there are waterspouts in case you get too hot or thirsty. There's just the trail, though. No fence. I walk right up against the canyon wall because it's scary. Dad's happy. His camera is bouncing against his chest as he walks.

"Tessa Bessa, look at that!"

He stops, heads to the edge of the pavement, and steps down onto a jagged ridge of rock. "Dad! It says to stay on the path."

"Yeah? And who's listening?"

He's right, really. People dot the cliffs. They crawl their way down stone ledges. One guy lays on a narrow, stone strip, his shirt off, hands cradling his head. "Dad, come on." I hate seeing him there, at the edge of that rock.

He turns sideways, eases farther down. I can hear the skid of dirt under his shoe.

"God, Dad, what are you doing!"

"This is gonna be a kick-ass photo," he says. He snaps a picture, uses a hand to balance himself on his way back up. We hike farther, and after a while, the pavement ends. There's only the curve of dirt path, down, up, around, until it disappears.

The well is so deep, you can't even see to the bottom. The trail is all earth and loose pebbles now. And narrow. Narrow enough to feel that plunge right there in your stomach. Narrow enough to feel yourself going down even though you aren't. It does not seem a mile down, or two, or three. It's ten thousand miles down, easy. More.

"Dad?"

He's up ahead, but I'm ready to go back. I'm not good at this kind of thing. This is all seeming like a very, very bad idea. I should be in biology right now, watching some stupid movie because school's almost out and there's nothing else to do. It's hard to see the beauty here; it's hard to take in the red rock, the pink and brown layers, the magnitude, when I'm suddenly aware that all the other hikers have backpacks and water bottles and hiking boots.

"This is fucking majestic! This is *life*!" Dad shouts. His voice bounces around. He holds his arms out, as if to embrace every bit of it.

My feet are slipping on the loose rocks of the path. I try to grab at a clump of green brush on the cliff beside me.

"Look at that hawk!" Dad says.

I can't take my eyes off of my own feet. "Can we go back?" I hear the panic in my voice.

"Here we are!" Dad says. "The perfect spot. Wait till you see. Your mother would love this."

I don't know what he's talking about. I can't even think about what he's saying right then. My mother wouldn't love any of this. She wasn't a hiking, outdoorsy person. She'd been camping only once. She'd be worried about us on this frightening path. This is how far apart my father and I are, right here. *This* is how we're struggling. It's hot, and my shoulders feel like they're getting burnt. My mouth is dry, and the gravel is so loose, and there is only down, down, down. I see a flash of yellow, Dad's T-shirt. He's climbing the craggy notches of the wall again, to another boulder perch, farther out.

"Dad!"

I need so much from him, I do. I need him to hear me calling his name, for starters. But this is apparently what *he* needs. He drops to his knees and sits. He fishes around in one of the side pockets of his cargo shorts. I creep down, grabbing at branches. "Tessa Bessa, check it out!"

He is holding something to his mouth. I say a prayer, even if God is apparently on a coffee break. If that something Dad is holding is a joint, I don't know what I'll do. But it isn't a joint—it's something bright. A pink bottle? And then there is a sudden release of bubbles as he blows, the luminescent blue-green-pink globes that lift and float and crash against the rocks.

I feel the roll of gravel beneath the slick surface of my shoe, and I scream as I fall. I grab for a branch, for a handful of desert scrub, but there is nothing. My feet skitter out from under me, and there is the *tick-ping* of pebbles tumbling down. I land hard on my knees, my palms, and my heart is thudding. I open my eyes and see the red ground beneath me, and just beyond, the drop-off, the endless layers of rock to the bottom. Gravel burns under my skin, and there's the warmth of blood. I want to sob, but no sound comes out. My chest just heaves, and I won't turn my head to look. No, I grip the ground and keep my eyes fixed, because if I look, I will see a space so vast and immeasurable you could be lost within it forever. I want so much to feel as if I'm not falling. I need this most of all.

"Tess! What are you doing down there?" my father says. "Christ, you missed it. You missed the best part."

By the time evening arrives, there are ten messages on my phone, split evenly between Meg and Dillon. They begin somewhere around lunchtime. Meg has gone over to my house. They are both sure something is terribly wrong. This speaks either to my usual reliability or to my current fragile state, I have no idea which.

In the film version, I am an outlaw on the run. I am riding a satiny black horse that gallops away, and I have no ties to anyone. In real life, though, horses kind of scare me. Those big teeth. Meg sounds near tears—that's how worried she is—and Dillon has taken on the firm, no-nonsense voice of his father. I text them both. *Sorry to worry you. Dad decided we needed a road trip. I'm fine. More soon!* The exclamation point seems overly cheery. *Sorry,* I type again.

Sorry, sorry, sorry. Oh, you can pile on as many as you want, but the guilt is still there, like that pea under all those mattresses.

We stay at the Piney Woods Lodge. The name makes you think of stone fireplaces and stuffed elk heads and downy beds, but it is actually one of those two-level motels you see in movies where someone always OD's. No one ever OD's in a La Quinta in the movies. It's always these places with windows looking out onto a parking lot and gold room numbers on the doors.

Well, of course it smells like cigarettes in there. Not a recent cigarette, but one that was smoked sometime in the 1970s. I think about sleeping in my clothes. I once read an article that said the bedspreads in motels harbor more disgusting stuff than just about any other object on earth, and my mind is now unraveling all of the sordid possibilities.

This can't get any worse. (Be careful saying stuff like that.)

"We've got to go to Las Vegas since we're so close," my father says. "Don't you think?" He is flipping channels on the television, which doesn't take long, because there are maybe three whole stations.

"I'm not really a Las Vegas kind of person." I'm still pissed at him for what happened on the trail. And he's still clueless about it.

"What kind of person is a Las Vegas kind of person?"

This is too obvious to deserve an answer. The pixiebell is a little limp from all that time in the hot car, so I water it and set it on the laminated table by the window. It looks so innocent there. It's as out of place as a virgin on the Las Vegas Strip.

"Don't jump to conclusions before you've even been there."

This doesn't deserve a response either.

"Come on, Tess. Don't be like this."

"Like what?" I say, but of course I know.

"This is supposed to be . . ."

"Supposed to be *what*?"

I swear, we're an old married couple. The sound of our toothbrushing contains barely suppressed rage. I keep on with my high-pitched, cool *I'm fine*-ness, and Dad keeps on with his pissed-but-not-pissed, ignoring-me-but-not-ignoring-me act until the next morning, when we are back in the truck. Then I just go for the silent treatment—always a classic—and stare out the window on the way to Las Vegas.

We check into a place called the Flamingo. Dad says it's a splurge. The bedspread is actually nice. You don't think of bodily fluids when you look at it. There's a pool with a slide. We explore the city. There are lights and crowds and the constant *bing-jing* sound of casinos. I feel like I'm inside a pinball machine. There is a fake rainstorm in one hotel and fake canals of Venice in another, and there are guys on every corner handing out flyers to strip shows. There are slabs of prime rib bigger than your head, though I have to admit, I sort of like those. I like the ceiling of blown-glass flowers in that one hotel too, although I don't tell Dad that.

"I can't eat another bite," I said, eating another bite. Banana cream pie. The meringue on top is tall enough to go on the rides at Disneyland. Everything here is oversized, and I do mean everything.

My mood is just starting to improve when, through a bite of pie, my father says, "Portland."

"What do you mean, 'Portland'?" I'm afraid to ask. I'm done, more than done, with this trip. I am ready to go home. It hasn't quite been the life-changing shake-up I was hoping for. Nothing has become more solid or connected; nothing has become more understood. I've had to erase several new follow-up messages from Meg and Dillon, who both now sound pissed off, and my father is becoming more of an alien the more time we spend together. Basically, he's driving me crazy. If you think a road trip is a good idea, just remember that strained family relationships plus long car rides equals homicidal impulses.

"I mean, let's go to Portland."

"Oregon?"

"Of course Oregon."

"Why Oregon? What's in Oregon?"

"I went to school in Oregon. I've got friends there."

"Since when?" You get to thinking you know everything about your parents. You have to think that. It's too unsettling otherwise.

"Since forever."

"I don't want to go to Portland." Summer is about to start, and my mind neatly erases all the loneliness and distance I've felt for the last three months and starts playing the shiny, green-grass and blue-sky film version—Dillon and me holding hands while leaping in the ocean, Meg and me playing volley-ball on a beach. And wait, there's Jessa Winters, too, spiking the ball in her tiny bikini, though I hate sports, and volleyball makes my palms sting, and Jessa Winters isn't even our friend. This is some bad teen movie where a shark's about to appear and turn the water bloody.

"You never want to go anywhere. You always do this."

"Always-never statements," I say. "One of the Ten Communication Killers." I read that in one of Mom's magazines.

"What do you want from me, Tess? I'm doing everything I can here!" Dad's voice is getting loud. Two women diners in shiny tank tops look over at us.

"When you talk to me in a raised voice, I feel frustrated." Always use *I* statements.

"Are you implying I can't communicate? Is that what you're saying? I'm an excellent communicator!" he yells.

Now we're that couple fighting in the restaurant. My father runs his hand through his hair. I sigh and study the saltshaker. People are looking away. The waitress glances over nervously. Pretty soon one of us is going to get up and stomp off, leaving the other with the check. I want a divorce.

I wonder how often my mother felt this way. This is why you're supposed to have a mother *and* a father. Parental failings are more easily swallowed when diluted.

We are sitting in the Paradise Garden Café of the Flamingo hotel in Las Vegas, Nevada, USA, geographical coordinates: 36.1161° N, 115.1706° W. I know just where we are. But it's quite clear that my father and I are lost.

chapter four

Proboscidea: devil's claw. The seeds of the devil's claw were adapted to hook onto the legs of large mammals, thereby spreading seeds over miles as the animal walked. Eleven to fifteen inches long, with a grip as firm as a fishing lure, the devil's claw is the largest and most obstinate hitchhiking seed ever.

I tie the last pixiebell back into my mother's shoe as we leave for Portland. I hope it'll be okay after all this moving and driving in the heat and sliding around on the floor of my father's truck. If it isn't, I don't know what I'm going to do, because keeping it alive is the one important job I have right now. It's my simplest and clearest mission, and that's the one thing I'm sure of.

I do more sullen staring out the window. Dad turns on the radio so that he doesn't have to hear everything I'm not saying. I am oh so close to Henry Lark, but I don't know that yet. It's one of the great and terrible things about big changes, the way they sit unseen just around the next corner, pleased and calculating, while you innocently get a new stick of gum out of your purse and fold your arms and watch the scenery pass.

The atlas says it's 755.29 miles from Las Vegas to Portland. I'd look on my phone, but there's no service in the desert. The trip will take sixteen hours and seventeen minutes, not counting food and bathroom breaks. We keep heading north until we finally stop in the dead of night in some town called Klamath Falls. If there really are falls there, it's too dark and we're too tired to see them.

The next morning, when we leave Klamath Falls, I am a cranky hostage. If my mother knew (knows) about any of this, she'd be *furious*. I'm having fantasies of leaving my father behind at the next gas station. But as we come to our first stop sign, right next to a Texaco and a David's Restaurant ("Home of the Brawny Burger"), there's this little old lady carrying her dog across the street. I swear to God, it's taking her fifteen minutes and she's barely halfway. All this waiting is using up my precious minutes before I'll need a bathroom break again.

"I'm gonna honk," Dad says.

"You'll give her a heart attack."

"She'd probably beat me up with her purse."

"She probably knows kung fu," I say.

"Or at least fu," he says, which cracks us up.

And just like that, the mad spell between us is broken. We are friends again. We are friends all the way until Eugene,

Oregon, when large billows of smoke start pouring out of my father's truck.

"Fuck," my father says.

For once, it's an understatement.

It's green here, way more green than at home, and there are lots of Victorian houses too, small ones and big ones. I might like this place, if Dad weren't whacking the steering wheel over and over again with his palm and swearing. This is bad. This is really, really bad. We're never going to get home now. Well, he's had that truck for a billion years. We should've taken Mom's (my) car, which is way more reliable.

My father runs his hand over his stubble; he hasn't shaved since we left home. He opens the car door, and I roll down my window and stick my head out to watch. The hood creaks as if in pain when he raises it. The stupidest things make you think of other things. The word "pain," for example. In your worst fears, you think of cancer and excruciating agony and moaning even. There wasn't time for that, maybe. Maybe we just didn't get to that part. I don't really know. She *had* lost her taste buds, and her throat had radiation burns, and she couldn't eat. There were other burns too, all over her chest and even on her back. Mouth sores and scary weight loss. Still, the first surgeon told us she would likely completely recover. The oncologist said this too, and so did the other surgeon who put in that stomach tube. They were all pretty self-congratulatory about it, actually, until there was *a series of unfortunate events*. That's what they also said afterward. Doctors say a lot of things, and you want them to say more, but it's never enough.

My father knows nothing about cars. It's warm out, and the sun is on my face as I watch him. He is staring down at that engine, stunned and nervous, as if someone's just handed him the scalpel and asked him to save the patient.

"What's going on?" I ask. I have to lean way out to see him.

"The radiator."

I snort. He doesn't know his radiator from a hole in the ground.

"What's that supposed to mean," he asks but doesn't really ask. He pokes his finger around in there, touches something hot, I guess, because he pulls his hand back and shakes it.

"Radiator," I say. I chuckle.

"I worked at a garage in high school, smart-ass."

Okay, fine. Another thing I didn't know. Parents should not be capable of surprises. *Tessa Sedgewick's Handbook of Good Parenting*, Chapter One.

"What do we do?"

"We wait awhile."

He slams the hood closed. He rummages around in the backseat. I know what he's looking for. A little tin with an American eagle on it. He doesn't know I ditched that stuff back in the desert at a rest stop. *Tessa Sedgewick's Handbook of Good Parenting*, Chapter Two: No mind-altering substances allowed.

He looks at me hard. "You're kidding," he says.

I don't say a single word.

"You didn't."

I shrug.

"Jesus. This is some road trip."

We wait. It's the kind of waiting where you look at the clock again and again and find that only thirty-five seconds have passed. It's getting hot, so I get out too. We're both leaning against the truck. We're both looking across the street. There's a cycle shop and a used bookstore and Diablo's Downtown Lounge, which has a few motorcycles in front and lit-up beer signs in the window. We stand there way too long.

"License plate game," my father suggests.

"Don't even." I'm in no mood.

"Twenty Ques—"

"No."

His profile looks sad. I start to feel bad. "Karaoke on Fridays," I say, and nod toward Diablo's Downtown Lounge.

"'Some say loooove, it is a river . . . ,'" he sings.

"'That drowns the tender need . . . ,'" I sing. Mom had the album.

"Reed," Dad says. "The tender *reed*."

"Whatever."

I look for more gum in my purse. He busts out a few more lines, about love and flowers and seeds.

"People are staring." No one is really staring. There's a dog tied to a lamppost by the bookstore. He lies down, as if settling in for the rest of the show. "Is it time yet?"

"No."

We keep waiting. A man walks in a drunken zigzag out of Diablo's Downtown Lounge. What is it, barely eleven o'clock? Sheesh.

"Dave's Drinking Took a Turn for the Worse," Dad says.

It's a game we have, and when another guy comes out of the cycle shop in shiny green bike pants, it's my turn. "Mark Had an Unfortunate Run-In with Lycra."

A woman passes with an enormous, bulging purse. "Sheila Believed You Could Never Be Too Prepared," he says.

Finally, Dad tries to start the car, but the little arrow that indicates engine temperature flies all the way to the wrong side. The truck's making a bad noise, too, sort of like that time Dad ran the lawn mower over a garden trowel.

"Darn it!" My father doesn't really say this, but I'm saving you from more of his bad mouth. He paces around a bit, runs his hand through his hair again.

"We can hitchhike," he says.

"We're not going to hitchhike! What kind of a father suggests something like that?"

He sighs as if I've given him no choice. He takes out his phone. He turns his back to me (why is he turning his back to me?) and makes a call. I don't like what I'm seeing, not one bit. His shoulders are hunched as if he's protecting a secret, and I hear him laugh loudly. It's a jovial fake laugh that puts me instantly on high alert. The WRONGWRONGWRONG sirens are going off in my head, because he's over there smiling.

He's smiling! What exactly is there to smile about in this

35

situation? He hangs up. He pockets his phone like it's a crisp hundred-dollar bill. He's awfully pleased with himself.

"Who was that?"

"A friend."

"What friend?"

"An old high school friend, Mary. She knows a guy around here who has a tow truck company. Isn't that great?" He says this very fast, so that it comes out "Anoldhighschoolfriend-MarySheknowsaguy."

"Mary."

"Don't say it like that. She's just an old friend."

I want to remind my father exactly how long my mother has been gone: six months and three days. Mostly, you hope for heaven, but at times like these, I sincerely hope she isn't watching.

"I am all for you moving forward and finding happiness, tra la la, but looking up the old high school flame six months after the funeral is just tacky."

"You got this wrong, Tess."

"Mary"—let her name have sarcastic quotation marks—has sent over her buddy Simon, who drives us the rest of the way to Portland with my father's truck on his flatbed. Several hours later, we're at Mary's. Mary's house is small, and all of the jobs a husband might do are undone—the grass is long, the porch slants, and lightbulbs that you have to climb a ladder to change are burnt out. It smells like cat inside, even though there is no cat.

Mary has long black hair and talks in an overly sincere way

that includes grabbing my arm at various intervals. She is trying hard, helping the girl with the dead mother, but she really
needs to stop touching me. I keep my hands behind my back,
which makes me look like a prisoner walking to the exercise
yard. I feel like a prisoner. I make a desperate move and place
a hostage call to Meg, but it's tough to communicate over her
screeching. *"Where ARE you! Where have you BEEN? How can
you just TAKE OFF before school is even out!"* In the state she's
in, if I tell her what's really going on here, state troopers will
get involved. I'll end up on the news. Instead, I reassure her
how fine I am and get off the phone as fast as I can. I try
Dillon. "Wherever you are, babe, I'll come get you." I hate
being called babe. I always think of that pig movie. If Mom is
watching, this is a good time for her to *do* something.

We spend the night, and then another as we wait for Dad's
truck to get fixed. If I have to sleep on that couch with that
musty-smelling quilt one more night, I'm going to make a run
for it. I swear I will. Dad and I need to have a talk.

"You're not having fun?"

Honestly? He thinks that the cookie making and Clue
playing is a barrel of laughs? Maybe Mary is nice; fine, she's
a little nice, barely, but she's under the impression that I'm a
nine-year-old orphan. She almost tried to tuck me in. I have
only one more book left, which makes this an emergency situation. But worse, my father stays up late, talking and laughing
with "Mary." "Mary" made us red sauce and Dad made his
meatball special, and it was all too, too cozy. Old Roosevelt

High. Remember Principal Berry who had that affair? Did you know that Evan Gray became a mayor? He flunked civics, ha-ha-ha. I'm surprised they didn't sing the fight song.

"I'm not staying here." My bag is packed, and I have the last pixiebell under my arm. I mean business.

"The truck is fixed. I got a call this morning."

"Good," I say.

But what isn't good is what happens next. My father, he keeps driving north. He doesn't ask me for my opinion this time. I really am a hostage. When he doesn't answer my questions, I consider opening the car door and rolling down an embankment like they do in the movies. That always looks so painful. Every time I see that, I wonder if I'd have the guts to do it if Mexican drug lords were kidnapping *me*.

"Where are we going?" I ask for the millionth time.

"Trust me," he answers for the millionth time.

Trust him?

It gets greener and greener. I see signs to Seattle. I've never been to Seattle. I wonder if my mother has ever been here. When I think about that album in my bag and the fact that the album and the last pixiebell are nearly all that's left of her, my heart rockets through my body, ripping and tearing as it goes. That feeling almost folds me right in half.

"Canada," I say.

"No."

We arrive at a ferry landing. SAN JUAN ISLANDS, the signs

say. My father hands over some cash at the ticket booth. I took a ferry once, with Mom and Dad, to the island of Coronado. My mother's brown hair blew in the wind, and we ate burgers on the other side, but there were palm trees and there was sand ▬▬▬▬▬▬ ees are dark, pointed evergreens, and the shore is rocky.

I am not going to jump out of the car now, because "Mary" and her cat-smelling house are long gone, and things are looking up. It's possible that my father has a surprise. He probably wants to pay me back for the miserable time in Portland. "Islands" equal "vacation." This is what I tell myself. Sometimes you forget that surprises can go either way.

The ferry isn't here yet. Dad turns off the engine and rolls down his window and gets comfy. I do the same. I take a big, deep breath of that briny air. People are walking their dogs on the beach or waiting in their cars with the seats reclined or their feet up on the dashboards.

I check on the pixiebell. The dirt is too wet, much wetter than Mom or I ever keep it, and I wonder if Mary watered it when it was on her coffee table. I have a flash of worry. I hope it's going to be okay. All this moving around after so many years in one place—poor Pix, it must be in shock.

The car engines start and I whack Dad's leg, because he's fallen asleep. He wakes and looks at me as if he doesn't know where he is, which makes two of us. This is not reassuring. On a road trip, *someone* should know where you are, especially if that someone is supposedly the parent.

The cars all pile on to the ferry, and then Dad says, "Come on!" and we get out. You have to yell to be heard, so Dad just swings his arm in an arc over his head to gesture which way to go. We walk sideways between the cars and then find the narrow stairwell. Up inside the ferry, there are wide windows and padded seats, and I feel almost excited.

"San Juan Islands," I say.

"Parrish," he says.

At the sound of the word, I know there's something familiar about it. It's not just a name I've heard before; it's deeper than that. It's felt, like a memory. A far in and distant memory. Maybe I've spent too many hours in that truck, or maybe the wandering has scrambled my head, but the answer doesn't come to me at first. It doesn't come to me when the ferry passes the silent mounds of islands and deep-green bays, or when we disembark, or when we begin making our way through the winding road of evergreens.

But then there is the mailbox, and on it, one name: Sedgewick. My father's name. My name. And the way the mailbox tilts toward the gravel road, that gate up ahead, that white house with flowers all around, it all tells me one thing.

I've been here before.

"Home." Dad announces it as if it's a fact. That's not how it feels to me, though. I'm nervous. Because, of course, Parrish Island is where Grandma Jenny, my father's mother, who he— *we*—haven't seen in years, lives. Why we are here right now I have no idea.

But there are lots of things I don't know about this place. Not yet, anyway. I don't know that Parrish Island has always been a corner of the world where lost people go to be found. I don't know that its warm, red clay soil is said to be magic and its deep waters healing. And I don't yet know that this expanse of sparkling coves with their slumbering whales is the one and only home of my first true love.

chapter five

Reseda odorata: sweet mignonette. The seed of this plant is sneaky and self-serving. It's hidden inside a delicious fruit, which mice gather in their little cheeks, and then run off to faraway corners to enjoy it. As soon as the mouse bites into the tasty, sweet fruit, though, the seeds inside release a mustard bomb—literally, they taste like Grey Poupon—causing the mice to spit out the seeds. A dirty trick has been played on the mouse so that the seeds can have a new home.

That vault. The seed vault in the frozen archipelago of Svalbard . . . The nearest town is Longyearbyen. Do you know what's even more perfect than the fact that Longyearbyen is home to a vault where everything in it is meant to last forever? Death is forbidden there. It's against the law. Yes, in that protective place, you're not allowed to die. This came about during the influenza pandemic of 1917 to 1920. Since the victims' bodies did not decompose in those freezing temperatures, the virus inside them stayed alive. So the officials there made a bold move. They simply declared that dying was not permitted in town. It still isn't. The cemetery has banned funerals, and anyone who is deathly ill must be shipped to the mainland.

This vault, buried in the side of a frozen mountain, is not only the protected location of what may one day be 2.25 billion seeds; it is a place where the town's leaders have said the one thing that's needed saying for years: Dying is wrong.

I love that. I love that so much. That place is—well, I know because I've seen it—a *mystical* place.

But we're not at that part of the story yet. I am not huffing air so cold it burns my lungs and freezes my own tears to my cheeks. No, we're at the part of the story where my grandmother, Jenny Sedgewick, comes outside to greet us as we arrive. She is carrying a small dog under one arm. She doesn't look how grandmas are supposed to look. Meg's grandma is the round, white-haired kind who sends Christmas pajamas every year, and so is Caitlin's, who I see at every orchestra concert. Still, my grandmotherly knowledge is on the slim side. My mother's mother died before I was born (long before even Grandfather Sully passed away), and Jenny wasn't in the picture. It was never clear why there was this thing between my parents and Jenny. The few times I asked, my mother's mouth would get tight, and she'd say something like, *I did all I could* or *No one would be good enough for your dad.* Of course, you stop asking. If I ever pictured Grandma Jenny, I probably thought she had fangs by how the mood would shift whenever her name came up. But today she's smiling, completely fangless.

She has gray hair cut short and stylish, and she's wearing jeans that have paint on them, a big white shirt, and silver earrings. She's at the car even before my father turns off the engine.

"Vito," my father says. "You're still alive."

The stupid thought that crosses my mind is that it's a funny nickname for your mother. But then the little dog starts squirming with excitement. He's wagging his tail so hard at the sight of Dad, you'd think they were twins separated at birth.

"He remembers you," Jenny says. I decide to call her Jenny, not Grandma, Gram, Nana, whatever, out of some kind of loyalty to my mom. If she had some kind of bad feelings toward this woman, it is my duty to have them too, same as I have her wedding ring and her photos and the pixiebell. Jenny looks harmless enough, but I know and trust my mother. She had good judgment about people.

Well, she could also hold a grudge. Even years later, Mom never had a nice thing to say about Jessica Sims after she stole the jump rope I bought with my own money in the second grade. When Jessica and I started hanging out in high school, Mom still brought up the Jump Rope Incident as a reason to Just Be Careful.

My father scruffs Vito's little head. "The little bastard stole that chicken I bought, remember? He sees me and thinks 'meat.' No wonder he's happy to see me."

Jenny heads over to me, arms outstretched. But I am doing the math. I thought the last time we were here was when I was

around the kitchen and get a déjà vu feeling at the sight of that cookie jar and at the canisters that look like chefs.

"I am so sorry about Anna."

Of course, that's what people say, and there's no real response to that either. *Sorry* begs for forgiveness, and death doesn't deserve it.

"We're doing okay," my father says. This is such a lie. His voice even wobbles when he says it. His voice barely ever wobbles, and I've seen him do the huge, heaving sobs only twice. That said, you should know in advance that this is not some story where he learns to let out his feelings and we have the film version moment where we cry together in our shared loss. People have their own of getting through things, and that's that.

"Tessa, I haven't seen you you were this high," Jenny says, and lets her hand hover her knees. Vito thinks he's getting something to eat and s r fingers.

"It's been a long time," I say lite.

"I bet you don't even rememl ther says.

There is an awkward silence y rehash years of family hurts and dramas in thei eads, as I feel ashamed for all the wrongdoings I You w about.

"Well," Jenny says. It's a little it was tin the silent rehashing. She stands. "Let me show you a fashi

She points out various places—l Jenny' can be seen out the back window; bathroo kind of a t then, upstairs, a small bedroom. This is whei homemade "rest

47

up." I don't really need to rest up, but okay. I think she probably wants to talk to Dad alone.

There is a towel on the bed, with a bar of soap and a bottle of shampoo. It looks like we're staying, and apparently it has already been discussed. I don't know how I feel about this. I miss my own room, if not my own life, but I also sort of love *this* room. It's a white and blue alcove, and it smells a little like lavender, and the bed has a quilt on it, and the floor has a great, thick white rectangular rug. I get excited for a minute, because there's a bookshelf. I'm down to the last pages of my last book, which qualifies as a reading crisis, but there are only art books and Emerson and some poetry.

It hits me. The pixiebell. I left Pix inside the truck. I'm an idiot. I'm as bad as the people who leave their dogs and babies in hot cars with the windows rolled down a crack. I sneak past my father and Jenny in the living room, because they are talking quietly. The long, awkward silence we all were so lucky to share earlier only means that big, hard words are waiting behind temporarily shut doors, and I don't particularly want to be around when they open.

I turn the doorknob oh so slowly and head outside to get Pix. I don't know if it's my imagination, but it doesn't look that great. It looks a little limp. I am on the front porch again, holding the plant in my mother's shoe, when I hear my father's voice rise. I can't make out what he's saying. I only know that he's getting loud. This is how he talked to the TV all those years that George Bush was president. I don't want to go back in now, so I just sit down right there, holding the last pixiebell and trying to listen in.

I hear *You can't just go—* and *I'm not! You said you'd do—* And then, some idiot starts a lawn mower and I can't hear anything, except *You* and *Go* repeated a lot by both of them.

I consider my options. I am seriously thinking about getting his keys and driving myself home. I imagine this in my head, and it's kind of great. The music is on in the truck, and I'm checking in to one of those places that has a restaurant connected to it, a Denny's or something, and I'm turning on the motel TV and kicking off my shoes and loving being alone, forgetting that driving Dad's truck is like trying to drive an office building, and that one night at a motel would practically wipe out my bank account. I'm happily flipping through channels on my Mental Motel's remote control when this boy rides up on a bike. He's got white-blond hair, and he's wearing a T-shirt and shorts, and for some reason, even though it's sunny, he's got this scarf around his neck. I'd have made fun of it back home because it looks like he's a guy in a perfume ad, but honestly, the scarf looks fashionable, and so do the shoes he has, these checked sneakers. He's got a leather messenger bag worn crossways over his chest, and there's a long scroll sticking from it.

He's in a hurry, obviously, because he ditches his bike on Jenny's lawn and doesn't even notice me at first. But then he sees my father's truck, and then me, and he stops.

"I'm just going to drop . . ." He points to the scroll and then to the backyard.

"Fine by me," I say.

He jogs around to the back. After a few minutes, he reappears.

"Is Jenny . . ." He hasn't spoken a complete sentence yet.

"Inside."

"Are you . . . new?"

"I'm her granddaughter."

"Oh. I didn't know she had one." He holds his hand out. It seems like a formal thing to do, private schoolish, but it fits him.

I set the pixiebell on the step and shake. "Tess," I say.

"Elijah. I'm one of her students," he says.

"Oh." I'm taking in his pretty features—the perfect cheekbones and the elegant manners—and I'm obviously unable to do that and speak at the same time. My brain freezes. I search around for something to say, but I'm falling out of a conversational airplane without a parachute, and there's nothing to do but crash in an ugly splat of silence. "Cool."

"You going to be around?"

"I don't really know."

"Okay." He waits for something more from me, but I've been struck dumb. I'm sure I'll have a hundred brilliant things to say to him later, when I replay this in my head. "Well, see ya."

"See ya," I say.

Thank God my father and grandmother don't seem to get along. We'll be out of here by morning, and I'll never have to see that guy again.

When it seems safe, I actually do go back to the white-blue room to "rest up." I fall asleep. There's something about being there that lets me sleep like a rock. I feel like I haven't slept in ages, maybe not since that day when my mother sat on the edge of my bed and told me that she had a lump in her throat that had to be taken out. When someone tells you they don't want you to worry, it generally means there's a lot to worry about.

I wake up to the sound of my father's truck. I look over at the clock, and it's after seven, and I smell something wonderful, a greasy, crackly frying chicken smell, and there I am in that white-blue room, and it's dinnertime. This is no Kraft macaroni and cheese dinner. I'm actually excited. My mother was a great cook, but my father's got his one meatball recipe and that's about it. He also makes these black-speckled scrambled eggs because he always cooks them in the bacon grease without washing the pan, and that's just wrong in my opinion.

I don't think too hard about where Dad's going. I figure he's off to buy a bottle of wine or something, an ingredient we need for the feast. I could really use a wake-up shower, but I don't want to miss dinner. Jenny might even have a little plate of crackers and salami circles and squares of cheese to eat beforehand. You'd think I'd weigh two hundred pounds with the way I eat, but I got my mother's "good metabolism." I don't know if anyone actually knows what a "good metabolism" is. It's probably one of those unprovable myths like being lucky or having a green thumb.

I wash my face and brush my teeth, and I'm feeling really good all of a sudden. A nap, a minty mouth, fried chicken, and life feels hopeful. As if maybe we *can* go on and the future really *is* out there. You get flashes like that—like you can go on after all—or else the opposite, a flash where it hits you that she's actually gone forever.

Downstairs, Jenny's back is to me. She clatters the lid back on the frying pan.

"Can I help?" I ask.

She startles. She turns around, and her face has an expression I can't read. It's sadness and sympathy and something else. It's frozen almost, as if there is too much to say that she has no words for.

"Are you okay?"

That's what it is. She looks like she might cry. She holds a large fork aloft. Vito is watching intently, as if he's in the orchestra and that fork is the conductor's baton. "I'm . . ." She struggles. "Maybe we should sit down."

The happy hopefulness I was feeling has fled the scene with the goods, and my stomach drops. I try to reassure myself. Maybe she's just going to spill their whole story now; maybe that's what this is about. But inside I know better. Inside, you always know better.

She sits. I sit. So does Vito, but he's got other motivations. She takes my hands. Her own are soft and warm, and that softness almost makes me cry. She doesn't have to say it. I can't believe it, my God, but I know it.

"He *left*?" I say.

"Tessa," Jenny says. She looks about a hundred years old suddenly.

"For how long?" For a night, let her say. To meet friends for dinner, maybe. To get a beer. To take a drive. There are a hundred possibilities.

"A few days."

"A few *days*? He just dropped me here with someone I don't even know for a few *days*?"

She winces. I know I'm being hurtful, but I don't care. They've both let me down. They've all let me down. You don't just *leave*. You don't just *let* someone leave. You don't just *die*, for that matter. "What did you say to him?"

"I told him he was an idiot. I told him you need him right now."

"*Before* he left. What did you say to *make* him leave? You two were fighting."

Jenny's silent. I need this to be her fault, but it isn't.

Finally she says, "He just needs a few days, I think, sweetie. To be alone. This has all been such a shock."

"And it hasn't been a shock to me? Was this his plan all

along? We'd come here, and he'd ditch me?" Maybe he didn't even care about the Grand Canyon.

"I don't think he's planning anything. I think he's falling apart."

"Well, someone needs to not fall apart," I say. "He couldn't *tell me* he was leaving?"

And it's that thought, that he *fled* me, that he was too much of a coward to even face me, that causes me to shove my chair back, scaring the innocent Vito so that he scurries backward. I run upstairs. I have never been more furious in my life. I grab my purse. My phone is in there, and that's all I really need. I leave the pixiebell, too. Screw it. I don't owe anybody anything.

I slam that front door. The logistical problems haven't hit me yet. For one, that I don't even know where I am. I run down that driveway, the rage filling me, spilling over, propelling me forward even though I don't know where forward is. The weather has changed. The fading summer day is leaving us, and dark clouds are rolling in fast, coming in over the water, covering the bittersweet twilight and turning the night purplish and dark.

At the end of the road, I look over my shoulder. She's probably going to run out after me and break a hip or something. I don't care. I run past tall evergreens, the enchanted-forest kind of trees that loom ominous in the dark, the kind of trees that talk and scare small children who are alone in the woods in fairy tales. I run and run until my chest burns, past the curve

question in a way that maybe you'd want to answer. He's wearing a white shirt with the sleeves rolled up and a loose tie, and there is another boy with him, that same boy with the bike, whose name I can't remember right then, because the black-haired boy with the wide, soft brown eyes is looking right at me. He looks deep into my eyes and he can see me, right into me, I can tell. And then, gently as a passing thought, or even as gently as a memory, his thumb moves across the soft flesh of the underside of my wrist. He is holding his breath, I realize, because he exhales and then lets me go, and when he does I can sense his fingers still there, their heat, where he touched me.

"You sure?" he asks. He even sets his bag down. It's heavy with books, but the setting down means he is willing to wait.

"Yes," I say.

"Jenny's granddaughter," the other boy says. He's forgotten my name, and that's all right, because I've forgotten his.

"Right."

"Well, if you're sure," the black-haired boy says. He picks up his bag, and they head toward the door. He waves to a woman behind the checkout desk, a woman with short spiky hair and round glasses.

"Later, Henry," she calls.

I watch his profile and then the back of his head, the thick wave of hair, as he descends the stairs, and I feel this energy between us, an awareness that we're looking at each other, only not looking. He feels it too, I know. He feels it until he must turn around. He smiles. I don't know exactly what this smile means, only that it means something. Something immense. It curls around me like smoke, or like the arm of true love, and I wonder then if it's possible to fall ten thousand miles into the Grand Canyon and be held safe at the same time.

chapter six

Malus domestica: apple tree. If you plant the seed from the apple you just ate, the tree that will grow will produce fruit that looks and tastes completely unlike your original piece of fruit. Without tree grafting, your favorite kind of apple would have disappeared centuries ago. That's because—even more so than humans—each apple seed produces an offspring that is an individual quite unlike its parent.

Here's what I do next: I sit in one of the leather library chairs, which is as soft as an old baseball mitt. The chairs are in a group like they're having a little chair party, and there are also several rows of long, dark wood tables with green glass lamps hanging down over them. No one is in there but me and a blond woman in a sundress, who appears and disappears with her fat bag of books. I can hear the rain on the roof.

I'm in shock. First my father and then that boy. I'm having one of those moments where you wonder who this is, this person whose body you happen to be inhabiting. I let it all—the pounding rain against the windows, the quiet, the soft chair—take me in and give me comfort. I'm surrounded by stories and answers and years and years of volumes of the right words. My heart, which has been beating fast, starts to slow. That great musty smell of the library speaks of solid, timeless things, old and lasting ones, and I know what I have to do, of course. I had wanted to run, but there are reasons to go back to that blue-white room.

Sometimes you don't want to go on, but you have to. You absolutely have to, because there are things waiting for you. Good can sit in the distance, just beyond your view, waiting, until you go toward it. You must go toward it. That's another thing I learned.

I try to find the number on one of the library computers. This takes forever, and so I give up on that plan. But I'm in a library. If you can't solve your problem in a library, good luck to you. I know there are old phone books in here somewhere. I could ask the spiky-haired woman behind the desk, who is looking at me over the top of her round glasses, but I decide not to. Librarians know just about everything, but they especially know how to mind their own business. She leans back in her chair and returns to her magazine. It's got a pink cover with a vinyl record on it and it's called *Bitch*. When she sees me looking her way, she folds it in half so I can't see the word. I'm a stranger, and so who knows? I could be one of those people who freak out when they hear profanity, as if they've just been deflowered by vocabulary. Personally, I think there are more important things to freak out about, like world hunger, for example, or violence, or bad parents, such as the kind who leave a daughter on a strange island far from home after her mother dies.

I find the phone directory. It's a slim volume. Not many people live here on old Parrish. I take it way back to a far corner. If I was in any mood to laugh, I would, because there's a chair with its back turned to everything else. Pinned to it is an official-looking sign, which says LEAVE ME ALONE. Maybe I should steal it and wear it on my back.

I sit in that chair and dial. I keep my voice low. She answers on the first ring.

"Where are you?" she says. And not three minutes later, my grandmother, Jenny Sedgewick, drives up in her old Volkswagen van and opens the door.

"Get in," she says. "You must be starving."

He might have been right after all, my father. *Home*, he'd said. And when we drive back to that gravel road with the tilting mailbox, I realize it. This is the closest thing to a home I've got.

That next morning, I am awoken by the sound of a ringing bell. A ringing bell that reminds me of another ringing bell. Do you know what they used to do when someone was done with radiation treatment? The nurses would have the patient ring this big metal bell on a stand that they kept on the front counter. It was a forced rite of passage. The poor, emaciated person would receive a certificate, too, like the ones you used to get in elementary school, with scrolly writing: *This certifies that* (name) *is a math fact champion!* But this one said *has completed radiation!* A lousy xeroxed piece of paper.

What if I don't want to ring it? my mom asked me after we'd just heard it again.

I wouldn't ring it.

Isn't it sort of . . . dark? There's something twisted about it.

Cancer meets rodeo ranch dinner bell or something, I said.

We started to snicker in that way where you're trying not to laugh but can't help but laugh. She actually snorted, which made us laugh harder. We elbowed each other to shut up so all the sad people in the waiting room didn't see us. And then the bell ringer and certificate holder who'd just finished his treatment left the office. His cheeks were sunken in and his clothes hung on him like there was barely a body underneath. He looked like the people you see in the concentration camp movies. And he was carrying a white, plaster bust molded into the shape of a head and shoulders. It shut us up fast, because that cast looked creepy, like the death him, the ghost him, the absent-bodied him. I didn't know what it was, or why he had it. I must have looked worried, because Mom leaned over and said, *It's okay. It's just . . . They make this mold of you, and you wear it. They fit it*—she demonstrated putting it on—*to make sure you stay still. It doesn't hurt. It's just really . . . confining. But for the record, I'm not ringing the bell. And I'm not taking that thing home.*

Good, I'd said.

Unless maybe I can put it in the passenger seat so I can fake a ride in the carpool lane, she said.

To be honest, I never really believed in death. I knew in my logical mind that it existed, but it seemed more like an idea than something real. I still sometimes feel that way. Because it's unfathomable that she's actually gone-gone. The sheets she folded are still in the linen closet, and her writing is in our address book, and she's the one I talk to when something goes wrong or right. A half-eaten pack of her mints is in the ashtray of her (my) car. Sometimes I catch myself thinking that she's just away and will be back. I'm even sort of calmly sure about the whole thing. And then it hits me—the forever of it—and each and every time that happens, there's a gut-sinking twist of shock. I am felled all over again. *Where* did she go? That's what I don't understand. I have no idea. I just want her back.

The bell I hear now—it's actually a phone. It's funny, but a ringing phone doesn't usually sound like a ringing phone anymore. Phones sound like jazz riffs or steel drums or chirping birds, but not bells. I can hear Jenny downstairs talking. I leap up, because I know it's my father.

I throw on my robe, and I rush downstairs, and I'm rude to Vito, who's excited to see me. I ignore his wagging and jumping. Jenny's wearing this great floaty robe with huge dragonflies on it. The phone has been hung up. It hangs on the wall. It has one of those curly wires. Grandma Jenny hasn't yet discovered the freedom of not having to talk while being attached to the wall by an electrical umbilical cord. But look. She's got a package of bacon in her hands. Someone's told her all my favorite foods.

"Someone's told you all my favorite foods," I say. "Bread, bacon, fried chicken."

"They're all *my* favorite foods," she says. "Thank God I've got a good metabolism."

"What did he have to say for himself?" I ask.

"Do you want coffee?"

I shake my head. I don't drink coffee. But I like that she asks.

"He said his phone died. He called with a number to reach him."

I am so relieved that I could laugh and cry at the same time. Maybe Dad wasn't ignoring my calls. Maybe he just couldn't answer. Maybe he didn't even know I'd been trying to reach him all night. I think all those crazy maybes. When someone ditches you—ditches you, leaves you, dies, whatever—you're always stuck with the crazy maybes. That's *another* thing I learned. All those maybes are just hope looking for a place to land. Every maybe is Maybe They Love Me After All. Oh, it's pathetic, that mind game of misplaced faith that you play when you've been left.

"When's he coming back?"

"He said a week."

"Wait, what? A week now? I thought you said a few days."

"Tess."

64

I can't help it. I start pacing again. I want to throw something. She's getting the wrong idea about me, because I'm not
the run-off-mad type or the throw-something type. I get upset
when I see strangers arguing. I can't handle aggressive talk
radio, or TV talent shows where someone gets told how bad
they are, or animal programs where the tiger is about to over-
take the injured okapi.

I'm furious. But fury and devastation are fraternal twins.
They may not look alike, but they're made up of exactly the
same stuff. I want to cry.

"What can I do?" Jenny says. "Do you want to go back
home? Stay with a friend? I'll take you. I'll do whatever you
think is best. But I'd really like to have you here. I would, Tess.
We have lost years to make up for. We can *use* this. As a chance
to get to know each other, right? Yes? A few days? A week?
And, you know, maybe you need a rest too."

The word "rest" is so beautiful that I want to fall down on
my knees and lay my head right on it.

"He . . ." My voice is hoarse. Her eyes are kind, and she's
got bacon, and she said the word "rest." I almost want to tell
her everything. I want to tell her I hadn't slept in weeks. I want
to tell her how sad things are at home. I want to tell her what
keeps going around and around in my head, even the thing I
am most guilty of. But I can't. And I can't manage to speak the
worst thing: *He didn't even say good-bye.*

The *He* just floats around in the air until Jenny finishes my
sentence for me. "He's an ass," she says. It's not quite where I

was headed, but I like her direction better. "He's my son, and I love him, but sometimes he's as selfish as a dog. Wait. My apologies to you, Vito. That was unfair."

I look at Vito, with his white whiskers and sincere brown eyes. "*Vito* has better morals," I say.

"I don't know about that," Jenny says. "You can't trust him for five minutes."

Vito keeps looking at me with those sweet eyes. "Vito has a soul," I try instead.

"Indeed he does," Jenny says.

"I have absolutely no artistic ability," I tell her.

"Well, so be it. You can watch if you want, but it'd be nice to have you join in."

I've declined Jenny's offer of her car keys, which she dangled from her index finger, in favor of staying around while she gives her art lesson. I'm not *uninterested* in exploring this island. It's just that the little inner manipulator that is in all of us (I hope it is in all of us) is moving the pieces around in my head, plotting and scheming like an evil queen. Elijah—I've remembered his name now—might come to this lesson, and if he comes, maybe his friend Henry will too.

If there's an inner manipulator in all of us, though, there's also his or her greatest enemy, the practical teacher's pet, the sensible doubter, who's generally a pain in the neck and ruins everything. I'm here for a week—it's stupid to think I'll have some monumental connection with a guy I saw for two minutes.

I mean, get real. They all have their own lives here, and I'm just passing through to buy the I HEART WHALES T-shirt.

Still. Those eyes.

Fate shouts.

"Who's in your class?" Oh, innocent me.

"Well, there's Cora Lee, from the Theosophical Society . . ."

"The what?"

"Don't ask. We've got a lot of woo-woo mystical stuff around here. Just be warned."

"Hey, I can shake my chakras with the best of them." I barely know the difference between Reiki and Rumi, but oh well. And if you gave me the choice between an organic carrot and a Big Mac, I'm going for three thousand calories of fat and salt all the way.

"Margaret MacKenzie, she's a widow. President of the Parrish Island Garden Society. Joe Nevins. He and his brother, Jim, run the ferry terminal now that the Franciscan nuns have all retired or died. Are you sure you want to stick around? You should see your face."

"No, I'm sure." I wasn't sure. Maybe this wasn't even the class Elijah took.

"Nathan, he's a sculptor. Likes to change it up. Elijah, he's about your age. Parrish High. Incredibly talented." Now we're talking. "He comes to lessons with"—*yes, yes, yes!*—"his sister, Millicent."

The film version plays in my head. We're all driving somewhere in a convertible, laughing. Henry's behind the wheel, and I'm in the seat next to him. Elijah's in the back, wearing his scarf, which is blowing in the wind, and Millicent—wait. Millicent is dressed like a pilgrim, or maybe someone Amish. A dark dress, a prissy mouth. She's wearing a bonnet and sensible shoes.

"With a name like Millicent, she should have a bun," I say.

"Oh no. She's got blond hair down to here." Jenny gestures to her shoulders. "She's beautiful."

Redo image. Henry is driving, and Millicent is beside him, wearing a body-hugging dress. I'm standing at the side of the road with my thumb out. They pass me by, not even seeing me through their chic sunglasses. I stop the film fast, before I start running after them and waving my arms.

"Oh," I say.

"Looks aren't everything," Jenny says, which, thank you for the life advice, is something I already know. I try to determine if she means something by this, if she's telling me something about Millicent or anyone else, me even, but she's unfolding the legs of easels and setting up for her class, and I can't see her face. She's old, but she's strong. She's flinging those things up and whipping out large canvases from cupboards and hauling chairs.

"You need help?"

"Drag that stool over here? I like to keep the space clear for my own work, but it means hauling everything out each time." She's huffing a little. Hopefully, she doesn't have a heart attack or something. The funny thing is, every now and then, she does something that's a little familiar. The way she tilts her head when she laughs, for example. It looks just like Dad. Or the way she sets her chin in her hand when she's thinking. I've been so busy hating him that I forgot how much I love him. He hasn't always been the father who ditched me on some strange island after my mother died, and he's not just an irresponsible pot smoker who left it to me to take Mom to her appointments because it was *too intense* for him. He took me for long bike rides when I was a kid and set up a taste test between Ho Ho's and Ding Dongs. He read me stories using all the voices and made us a blanket fort that took up most of the house, and later, he helped me with my history homework, because he loved that stuff. *His-story,* he'd said. *Or her story. Point is, it's all great stories.* He took me to the bank to open my savings account, although I think Mom made him do that. He taught me how to change a tire.

"Who was Dad's dad?" I ask. I don't know why I've never stopped to wonder about this before. It's like this whole side of the family didn't exist. We never even really talked about any of these people, and it was one of those weird things that become so normal that you forget it's weird. The question is out of my mouth before I consider whether it's intrusive or not, but Jenny doesn't even flinch. She just goes on taking jars and stuff out of cupboards and setting them on the long counter at the back of the studio.

"Maxfield Sedgewick. He left us when your dad was in kindergarten."

"Oh," I say. "That's too bad."

"I don't know. What if it was a worse too bad if he stayed?"

I'm not sure how to reply, so I keep my mouth shut. "What's that one?" I nod my head toward a large painting against the far wall. It's as tall as me and twice as big across.

"What do you think it is?"

Great. Trick question, I'm sure. Abstract art and poetry—they always involve a trick question. Honestly, I don't get it. I like those very realistic paintings that look like photographs, or novels that are so much like actual life that you feel understood. But poetry—all those wombs and leaves falling and oranges on plates—whatever. Same with modern art. Splotches you're sure you could do yourself if someone gave you a couple of cans of Benjamin Moore and an afternoon.

I take a guess. "A tree." I don't want to be impolite. What I think is that it's brown and green smears, but I kind of like it anyway.

"It *is* a tree. And ground. Earth, life, renewal, all that."

"'The Circle of Liiiife . . .'" I sing that Disney song.

She smiles. Does Dad's head tilt. "Pretty much."

"That's no tree." I point to a thin sheet of canvas rolled out across a small desk at the back of the room. It's held flat by a glass paperweight and a cup of pens. The image is of two faces, I think, nose to nose. Beautiful faces. A mirror image, anyway.

"That's Elijah's."

It's interesting and odd. But I don't have much time to think about it. "I hear a car," I say.

"They're here. Do you mind running in and grabbing me a water bottle from the fridge?" she asks. "That bacon made me so thirsty."

"No problem."

I want to run back to the house anyway, do an Insecurity Check on my makeup. I've barely worn any since Dad and I started out on this trip, but the whole Henry hope-thing made me do it up this morning. Now I'm just nervous to see Elijah again and to meet Millicent. In spite of the fact that I've been rudely ignoring all calls from home, I'm actually excited to be with people my own age.

I dash upstairs, brush my teeth again. I run back down. I give the abandoned Vito, who's lying on his hairy dog bed, a pat on his head. I grab a couple of water bottles from the fridge. I'm on my way out of the kitchen when I see it. A piece of paper. It's got a phone number on it. Dad's number. But there's also a second number written there, under a name. I don't know what I'd been thinking, because I'd imagined him at some log cabin or something, sleeping and getting high and staring at nature, I don't know. Having time in the wilderness to think about what it means to lose my mother and where we'd go from here. And so I now must add another member to the inner crew. There's the manipulator, the teacher's pet, and, let's not forget, the utterly deluded big fat fool.

Mary, the note says.

They are all painting wildflowers that Jenny has hastily shoved into a glass jar. It's a painting class cliché. I want to elbow someone and crack up, but there's no one. Mom would get this joke. I'm in this painting class cliché all by myself, and it gets worse, because I'm holding a brush. I'm sitting in front of an easel. I'm sitting in front of an easel with a big smeary splotch on it, made by yours truly. Sometimes you just have those moments when you wonder how in the hell you got where you are.

She looks over my shoulder. "Rule number one," I tell Jenny. "Colors mixed together equal brown."

"Just have fun with it," she says.

"Fun is my middle name," I say, which isn't exactly true. I'm showing off a little for Elijah and Millicent, who are sitting next to each other, painting with concentrated expressions. Millicent held her hand out to shake mine when Elijah introduced us, same as he had, and now she is biting the end of her brush. She does have long blond hair and blue eyes and tiny, perfect features, and green shoes with little embroidered flowers, which means she has the money for green shoes with little embroidered flowers. She's wearing a blue skirt and a red

T-shirt, and none of this sounds like it goes together, but it does. I never know how people manage to create those don't-go-together outfits that actually do go together. When I try it, I look like I've been in a Marshalls dressing room during an explosion.

I laugh a little too loudly in a shameless move to get Elijah's attention. The plan is, they'll notice what a great time we—me and Henry and them, of course—could all have together. But they don't even look up. It's starting to remind me of those horrible paint-your-own-pottery birthday parties you think are going to be fun until everybody suddenly acts like they're creating the Sistine Ceiling.

Elijah is wearing white pants—bold move in painting class; let's give him that—a bright blue T-shirt and leather sandals, and a watch, which is actually kind of cool, because no one wears watches anymore. His blond hair is gelled artfully to one side, and those model cheekbones he has look like a pair of perfect sand dunes rising from a magazine desert. They *both* belong in a perfume ad. And here's another thing. Elijah's not painting the wildflowers in the jar. It's something else. Something new. I can't quite tell what yet, because right now it's only a sketch. There are pencil marks and white paint, along with some yellow he's laying down.

"Max told us he didn't want to go to sleep because it's *boring*," Nathan says. "He obviously doesn't remember his dreams. Last night, I was in a parade in a mall with Paul McCartney and Snoop Dogg right before a tornado hit." I like him right off. He has a rumpled-bed look—old Levi's, T-shirt with the sleeves cut off, shaggy brown hair. He's slipped off his shoes, so his bare feet are on the canvas drape below him. He's pals with Margaret, the old lady with the sweet blue eyes and fluffy hair; they drove in together and sit next to each other. Nathan helped her find a place for her purse and gave her a hand taking off her sweater.

"Dreaming is lovely," says Cora Lee, who is about a million years old. Her voice sounds like fluttering leaves. Her hand is shaking so hard, she has to hold it with the other one to keep it still. Yet I can see from where I sit that her painting is precise, and each purple petal looks like a purple petal. She's even put a chip in the neck of the jar exactly where one really is.

"My Eugene used to sleep like the devil," Margaret says. "A freight train could barrel through the room and he wouldn't stir."

"That's how Jim is," Joe Nevins says. "Even when we were kids." He's got a plaid short-sleeve shirt stretched over a round stomach.

Then everyone is silent again. Jenny walks around and murmurs advice. She points her old finger and says, "Good" or "Balance" or "Fullness" or "Notice how . . ." as I sneak glances at Millicent's manicure, the kind where the nails are white at the tips, same as candy corn. It has a name, but I can't remember it. My manicure knowledge is on the slim side.

Wait. *French.*

"French?" Elijah says.

74

Did I speak out loud? Tell me I didn't speak out loud. Jenny has placed me next to Elijah, which is so helpful, because that allows him to see the extent of my artistic talent that much better.

I think fast. Thinking fast is not something I'm great at. "The flowers," I say. I am such an idiot.

"Provençal," Margaret says. "Giverny."

"*Majolica Jar with Wild Flowers*, Van Gogh," Nathan says. "French, absolutely."

I want to kiss them both. I think I love these people.

"Purple is the color of the spirits," Cora Lee whispers.

"*Oui*," Jenny says, and winks at me, as if we are sharing a joke. I don't know if we are sharing a joke, though. I don't really know her. I don't paint. I've never been interested in painting. I am suddenly filled with the most intense longing for home. Home the way it doesn't exist anymore. Home where Mom would come home from work with a couple of fat bags of groceries and we'd unload them together. She'd say, *I got that yogurt you like.* I'd give anything to just hear that.

I stare at my painting as if pondering my next creative move, but I am really counting up how many minutes my mother lived. Sixty minutes in an hour; one thousand, four hundred, forty minutes in a day; and 525,600 in a year. I dip the brush in the paint and do the math on my canvas. Forty-two years, which is 22,075,200 minutes or so. I write the number 22,075,200 again in purple, the color of the spirits. It looks so large, but it isn't. It's not nearly large enough.

Jenny claps her hands together. Everyone is coming out of their trances and shuffling things and standing up. Elijah stretches as if he's just run a mile, but his painting doesn't look all that different from when he began. There is the snapping of paint-box clasps, and Millicent has her perfect back toward the room as she stands at the sink and cleans up. "If I have to paint another flower, I'll scream," she says. Funny, I didn't see the armed gunman who was forcing her to use that brush, but maybe I missed him.

Elijah holds his canvas carefully between his palms and carries it to the long counter, where he sets it beside the others.

"So weird running into you last night," I say to him.

"Parrish Island, population three thousand, and a good lot of those don't live here full-time. You always run into people."

"Oh," I say. He's smashing any image I had of a Meaningful Coincidence. It's starting to happen again, the vast conversational wasteland. I realize something, though. It's happening not only because those perfect blue eyes intimidate me, but because he's not all that friendly. Truthfully, he and Millicent are a pair of icebergs. Still, I can't forget another set of eyes, ones I've been seeing every time I shut my own. I can feel that hand around my wrist right here and now as I stumble for something to say to this boy, who happens to be smiling a billboard smile—large and perfect, but fake. "Your friend Henry seems nice."

"Henry is weird," Millicent says without turning around.

"Henry's not weird," Elijah says.

"I like weird," I say.

"Mill, hustle up. I've got to be at work in ten."

I try again. "Where do you work?"

"Hotel Delgado?"

I shrug my shoulders. I've been here all of two days.

"He's a waiter," Millicent says. She holds her hand in the air as if she is carrying a tray. "Baked potato or fries with that?"

"Fries," I joke, but they are too involved in their own sibling rivalry to notice.

"At least I have a job, loser," Elijah says. "I don't sit around all day reading magazines and slathering on more sunscreen, my hand out to Mommy and Daddy when I need a little cash."

"Who's the loser? Summer is for rest and relaxation, not for hot grease and cleaning up gross stuff under high chairs. Stupid brother." She flicks him with her thumb and forefinger. "Well, see ya," Millicent says to me.

"See ya," I say.

"Later, Jenny," Elijah calls.

So much for hanging out tonight. So much for us all going over to the Hotel Delgado, wherever that is, to share dessert. So much for a chance to see Henry again.

Margaret is struggling to get her sweater back on, the one lone sleeve darting around like a fish on a line. I catch it and help her aim. That old arm has a map of veins on it. Maybe it's all the turns taken and not taken over a lifetime.

77

"Thank you, my dear," she says. She actually says "My dear," just like you think old people do. "It was a pleasure to meet you." But then she crooks her finger, and I lean down. "Don't let it bother you," she whispers. "Those two think their you-know-what doesn't stink."

I'm on a roll. Jenny will get the wrong idea of me now, because I'm trashing her students, whom I just met. Generally, I'm an open-minded person. A benefit-of-the-doubt-giving person. Death has made me easily fed up.

"Would it kill them to be friendly? Could you get your nose higher in the air? I mean, why does she even take the class if she doesn't like it?"

"I think she likes it a lot. Terminally bored is just her way of being in the world."

"Her way of being *superior* in the world! And what's with the two of them, anyway? They seem awfully close. Close-close. Hey, I read my mother's old copy of *Flowers in the Attic*."

"It's nothing personal, Tess," Jenny says. "You have to remember, hundreds and hundreds of tourists visit during the summer. They go on their whale-watching tours and stay in our B and Bs and then they go home and we all go about our regular lives. You don't expect to *bond*."

"'We,' 'they,'" I say. My voice sounds too sarcastic, even to me. But I don't like her tone either. Or maybe I don't like that she's joining them in "we" and leaving me all alone out here.

She holds up a hand. She actually steps away from me. "I'm not your enemy."

"Could have fooled me."

Jenny gives me a long stare, the kind Mr. Shattuck used to give the mouthy potheads in Algebra II. We're still in her studio, and she heads over to her desk and starts shuffling stuff around, as if she's done with this conversation. She puts on the glasses she wears on a chain around her neck and studies a small stack of glossy photos of what looks like her own art. Well, sure. Of course she's loyal to these people. This is her life. She's known me, her own flesh and blood, all of five minutes.

This is not going the way I expected. Jenny is obviously not the fountain of grandmotherly love and understanding I thought she might be. And she is not bowing at the altar of my grief like she's supposed to either. Her jaw is a granite slab, immoveable and almost defiant. It's Dad's look. It's my own; I hate to admit it. We're a generally optimistic lot, but we're fond of our own views, let's just say. Sure of our own position. "Stubborn" is another word for it.

Well, my mother was too. She and my father could face off like a pair of boulders.

"I'd like to get out of here, if I'm allowed," I say.

She opens her desk drawer, grabs her keys, and tosses them to me. In the film version, I catch them neatly and stride off, with my hair flowing out behind me and my shoes *clip-clip*ping their displeasure. In real life, she makes a bad throw, and I make a worse catch, and the keys go sliding across the floor and I have to retrieve them from under Cora Lee's abandoned chair.

"There you go, Rapunzel," she says. "First gear sticks."

It's official: I hate it here.

chapter seven

Sesamum indicum: sesame. The sesame seed is one of the oldest spices known to man. The most famous reference to sesame seeds came in the tale of Ali Baba and his forty thieves. "Open sesame" was the magic password, which unlocked the door to the robbers' den. The phrase was used because ripe sesame pods are so delicate that they can burst open and scatter their seeds at the slightest touch. Call them overly sensitive.

Inside the house, I grab my purse. I swipe the piece of paper with my father's number on it and tuck it into my pocket. I want to go home. Vito hears the keys jingle and thinks we're going somewhere.

"See you later, alligator," I say to him.

But I say this sort of meanly. Sorry, Vito, but I feel the sort of pissed that makes you want to step down hard on the accelerator, and when I do, the old Volkswagen van sputters and dies. Apparently, it's one of those days when even objects—stuck closet doors and cold showers and old cars—have lessons of philosophical importance to impart upon you. Thanks, got it. I try again with less road rage and make it down the driveway and out onto what seems like a major street. I spot a sign: DECEPTION LOOP. Roads named after lies, very comforting.

But it *is* comforting, because it's beautiful. The road curves high and winding around the outer edge of the island, so it's good that I'm basically driving a sluggish tin can. The car rattles as it inches along, but it somehow fits this road. Cliffs drop down into the sound, and those waters are wide and sparkly, and I get that great Nature Feeling, that great and *important* Nature Feeling, where you understand your smallness and you sense God, even. I'm glad for that feeling. God is such a relief.

I roll down the window of the van, which you do manually with this tiny, round handle I can barely get my fingers around. It smells like the ocean out there, and I suck in a big lungful of that air. The sound sneaks out of view, and then it is back, and then I find myself beside a wide meadow that dips down to the sea. There's a Victorian house in the distance and another small, shingled house next to it. I pull over by a row of mailboxes, because it's one of those places that make you imagine living another life. You picture yourself there, with a bowl of lemons on the table and a golden dog who follows you wherever you go, and for a minute, you're so happy. All of life stretches before you then, all the possibilities, the thrilling power of your own future, which means it's a good place to try to phone my father.

I spread the piece of paper on the dash. My heart is thrumming. I hear the trill of the phone, and I wait, but it just rings and rings and rings. And then there is "Mary's" voice, the traitorous, cat-hair-covered Mary, the "Mary" of spaghetti-sauce-stained Tupperware and cobwebby ceiling corners, asking me to leave a message.

"Dad," I say. I don't want my voice to sound pleading. "Dad. You need to call me. I don't want to be stuck here with your mother. This is wrong. I want to go home. You need to come back and get me out of here."

I hang up and am instantly filled with regret, with the sense that I've played this very wrong. It's the same regret of the e-mail that can't be unsent, the button that can't be unpushed—events that spool out in ways that can never be different now.

The butter-colored grass in that meadow sways in the breeze, and a girl bicycles up the road to the house. It's stupid, but I wish for some kind of sign from my mother. *Please*, I say. I just want to know she hasn't forgotten about me. We didn't have time to discuss a plan. You know, like, I'll send you rainbows or butterflies or shooting stars. She wouldn't have gone for those clichés, anyway. Everyone who's lost someone starts seeing butterflies. My father says it's the same thing as when you don't notice mattress sales until you need a mattress and then they're everywhere. I say take your comfort where you can get it.

I hear an odd sound then. It's a sudden gust of rattling and quaking, like a storm under that clear blue sky. There is rising rhythm, tribal beats, clattering gourds, a chorus that's joyful and triumphant and ancient, and it's coming from that shingled house. I squinch my eyes to read the words on the mailbox. RUFARO SCHOOL OF MARIMBA.

If this is my mother's sign, she's picked something you can dance to. I smile. Parrish Island, it's a strange place, all right. Damn, it's strange and kind of wonderful. And I can't shake the feeling that it's coming for me, drawing me in, like it or not.

Deception Loop connects to an inner road, the Horseshoe Highway. I try to map where I'm going on my phone, but this town resists technology. The service is spotty. I like how the big, grand places—forests, oceans, islands, mountains—make it known how they feel about our need to talk, connect, sign on. They say, *Not here.* They're the wise elders that make you sit still and be quiet.

I have to find where I'm going by getting lost. Someone has made a sign on this street that says BOBCAT ROAD. The words are etched into a wooden arrow and painted black. But when I look at the map I find in Jenny's glove compartment, I can't find a Bobcat Road anywhere on it. I drive in circles until I recognize an old oil tank with a huge banner on it, CONGRATULATIONS J & J! And then I see Point Perpetua Park and a corner where three roads merge. This is the way to town.

And all at once I am on the now-familiar street. There's the bookstore and a store called Quill, Sweet Violet's Chocolates and a tavern called Bud's. It is only a bit farther to the long, wide stone stairs that lead to the fat columns of the Parrish Island Library.

Outside the building, I recognize the spiky-haired librarian, who's leaning against a car in the lot and smoking a cigarette, which she tosses to the ground and stubs out with the toe of one black high-top Converse. She looks upset, like maybe she's been crying. I hate to see people crying. Sometimes I think the invisible barrier between me and other people is too thin. Their emotions come right in and become mine. Maybe I stand right outside my own fortress.

I go inside the library, and she follows, but we don't speak. Of course, I've known all day I'd be coming here. Snippy back-and-forths with Jenny were just an excuse.

Usually, I set one foot in a library and I feel my own internal volume lower. A library is a physical equivalent of a sigh. It's the silence, sure, but it's also the certainty of all those books, the way they stand side by side with their still, calm conviction. It's the reassurance of knowledge in the face of confusion. But now, even in my most favorite calm place, my heart is like a racehorse thundering down a track, because I'm looking around for a certain slim boy with a swoop of black hair. I'm looking for the owner of those fingers, which have marked my wrist in a way that feels lasting.

It's stupid to think I'll see him here again. School is out and it's a beautiful, warm day. Why would he be here of all places? Because I saw him here once? Because I'm willing him here now?

I've finished my last book, so the reading crisis has turned into a reading emergency, regardless. If I have to be stuck with my father's mother, I need some books to get me through it. So I wander toward the fiction and meander up and down the aisles. I can hear a mother reading a Babar book to a toddler who keeps asking "Why, Mama? Why?" A man is perusing a newspaper next to the B-through-Ds, where I want to look. A tall, thin guy with a scrappy goatee wheels a cart around and reshelves things, and I snoop on it, because stuff always looks better and more interesting on the cart. For a while, I forget that I'm there to see that boy.

But then, voices. I pop my head out of P-through-S to look, but it's a guy and a girl about my age, probably here only to make out where no one will find them. I wander back to the Leave Me Alone chair and sit for a while, trying to decide what order I'll read my new books in. The only person I can see is a very short uniformed policeman in True Crime, holding a book with a cover featuring a knife dripping blood.

This is pointless. This is how lonely I've become: ten thousand miles lonely, lonely enough to think some two-second encounter with a guy is going to change my life. I take the whole story I've created in my head (and, wow, what a story—you should have seen the fun he and I had, what a fine person he was, and how he made me laugh), and I toss it. I toss the whole thing.

"It's *you*," I say.

He looks at the librarian, hard. And I realize this magical, fateful appearance is not because of our shared destiny playing itself out. This is why he's come. Not for me, but in a convergence of events both lucky and unlucky, for her. "So, she didn't . . . ," he asks the librarian.

"She didn't."

"You smell like cigarettes. I can tell from here. Sasha, Jesus. Thirty days without, and now you've got to start all over."

"Just one. For God's sake. I deserve just one."

"You can't give up," Henry says. But he is looking at me when he says it. His sweet, large brown eyes are staring into mine. "You can't."

A book slips and drops from the counter. There must be fifteen of them, and I'm trying to take in the titles to find a common theme. There is one about Rome, with the half circle of the Coliseum on it, one called *Man's Search for Meaning*, and something about the Arctic. . . .

"Did you *read* all these?" I ask.

"Well, this one was boring." He holds up *The Roots of Latin Roots*. And I read the whole first chapter of this"—he picks *The Secret Life of Oceans* up off the floor—"before I realized I'd already read it."

"Henry reads more than anyone I've ever met in my life, including me," the librarian says. "He can't stay away from here, even on his days off. You miss pushing the cart, don't you? You love the cart. Admit it."

Visions of destiny and happenstance meetings evaporate fast. He *works* here.

"She's going to think I'm a geek."

"I don't think you're a geek," I say.

"He's not a geek." The librarian wipes her nose with the back of her hand.

If he is, he's the most beautiful one I've ever seen. His hair is short, but a swoop of bangs almost drops into his eyes. His face is narrow, breakable, but strong, and I am watching his mouth move, I realize. It's a lush mouth, with perfect lips. He's wearing plaid shorts with a crisp white shirt, sleeves rolled up, and his hands are now shoved into his pockets. I'm staring. He is maybe staring too, but it's hard to tell if it's all-on-his-own-staring or staring-because-I'm-staring staring.

"*Henry*," the librarian says. The word is a reprimand. "This isn't about *you*."

"You're right. I'm sorry. Sasha needs the love doctor," he says. "Oh God. That sounds bad. I'm just joking! I'm the farthest thing from a love doctor. I'm not even a love nurse. I'm not even a love, what, the ones that empty the bedpans." He turns his gaze toward the librarian. "She's going to think I'm a creep."

"I don't think you're a creep."

"He's not a creep," Sasha the librarian says.

I smile. But it's clear they have things to talk about, because Henry moves behind the desk and retrieves what I gather is his own coffee cup. "I'd better get going," I say. I think I'll just fly on out of here on wings of joy and happiness.

"Happy reading, Tess," he says.

I head out, look over my shoulder, and wave. He's watching me. I feel it. I catch this quickly too: He knows my name, so he and Elijah have discussed me. Now I'm sure. I don't know *how* I'm going to see this boy again; I only know that I *will* see this boy again.

They think I'm gone, but I hear her say it. I hear it just as I push open the heavy, important door of that library.

"Goddamn it, Henry. You can't go falling for someone right in front of me after I got my heart broken. It's just plain rude."

At the librarian's words, well, now I am also sure that the VW van is a van of goodness and that the waters of Puget Sound that I can see from these steps are twinkling a million diamonds that are mine for the taking. My emotions are rising, ready to overflow. The sun is smiling just for me. I am sure of this all the way back to Jenny's house. I word my apology to her nicely in my head. It's easy to give with my heart soaring with generosity. I watch it all: She accepts my apology. She cooks something great and we eat it together. Wow, look—Jenny and I are bonding. She's showing me the old family photo album. She's writing me into the will. Now I am in her next painting class and, man, I've improved. You should see my jar of flowers. It could go in a museum.

Thanks, Mom, I think, which I know is stupid. Talk about having a relationship with someone in your head. But it helps me to think she's Up There, supporting me like she always has. That even *dead* doesn't change some things.

It's a confusing game, though, because if I give her credit for Henry, do I blame her for what happens next, when I arrive home?

No. Mom would never destroy something she had handled so gently and cared for so dutifully and *loved*. It meant so much to her. It means even more to me.

I shriek when I see it. I can't even believe I'm seeing what I'm seeing. Someone has destroyed the most important thing I own right now. That someone is about twelve inches tall. He's wearing a guilty expression, and darts under the desk when he sees me.

"Vito! What did you *do*?"

The last pixiebell has been pulled off the windowsill, and there is dirt everywhere, and a small sausagelike dog treat that Vito's likely tried to bury in the only real dirt in the house lays near the empty pot. The plant itself has been flung or dragged to the other side of the room. It looks like a crime scene, with Pix's poor mangled body limp and dying.

"Goddamn you!" I scream. Vito makes a run for it. There's the sound of heavy footsteps dashing up stairs and Jenny calling my name.

I kneel down and try to scoop up the spilled dirt and shove it into the pot. I pick up the dead plant. I've never seen its roots, and now that they are exposed, it is hard to believe how delicate and insubs

"Tess," Jenny says from the doorway. Her voice is distraught, and she looks confused. She has no idea what this plant means to me.

I start to cry. She crouches beside me. I was at the library. I was driving. I was happy. I was not here when this terrible thing was happening.

"It's okay," she says. "We'll replant it, Tess. It'll be fine."

She cannot understand this. I may not fully understand it myself. It's just something I feel. The importance of it, the way this plant matters. It has been entrusted to me. Grandfather Leopold planted that stolen seed more than sixty years ago, and it has stayed alive because of my mother. She watered this plant and she stroked its leaves, and she moved it toward the sun when it needed sun and toward the shade when it needed shade. And now it is my job to keep it alive. It's the living link between us.

That link sits in my hands, and it doesn't look good, no, not good at all. The cloverlike leaves are already soft and weakened. Stems have been broken in parts. Bits of roots are scattered and wrecked. I don't know what to do but hold it gently. Jenny sets her arm around my shoulder, and at her touch, my emotions spill. Sorrow and guilt wrench inside, and I am struck with the horror of loss all over again. *I'm sorry*, I sob. *I'm sorry, I'm sorry*.

chapter eight

Lodoicea maldivica: coco-de-mer, otherwise known as the sea coconut or the love nut. This is the biggest seed in the plant kingdom. It grows up to twenty inches across, can weigh up to forty pounds, and is thought to resemble the buttocks of a large woman. Until the true source of the nut was discovered in 1768, it was believed by many to grow on a mythical tree at the bottom of the sea and was displayed in private galleries. Another myth: It traveled for miles and miles by ocean to plant itself into a new home. But no. It's a nut from a palm tree is all, a big, giant nut, and any found in the water are only floating around because they're rotten inside.

There are two major theories about the way life operates. You've got your Random Acts of Chaos model, which basically says we're all just leaves in a windstorm and who knows why we blow one direction or another, why some of us end up on a pleasant rooftop or swept into a yard waste bin. And then there's its opposite. This theory says life is all planned for us, every channel change or class schedule or stoplight, piece following piece. The way, for example, my father chose the exact same sociology class as my mother and then the way they saw each other again when Sedgewick and Sullivan had appointments with their advisers at the same time. If my mother's name had been O'Sullivan, I wouldn't be here. And *that* happened when Grandfather Leopold's own father changed his name just before setting foot on Ellis Island.

But as Jenny and I sit in her living room on her big, squishy couches, looking at the replanted pixiebell on the coffee table, I believe in another theory. This one is more like those horrible obstacle courses we had to run on Field Day in the sixth grade, deliberately laid out by the sadistic Mrs. Plemp, who also made us play flag football at recess. I hated those obstacle courses. You had to weave through the orange cones, which were set in front of the monkey bars, and after the monkey bars came those tires in rows, and after that, the long, narrow beams, and it all happened before crazed and screaming sixth graders, who wanted blood like the audiences at the Roman Coliseum. I ran my heart out as my shoe came untied, racing against Sophie Ekins, Mrs. Plemp's pet, the best athlete of both the boys and the girls, who once made fun of my Toucan Sam T-shirt, my favorite.

One hurdle after another. Obstacles both large and small to get past.

That's my latest life theory, and I am busy developing it as we sit on that couch with fingernails dirtied by potting soil.

We have tucked Pix back in as best we can. But it bothers me, this new, foreign earth, after the old had been Pix's home for so many years. I can't shake the feeling that this is just one more terrible thing on top of other terrible things. A sense of doom can become habitual; also the sense that God is like Mrs. Plemp and that there will always be more orange cones.

I am trying to tell myself otherwise, but the last pixiebell doesn't look good. It is not a plant that has ever grown much in height, and it's rather delicate for starters. In all the years that my grandfather had Pix and then my mother and now me, it has stayed about seven inches high, and its delicate leaves have fanned out only an extra inch or two. It isn't a particularly remarkable-looking plant, but that's not the point. It's *lasted*. Now its one long stem is still intact, but several of its smaller shoots have been bent and broken, and the cloverlike leaves are curved downward.

Every single thing is not some big death metaphor, but still, I think it. I think about Mom under the quilt, lying on the living room couch. She had caught a cold. You get a billion of those. And, sure, she looked bad from her treatment, with her thin, sucked-in cheeks. She'd lost so much weight—not only due to her burned throat, but because all food tasted like tin after her taste buds had been obliterated. But still, a cold is a pretty regular event. A cold doesn't kill you. A cold plus her kind of cancer doesn't kill you. She was tucked in, and the TV was on, and she'd made herself one of those awful chocolate nutrient shakes, but she let it sit there separating, and I had a bad feeling. I did.

It's the same feeling I'm having now, with Pix. I'm supposed to have faith that it'll be fine, but what I see doesn't look fine. In fact, it looks so un-fine, I almost don't want to look anymore. I feel bad about this, but I so much did not want to look at my mother on that couch that I volunteered to go to Rite Aid to pick up the codeine-laced medicine that was supposed to help her nasty cough. Outside, there was daylight and motion and the brightness seemed almost surprising. I stayed in that store a long time. I walked up and down all the aisles with the Christmas stuff. I just wanted to be with the boxes of tinsel and shiny round ornaments and lights and tacky decorations, like the Styrofoam snowmen with so much glitter you were permanently marked with it just by strolling past. Weeks later, I saw glitter on the sweatshirt jacket I was wearing that day, and the guilt almost sunk me. That day, I'd wanted to flee. I kept walking around Rite Aid, soaking in the Bic pens and Dr. Scholl's, because it all seemed so normal. Maybelline mascara was regular life, and it wasn't so *sad*.

"It'll be back to normal before you know it," Jenny says. She doesn't look too sure. "Anytime you replant something, it always looks a little . . . unwell. At first. Until it gets going again."

It has to. Maybe this isn't something anyone can understand, but it has to.

"Try not to worry," Jenny says. "You worry a lot, don't you? I see it in here." She points to her own shoulders.

I try to imagine letting go of worry, but this feels akin to jumping out of an airplane. Worry lets you hold on so that you, so that *no one*, falls.

"I know," she continues. "Worry makes you feel like you're *doing* something, but it eats at you."

But then again, worry can propel you to *actually* do something. Worry can propel you to make a plan for when global catastrophe strikes, a plan that involves our basic, most simple life-giving seeds such as corn, wheat, rice; a plan that unfolds inside the deepest layer of an icy mountain, in a structure constructed of reinforced concrete with rock caverns and doors of steel, situated high enough to allow for major climate changes and a seventy-meter rise in sea level—the equivalent of the simultaneous melting of all the ice in the Antarctic, the Arctic, and Greenland. Worry is not all bad. But we're not at that part of the story yet.

"Are you saying that you don't worry, Jenny? You should see *your* face." I don't particularly like Jenny noticing the way I operate. I don't want her hands tinkering with my personal machinery. It's time to switch the focus to her, and quick.

"Do as I say, not as I do." She chuckles.

"Dad obviously doesn't take after you. He's all about life in the moment, cha-cha-cha."

"It's all that—" She puts her thumb and two fingers to her lips and inhales.

"You know about it?"

"Since he was sixteen."

"I hate it," I say.

"I hate it too," she says.

Our mutual defection makes me feel bad. "He's not irresponsible about everything. I mean, he's a good father."

Jenny has her bare feet up on the coffee table. She folds her arms, purses her lips, giving her face a bunch of little wrinkles. She's keeping her mouth shut.

"He's consistently inconsistent," I try, and when she's still silent, I say, "Fifty-three percent of people ages thirty-nine to fifty have smoked pot. Thirty-six percent of those are chronic users."

She raises her eyebrows. "They say it freezes your mental growth at the age you start using it."

I think about this. "So, he's perpetually sixteen?"

"Well."

"I love him no matter what," I say.

"*I* love him no matter what," she says.

I may have a lot in common with this stranger after all. I almost feel a bond between us. Female solidarity, all that.

"What's that one?" I nod toward the large painting in front of us, four brown smears rising toward blue. "Trees? Earth, life, renewal?"

"I repeat myself." She shrugs in apology.

"Why did I not know you all these years?" I ask.

"Misunderstandings."

I wait for her to say more, but she doesn't. Something is poking my back in that couch. It's jabbing me. I feel around. Sticking out between the couch cushions is a rawhide bone. I hold it up.

Jenny shrugs in apology again, and then she smiles. "He loves to bury."

It's kind of funny, but I'm not ready to forgive Vito yet. He's forgotten all about his crime spree and lies in a doughnut circle by Jenny's chair, farting something awful every now and then.

"He is who he is," Jenny says.

My father calls me that night. Jenny and I are just putting away dinner dishes. I look down at my phone, expecting it to be Meg. She's left me three messages today, each increasing in panic. Something about Dillon breaking up with me. The messages make me feel like I'm watching a predictable movie. But it isn't Meg.

"Speak of the devil," I answer. Jenny was just telling me about my father in junior high—how he made a chessboard in wood shop and then decided he was going to go pro, studying books like *Bobby Fischer's Master Class*. I head for the stairs, plugging one ear as if there's a racket over here, even though Jenny has stopped rattling dishes in an obvious attempt to listen in. In the blue-white room, I shut the door.

"It's about time," I say. But there's no response. I think maybe he's hung up. "Are you there?"

"I'm here."

"What the hell, Dad? I mean, how could you do this? When are you coming back? This was supposed to be a short trip to the Grand Canyon! I don't even know where I am!" I hope Jenny doesn't hear this. I need to lower my voice. I sit on the edge of the bed, run my fingers along the lines between the quilted squares.

"Remember when we were in the Luxor? In Vegas? The place with the pyramid?"

"Of course I remember. What, I've been suddenly struck with amnesia?"

"Tess, something happened there. Surrounded by all those big sarcophagi, King Tut, whatever."

"King Tut in a hotel."

"A pyramid is a *burial place.*"

"I know that."

"It hit me. I was standing there, and the whole year, it caught up with me. We're in this burial place, and I'm thinking life, death, the fucking timeless shitty deal of it, and I'm lost. Suddenly fucking *lost.*"

"It was a *casino*, Dad. You had a crisis in a *casino.*"

"I tried to be okay, you know? We went on that roller coaster after? But it all felt pointless. I met your mom when I was twenty-one. I don't have a shirt in my closet she hasn't picked out."

"You've got that Bob Dylan T-shirt you bought at the concert. You've got Goofy playing golf from when we took that trip to Disneyland. You totally picked it out yourself. Mom would never buy Goofy. We weren't even in the store with you."

I don't have the patience for his dramatics. Couldn't he have told me any of this at the time? Couldn't we have discussed it over a slab of prime rib? Because, I'm sorry, he had both hands in the air on that roller coaster. He was shouting *Yeah, baby!* He bought the picture they took of the two of us in the front car, me clutching the bar looking like I might puke and him with his raised arms and wild-eyed joy.

Now I pace the floor; I trace the perimeter of the rug with my steps, heel to toe, heel to toe, all around the rug and back again. I don't understand where he's going with this, honestly.

But then he tells me.

"I realize . . . It's nothing. It's all pointless and meaningless without love."

I think of Cat-Hair Mary. Life's pointless and meaningless without someone to take care of you, more like it. In my heart of hearts, I don't believe this is about a crisis of faith or love or loss. I think it's about other things, like being a man, things I don't understand, needing sex, or some kind of physical comfort in the moment, even. "I want you to tell me the truth. Was this the plan all along? You'd get me to go away for a few days, and then we'd keep going until you got to Portland? How long have you been having the Classmates Reunion with old Mary? Because this is disgusting."

"No," he says.

"No, what?"

"No, this wasn't the plan all along."

I don't press for an answer about how long he and Mary have been communicating. I'm afraid to know.

"When are you coming back? I can't stay here forever. Meg has a job waiting for me at the day care where she works." This isn't exactly true. Meg has mentioned it only once, and I have no intention of taking that job. Meg is great with those kids. She loves every sticky, grape juice minute there, but I'd hate it. That sounds bad. Who hates being with toddlers? But I wouldn't be able to keep up the cutesy, high-pitched persona they require. Ten minutes would drive me to drink, and beer and graham crackers would get me fired for sure.

"Just give me a few weeks. I need to sort some things out."

"A few *weeks*? Now it's a few *weeks*?"

"Tess, come on."

"Come on, what? You can't just ditch me like this! You're supposed to be here for me, Dad. You're the parent. Even if you're confused and hurting, you're supposed to be here for me when I'm confused and hurting."

"It's the airplane thing, Tess. You know the airplane thing? I can't put the oxygen mask on you unless I put the oxygen mask on me first."

"That is such bullshit, Dad." I'm not the swearing sort, but my fury is rising up. It is one of Jenny's huge trees, a brown smear in a black paint storm, branches whipping and cracking. "That's just bullshit. I hate psychobabble bullshit like that."

He's silent. I can hear him breathing. My heart is pounding. I'm too furious to speak. We're both silent for a long while.

"I may never forgive you," I finally say. I feel like this might be true.

And then I remember that the pixiebell is still downstairs, and so is Vito. "I gotta go."

"Tess." He is asking something of me. Whatever he wants, I can't give.

"I've really got to go."

I hang up and run so fast down the stairs, it's lucky I don't break my neck. But the pixiebell is right there where I left it, slouched but undisturbed.

Jenny and I wait for a peach pie to cool. She wants me to stay with her as long as I want to stay. I don't exactly have a lot of other options, but I think that'd be hurtful to say. She cuts that pie, finally, and my phone bleeps. Dad has sent me a photo. It's a picture of a tall guy outside what looks to be a Mexican restaurant. The guy is leaning against a concrete wall, which is painted to look like a desert. The guy has tall hair. Really tall hair.

Jarvis Believed That Even Hair Could Get to Heaven, Dad's text reads.

But I don't respond. I don't respond because all I can see is Dad and Mary sharing a basket of tortilla chips as they drip salsa on plastic-covered menus and wait for their margaritas to arrive. And I don't respond because I know that if I were on a plane and the yellow masks popped out from the ceiling, I'd put the oxygen on my kid first. I would. I don't care what they say.

chapter nine

Amaranthus caudatus: love-lies-bleeding. The seeds of the amaranth, the most important Aztec grain, are ancient. At one time, they were so critical to the culture that each year, a month-long festival celebrated the blue hummingbird god that alighted upon the plant. A huge statue of the god was made from the seeds, and at the end of the festival, everyone was given a piece of the god to eat. In Victorian times, though, the flowers from the love-lies-bleeding plant meant only one thing: hopeless love. Giving them was a declaration that your heart was in over your head.

The pixiebell has not recovered from Vito's mauling. Two days later, I think it looks worse. It makes it hard to concentrate on what Meg is saying.

"—his *house*. What's she doing at his house?"

"Whose house?"

"For God's sake, Tess! *Dillon's!* Who have we been talking about for the last fifteen minutes!"

"So, he's moved on. Good for him."

"Don't you even *care*?"

"Remember when we used to wear pajama bottoms to school? We liked it at the time, but looking back, you realize how stupid it looked."

"Okay, okay. Fine. I shouldn't care about this more than you do."

"When he kissed me, I'd be planning my outfit for the next day. I'd be writing my thesis statement for a paper. Dillon and I had the kind of relationship that's more like trying out a relationship." I think I hear a car coming down the road. "Hey, can we talk later? I've got to go."

Jenny made an emergency call to Margaret MacKenzie from her class, who is also one of the leading members of the Parrish Island Garden Society. If anyone will know what to do about Pix, it's her.

"Okay, but it's weird having you gone," Meg says. "I miss you! And what your dad is doing . . . My mom won't stop talking about it. You know how she can get. She loves you. She's worried. You heard me, right? You can stay with us? For as long as you need."

Vito is barking up a storm. I can hear Margaret's voice. "Kiss you and hug you," I tell Meg. "Hug your mom. I love your mom."

"She never even uses her sewing room."

"I'm fine. See you soon," I say.

"I've never heard of a pixiebell," Margaret says. She is sitting close to me. Her perfume is flowery sweet, and her sweater is purple like a lilac, and her tennis shoes are buttercup yellow, and her eyes are blue as a forget-me-not. She's a walking flower. She's a walking flower, and she's old, and she's the vice president of the Parrish Island Garden Society. I feel a rise of hope. Pix is going to be all right.

"This may be the only one." The pixiebell is on the kitchen table in front of us, like a patient in the doctor's office. "The *last* one," I say.

"Really?" Jenny says. I've never told her that part—how rare this plant is. How one of a kind and important.

"Oh my," Margaret says. "That's remarkable. How did you come to possess it?"

"My grandfather had a friend who was a professor of botany. He stole the seed from the professor's rare collection during a Christmas party. The plant was extinct, but my grandfather grew the seed, and now we have the last pixiebell."

"Wonder if he ever got invited back," Jenny says.

"Well, I'm speechless," Margaret says, but she sticks one finger in the soil, then pulls it out. "Soil seems fine enough. What's happened to the poor dear?"

"'Mary' overwatered it in Portland before Vito tore it apart."

"'Mary'?" Margaret says. She even puts the sarcastic quotation marks where they should be.

"Don't ask. And then there's all the moving around we've been doing. It's been riding in Dad's hot truck and ending up all kinds of weird places. . . ."

"Hmm." Margaret clucks. "A plant needs stability. Let's

keep it in one location for a while. Somewhere sunny, where it can recover. Water judiciously. Look, these leaves are yellowing." She puts her crinkled finger to them.

"What does that mean?"

"Lack of nutrients, most likely. I'm not sure."

"You're not sure?" Jenny asks. She looks worried.

"I grow roses."

"Maybe someone else in the Garden Society might know?" Jenny suggests.

"Well, our president, Ginny Samuelsson, also grows roses. You know Ginny. She and Frank live out near Little Cranberry Farm?"

"Maybe one of the other members?" I say.

"There's just Ginny and me, dear. Now that Miss Poe has passed on, there are only the two of us. Wait a minute. Stay right here." She scoots back her chair and heads out the front door again. Jenny looks at me from over the table.

"My confidence is lagging," she says.

"Mine too," I admit. It's not just lagging; it's become like those sorry blocks of wood our neighbor Bennie Milstone used to tie to the back of his bike, pretending they were hydroplanes. They'd bump along nicely for a while until they busted. We wait. And wait. "She's been gone a really long time," I finally say.

"Maybe I should check on her," Jenny says. "She might have . . ." This starts us giggling. We're both having the same wrong thought.

But Margaret comes back alive and well and singing, "Here

I am!" as she returns. Vito barks up a storm again as if he's never seen her before, which unfortunately speaks to his intelligence level. "I walked out to my car, and when I got there, I forgot why I went."

"That happens to me all the time," I lie.

She plunks a box on the table. "Well, this should do the trick."

Rose and Flower Food. Jenny and I lock eyes. I roll mine. Of course, Pix is neither rose nor flower.

"That's it?" Jenny says. "Water, light, soil, a box of food?"

"It's not rocket science," Margaret says, pretty snippily too.

It's become abundantly clear. This is up to me. If I don't do something, and fast, the last pixiebell will be gone for good.

Jenny's Internet connection is from the caveman days. "I think I'll go and make lunch and eat it and then take a drive in the country and then come back and then maybe this page will have loaded," I say.

"Technology." She shrugs, as if she could take it or leave it.

Well, I could use some cyberpower right now. I need knowledge and information at high speeds. There's got to be more I can do for Pix than the plant equivalent of unplugging your computer and plugging it back in again. Less water, more light. That plant is going to *die*. "I'm heading out," I say.

"*I'm* heading out," Jenny says. "I'm meeting with the gallery owner where I show my work."

"Oh." I forgot for a minute that Jenny has her own life.

"I can drop you off or you can take the bike."

"Bike," I say.

"In the garage. See you for dinner?"

"Not sure," I say. Jenny raises her eyebrows, but says nothing more. I shut Pix away in my room, safe from Vito. I say the simplest, CliffsNotes version of a prayer: *Please*.

Jenny's garage has that dusty-musty smell, and there's all kinds of weird stuff inside—old wood chairs and a tin drum and a store mannequin that makes me startle before I realize it is not a psycho killer. The bike is in a spiderwebby corner. It shouldn't even be called a bike, which is something one associates with a mode of transportation used by Lycra-clad athletes, a sleek object that zips and speeds a person to their destination. No, this is a *bicycle* with a half-flat tire and a *basket*. I think I saw this thing in *The Wizard of Oz*. I roll it outside.

Vito is sitting on the front step, waiting for his life to get more exciting. "Forget it, Toto," I say to him.

The bike has only one speed, and so by the time I get to the library, my calves are burning like I've just climbed to base camp carrying the yak. I set the bike down on the steps. I suppose I should chain it up, but this town seems to be the type of place where you could walk around dressed in hundred-dollar bills and people would only nod and smile. The bike isn't exactly screaming *Steal Me*, anyway. It's missing a kickstand.

The last time Jenny rode it was obviously before the invention of helmets.

"Henry will be here in ten," Sasha says. I didn't see her over there, huddled by the Dumpster. She tosses down her cigarette stump, twists the toe of her boot back and forth to put it out.

"I'm not here to see Henry," I say.

She snorts. She has a pinch of her T-shirt and is fanning it back and forth. "This"—she taps the cigarette butt with her toe—"is between us, right?"

"Right." I'm on Henry's side about the cigarettes, but it's none of my business. She's not going to be able to hide her crime, anyway. No matter where a person smokes, they stink like they've been sitting in a tavern, listening to Kenny Rogers music and waiting for their turn at the dartboard.

Inside, the guy I saw with the cart last time is behind the desk. "Larry," Sasha calls to him. "Jenny's granddaughter."

"Hey, Jenny's granddaughter," he says. His T-shirt says SAVE THE MALES, and he's got scruffy chin hair that may one day, with hard work and dedication, grow up to be a real beard.

"Tess," I clarify. "I'm looking for stuff on plants."

"Cool," Larry says. He steps from behind the counter, motions me to follow.

"Plant care?" I say. "I've got a sick plant."

"Righto." He's a man of few words. I can tell we're getting close, though, because we pass books on volcanoes and the universe and forests, and now the spines have all turned shades of green.

"I don't know anything about it, and I really need to know."

Larry is flicking out volumes expertly with the tip of his finger. They are stacking up in my arms. *The Big Book of Plant Care. The Houseplant Survival Manual. The A to Z of Plants.*

He stops. "Wait. What kind of plant?"

"I don't know exactly. A rare kind."

He thinks. He tosses *How to Keep Almost Any Plant Alive* onto the pile. "Ba-da boom," he says.

"Thank you."

"You oughta ask Henry." He gestures to the desk, where I am thrilled to see that Henry has arrived, just as Sasha promised. My heart starts thrashing around. He's just as beautiful as I remembered. Those cheekbones! Sweet, vulnerable cheekbones! He is poking Sasha in the chest with one finger. He knows a bad tavern when he smells one. "The excellent Mr. Lark has a mind like an encyclopedia."

"Okay. Thanks again."

I settle myself at the table where I saw Henry for the first time. I keep peeking over at the desk. Henry, in his thin-framed, elegant, odd way—he's got an unusual charisma. I open the first book, but I'm not concentrating very well. I forgot to bring paper and pen to take notes, and the print in the book is small, and the words in the table of contents might as well be written in a foreign language for all they sink in to my poor, overcome brain. I turn the page anyway. I'm such a faker. The words on the page say something like *Henry, Henry, Henry.*

He doesn't see me, or if he does, he doesn't come over. He's sipping from a coffee cup, his hair falling over his forehead when he leans in. He's laughing at something Sasha says. It's one of those full laughs, not a heh-heh laugh, but a soul laugh, a spirit laugh. It makes me laugh too, as I sit there reading "Make the most of compost" again and again. The line sings.

He'll be coming over. I'm sure of it. How can he not notice me? But there are library manners at work, the unspoken agreements that happen here—having your nose in a book conveys a request for privacy, and in this place, it's a request that will always be respected. I will have to catch his eye, give the visual cue that lets him know it's okay to interrupt.

I'm plotting and scheming as passively as a heroine in a Victorian novel when the library is overtaken. It's like a SWAT team invasion of mothers and toddlers and babies and strollers and commotion. I think about getting under the desk like we used to do for the earthquake drills in California. Okay, maybe there are only six or so mothers, but all that struggle with doors and equipment and squirming bodies and bags slung over shoulders and bits of conversation and one kid falling and crying and suddenly it's like you might as well surrender with your arms up.

Well, sure, I missed the sign. STORY TIME, 2:00 P.M. Every mother on the island must be here. And, wait, a father too. I recognize Nathan from Jenny's art class. He's got a little girl on one hip, as a bigger boy walks behind, dragging his feet as if he is being sent off to camp to do thirty years' hard labor.

"Max, my man," Henry says when he sees him. A smile starts at the corner of the boy's mouth. "Glad you're here. Couldn't manage all these little kids without you." Nathan looks grateful. A toddler with blond ringlets sees Henry and runs up to hug his leg. He pats the child in a way that's both shy and game, the way you'd deal with an unfamiliar but affectionate relative at the family reunion.

This I have to see.

I keep my nose in *How to Keep Almost Any Plant Alive* by Dr. Lester Frank for as long as I can: *True for every living being in this world, excessive amounts of any one thing is often detrimental, even if that substance is necessary for survival. Plants need the essentials that we do: water, food, light, a good place to be grounded, and loving care, which encompasses the spectrum from attentive tending to leaving alone, based on what the plant most requires.* The noise in the library appears to die down; the squirming bodies settle, and the cries and whines are appeased with comfy laps and Baggies of crackers. I push my chair back. I do not look over at Sasha, as I don't want to catch her catching me. Well, certainly I can browse the plant care shelf myself without it being some big deal, can't I?

I give my face what I think is a concentrated, studious look, one that conveys how I need, and will now seek, a particular piece of information. There is a great view of the children's section over by the plant books. A perfect view. If all of life is designed in advance, piece following piece, then old Mr. Dewey Decimal one day had an idea that would eventually, years later, allow me to see Henry Lark from the perfect vantage point between 570—Life Sciences and 580—Plants.

Henry Lark sits in a child-sized chair, his knees high. He holds the book in front of him so that his audience can see the pictures, and he is making the sound of a duck if a duck could talk. Nathan's boy, Max, is in front next to him, legs crisscross applesauced. He wears an expression of importance, Henry's right-hand man, but this expression quickly fades as Henry reads, and Max twists himself to see the pictures better. Henry's voice plays all of the big emotions, duck worry and then duck fear and then, finally, duck joy. The whole scene—Henry with those high knees and the toddlers solemnly munching fish crackers and a baby drinking juice out of a bottle while patting her mother's cheek—well, I reverse my ungenerous feelings about small people. They are earnest and their hands are chubby and, aside from the bottle drinker, are so focused on Henry that even I feel that the duck's story is the most important thing in the world right then. If that duck doesn't find his way home, I will be heartbroken.

The story finishes and there is a smattering of applause. It's so sweet, you want to cry. And then comes a second book. This reading includes puppets, I hate to say. Henry would kill me for telling that part.

Story time is over. Henry reaches his hand out to a pregnant woman who can't quite make it up from her position on the floor. Babies grasp his index finger as he says good-bye. He is ruffling the hair of kiddies, and that's no exaggeration.

He is the sincerest politician, the one-man army of goodwill. He doesn't gush—he actually is holding a piece of himself for himself, you can tell. It's self-respecting. The mothers love him. I have given up hiding. I am leaning openly against the outer edge of 500—Natural Sciences and Math. I've been wrong not only about toddlers but also about what life itself has to offer, and this is a change of feeling so intense that I understand already that Henry is a force my poor sorry self will now have to reckon with.

Henry slumps in the chair across from me. "The puppets," he says.

"What happens in the library stays in the library," I say.

"You hold the power to blackmail."

"Hmm . . ." I consider. "The photos are valuable, then."

"Larry says you have a plant emergency."

"Larry says you're an expert."

He laughs. "God, no. I've read a few books, is all."

"On everything."

"Barely scratched the surface," he says. "What've you got?" He leans across the table, and I slide the book in front of him. The leaning—it brings him close to me. I smell evergreen boughs again and something that is just Henry. It shoots me some pheromone arrow and I am felled.

"Food, water, light. I need more than that."

"After the basics are covered, it's helpful to know exactly what you're dealing with. What *kind* of plant. The name. Then we can find out how to care for it specifically, heal its particular issues. Varieties of plants have their own problems, et cetera, et cetera. . . ."

"I know its name. It's a pixiebell."

He leans back. "Hmm . . ." He runs his hand through his hair, then fixes those eyes on me. I hold back a shiver. "Okay. Well, then. Come on."

Lead and I'll follow. But unfortunately he's only heading to the two computers that sit on a long counter. It's funny, because in San Bernardino there are twenty or more. Henry stands, hunching over, and I hunch beside him. Our sleeves meet, have incredible chemistry, and find out that they could live happily together forevermore in a laundry basket or dresser drawer.

"Pixiebell," he types and then waits. "Slow," he apologizes. But I don't mind the bad Internet connection now. Take your sweet time, oh leisurely loading pages. Let us curl up here as night arrives, while the information makes its way across the web-desert by camel.

"Damn," Henry finally says. The results show thousands of possibilities.

"Children's clothing, screen names, songs . . . Should we try 'pixiebell plant'?"

He does. We wait. He turns his head to look at me, grins, and shrugs. His lips are impossibly lush, pouting without pouting. But it's the eyes that get me. Brown eyes so sweet, they just melt me at my center.

"Wait. Here," he says. "Found it." He pulls up an article about a trailing plant. Part of it is in French. There's a photo. The plant has wide, stout leaves and white flowers.

"That's not it."

"No?"

"Not even close. Maybe we should try 'rare.' Or even 'extinct.'"

He stands straight. Looks at me full on with new interest. "Really?"

"The last one of its kind."

"Wow," he says.

"I can't let it die."

"Yeah," he says. It's a *yeah* with an *of course*. A *yeah* that's final. This yeah tells me that he understands the weight of the situation without me saying more.

"No results," I say. "How can that be?"

"This might be more challenging than we thought," Henry says. "Let me do some looking. Or come back tomorrow and we both can. We've got to be able to find 'pixiebell' somewhere."

"'If we know who it is, we know how to love it,'" I say. And to Henry's baffled expression, "Dr. Lester Frank."

"Right," Henry says.

Having made no real progress, I'm worried about Pix, but I'm happy, too. *Come back tomorrow*, Henry said. It's good enough for me. It's more goodness than I've come to expect in quite a while. But then he says something else. "I work a half day today. Done in"—he looks at his watch—"three hours and fifteen minutes. There's this burger place out by Hotel Delgado. The name sucks—Pirate's Plunder. But the burgers . . . It's one of the best places on the island. You been out there yet?"

"No! I haven't really been anywhere yet. That sounds great." *So* great.

"Burgers okay? I mean, meat?"

"There's something you should know about me," I say. "I've never met a beef product I didn't like."

"People around here . . . *Tofurky*."

I pretend-shudder. "After I watched that documentary about cruelty to tofu, I gave it up forever."

"Free-range soybeans only for me," he says. "It's more of a natural life for them before they're—" He slices one finger across his throat. We are cracking ourselves up.

"Six? Here?" he says.

Six, here. Seven, eight, nine, anywhere.

chapter ten

Chamerion angustifolium: fireweed. The seed of this plant uses its lightness and a set of wings to ride the wind to new places. It is also known for its ability to transform the most desperate locations. This seed will choose lands destroyed by fire and oil spills and war, blanketing them in no time with color and life.

Jenny is not my mother, but still. It seems only polite to call and tell her where I'll be. After all, she might worry, same as Mom does (did). Since I got my driver's license, every time I drove two blocks to 7-Eleven, Mom expected to get a call that I was in a fiery crash. I'd always tell her not to wait up when I went out, but she always waited up anyway. She didn't want me to *know* she stayed up, though, same as she didn't want me to know she followed behind me in her car the first time I walked to school alone when I was in the third grade. Still, I'd hear the toilet flush or the porch light would go off not long after I got home.

My instinct is on target about Jenny, because she answers the phone with, "Is everything all right?"

"I've been abducted," I say.

"Aliens, I hope," she says. "We can make some money when you sell your story to the media."

"I'm going to hang out down here and then have dinner with a friend."

"What friend?" she asks. I've forgotten that she knows everyone on this island.

"Bud, who owns Bud's Tavern," I say. "I know he's fifty and has a little problem with the bottle, but love conquers all."

"Bud wouldn't touch anything stronger than an Orange Crush. They hold the Beer and Book Club there, and he has an iced tea."

"Henry Lark," I say.

"Henry Lark?"

"You sound surprised."

She doesn't respond to this. "Is it a date-date?"

"We just met. At the library. But yeah. I mean, he isn't coming over in his suit and tie to talk to my father about his 'intentions,' but we're getting a burger."

"Oh," she says.

"What? What does that mean?"

"I said, 'Oh.' It means 'oh.'"

"It was the *way* you said 'oh.'"

"I just thought Henry was . . ."

"You just thought Henry was *what*?"

"Um . . . busy with other things. People. People and things."

"Not as busy as you thought, I guess." I sound smug, even

to me. I rather love feeling smug. Smug is kind of terrific, which is why it gets us into so much trouble.

"Can Henry give you a ride home? I hate to have you bike in the dark. Deception Loop is pitch-black at night."

"Glad to see you're making friends, Tess," I say in a Jenny voice.

"Glad to see you're making friends, Tess," Jenny says.

Three and a half hours sounds like no time to kill, but it ends up feeling like three and a half days. I keep checking the time, and five more minutes have passed. Of all objects, clocks are the cruelest. Beds, second.

I stay in Randall and Stein Booksellers for a long while, and then I head to this chocolate shop, Sweet Violet's. I have the great idea to buy some caramels for Henry and me tonight, but I end up spending a ridiculous amount of money. I could have practically bought a used car for the price. They pack them in this box with a big, fancy bow, too, and it looks like more of a gift than I intend. Then I sit on this hill in a park that over-looks the water, and I read *How to Keep Almost Any Plant Alive* by Dr. Lester Frank. *Like all living things, plants require you to understand their personal language. Misunderstandings can have dire consequences. You must listen hard to what a plant is silently saying.* Dr. Lester Frank sounds a little crazy. I look for his photo in the back of the book. No luck. *Plants, animals, and children are the only beings who deserve unconditional love and the only ones you can trust to return it.* He sounds crazy *and* bitter. I can picture Dr. Lester Frank, lovelorn and alone, in his green-house loft, surrounded by spider plants and violets and delicate orchids that only he understands.

The park I'm in is a little creepy—one of those dark, foresty sorts, with tall trees and grills set in concrete squares and empty picnic tables. The film version shifts: Now Dr. Lester Frank is burying a rejecting lover in his backyard with a gardening trowel. It's time to get the heck out of here.

I am wishing for a shower and a toothbrush. At the thought of my date with Henry, my heart is back on the Las Vegas roller coaster, alternatingly plunging to the pit of my stomach and then rising high with victorious hands in the air. The old me thinks about calling Meg and telling her about my upcoming date, but the new me decides not to. Instead, I ride my bike a block over and find a pharmacy. By the back counter, I see a familiar violet sweater and white head. It's Margaret, filling a prescription. I dart around, trying to avoid her, and buy a small fortune's worth of travel-sized products: deodorant, toothpaste, lotion. My purse is bulging with tiny boxes.

The little toothbrush actually unfolds. Cool. I was never this nervous for a date with Dillon. I freshen up back at the creepy park's creepier bathroom. I confess I even shave my legs, which is an awkward and disturbing thing to do in there. I hope I'm not murdered before my date with Henry. It'd be easy to do me in with a gardening fork when I've got one foot propped up on the park bathroom's metal sink.

Finally, it's time. I walk my bike back to the library instead of riding it, so that the wind whooshing past doesn't mess up my hair. I am waiting for Henry on the library steps when he puts his hands on my shoulders from behind. I didn't even hear him coming. He gives me a little shake. It is the second time he's touched me, and I want a third and fourth and fifth time, more times, until I stop counting.

Henry's got a satchel over his shoulder, and it's bulging like a fat man in a tank top. "New books?" I ask.

Henry shrugs. "I'm an addict."

"Are you interested in *everything*?"

"Hmm. Not football. Not . . ." He thinks. "Eighteenth-century porcelain?"

"Basically everything."

"Okay, yeah," he admits. "Hey, do you mind if we stop at my house? I forgot my . . ." He pats his back pocket where his wallet would be.

"No problem. I've got my bike, though. Should I leave it here?"

"Nah. Kenny Travis will steal it. Kenny Travis will steal anything. He once stole the Jarvises' Saint Bernard when it was tied up outside the bank. Anything goes missing, you head over to Kenny Travis's house and his mother will give it back."

"His mother?"

"Kenny's eight."

I am in Henry's car, and I am having a hard time believing I am in Henry's car. It is an old Mercedes, but don't get the wrong idea. The car is about a thousand years old, and it's yellow and boxy, and every now and then it backfires and I think we've just been shot.

"Car mechanics," Henry says. "I'm not interested in car mechanics." We've wedged Jenny's bike into the backseat, and the front wheel is spinning near our heads. I watch Henry's profile. I'm engrossed, because this is Henry driving a car. His elegant hands shift into third. I am on a fact-finding expedition in a new country that is Henry. There is a string of wooden beads hanging from his rearview mirror. There is an orange water bottle by my feet. A notebook with a worn leather cover is shoved partway into the fold of the front seat.

"Journal?" I gesture to it.

"Nah." Henry blushes, though. Even the tips of his ears are red. This is what happens to Henry when he lies, although I don't know that yet. "Just stuff. To do. Thoughts, whatever. Here we are."

It isn't where I pictured Henry living. He has turned into a neighborhood with a sign marking its entrance: WHISTLING FIRS. It's a regular suburban-type street, with regular houses that all basically look the same. It's the sort of place where someone's bound to have one of those outdoor banners that remind you what holiday it is. And, yep, there it is. Decorated with a beach bucket and sunglasses, so we'll all know it's summer.

But wait. What's this? There's a guy washing a car while wearing a kilt. Maybe I've been out in the sun too long.

"Is he wearing a kilt, or am I seeing some sort of Scottish mirage?"

"He's wearing a kilt. That's Jackson. He went for a hike once on Mount Conviction a few years ago and got lost. Like, about-to-die lost. But then he heard the sound of bagpipes and followed it to safety. Now he wears a kilt."

I make that *heh* sound in the back of my throat that means *Are you kidding me?* But Henry's serious. He beeps his horn and Jackson waves and Henry waves back as we turn in to a driveway. I've learned my lesson: Don't let a suburban ranch house fool you. *Nothing* is regular on Parrish Island.

Inside, Henry drops his bag by the door. I snoop around on my Henry fact-finding mission. There's a grandfather clock and a bench to sit on while you take off your shoes. Past the hallway, there's a staircase and a living room with a plaid couch and a rocking chair and a table with lots of magazines.

"Hell-o!" he calls out, but no one replies. "I live here with my mom. My dad lives on Velveeta."

Well, this is what I hear him say, anyway. I am thinking this sounds like a very limited diet when Henry notices my puzzled expression.

"It's a boat. *La Bella Vita*? 'The Good Life'? He usually docks it down by Hotel Delgado, but he's taken it to Tortola for a while."

"Oh, wow. Cool."

He takes the stairs two at a time, and I'm not sure what to do, so I follow. And then there I am in Henry's room. I am hoping his mom doesn't come home right now. It'll look bad if we're in there alone. In the film version, my shirt is buttoned wrong and Henry is tucking his in as fast as he can, but it's only the wish-fear of my imagination, because Henry is focused on the task at hand. He is searching around his desk for his wallet and feeling in the pockets of jeans, which gives me a minute to take in his room.

Books. Books are stacked and tumbling. Books are packed into bookshelves. Books are lying open on his unmade bed and are piled up to create a nightstand. There is also an old, sepia-toned map of the world on one wall, and on another, an elaborate boat in a rambunctious sea. I recognize that boat.

"Hey, the *Dawn Treader*," I say. I am so happy to see the *Dawn Treader*, I can't even tell you. I loved that book. The Chronicles of Narnia are my very favorite books ever. "Those are my very favorite books ever," I say.

"I knew I liked you for some reason," Henry says. He is kicking a pair of boxers under the bed so I don't see. He is feeling around in his sheets. "Aha," he says. He holds up the wallet and gives it a look that says that sneaky bastard has nothing on him.

"Great job, Encyclopedia Brown," I say. Why his wallet is in his sheets, I'll never know.

"We're outta here," he says.

And we are. But not before I see it. On his desk, there's a picture frame. It is not odd that he has a picture frame on his desk, of course. The odd part is that it is facedown. At the sight of it—well, I know right then that there is more to be found out about Henry Lark than I first thought. More than favorite books, or fathers on boats, or boxers. A photo too special to get rid of but too painful to look at means one thing and one thing only—Henry Lark has had his heart broken.

On the way out of Whistling Firs, Henry waves to an old lady whose house has a FOR SALE sign out front.

"Mrs. Martinelli," Henry explains. "They're moving. She and her husband bought a cocoa plantation on the Ivory Coast. I've known them since I was, like, seven."

"Does anyone around here just do anything . . ." I was going to say *normal*, but that sounds bad. "Usual?"

Henry looks at me with a baffled expression. He has no clue what I mean. The car deodorizer hanging from his rear-view mirror is shaped like a Twinkie and smells like vanilla, and nothing in this place strikes him as odd.

"Everyone has a story, I guess," he says. "And every person's story is either a little crazy, or a lot crazy."

"I guess that's true."

"You too? I mean, what are you doing on Parrish? You've never exactly stayed with Jenny before, at least for any length of time."

"Does everyone know everything about everyone else here?"

"Pretty much," Henry says. He is a careful driver. Or else, his car just can't make it over thirty. Every time he turns a corner, the bike wheel starts spinning by my head as if it's in the lead and rounding the last bend in the Tour de France.

"I didn't *know* I was coming here."

"Surprise trip?"

"You could say that."

"Got it. It's private."

"No, it's fine. I don't mean to be mysterious, but we're having a happy evening, and in this particular story there's a dead mother and an AWOL father."

"Oh."

"See what I mean?"

"Jesus."

"So let's talk onion rings for now. First thing I should know about you. Onion rings or fries?"

"Both," he says.

"I knew I liked *you* for some reason."

The Hotel Delgado overlooks the sound. It's a stately, old white building with a huge porch and green shutters. It's something you'd see in Key West, and I know this because we went there once, Mom and Dad and me. Dad wanted to go because he read that the town celebrated the setting of the sun every night. He thought we shouldn't miss a place like that. The celebration turned out to be touristy, with people selling conch shells and T-shirts and handing out pamphlets for discount marlin-fishing trips, but this did not dampen my father's enthusiasm one bit.

The Hotel Delgado, though, is surrounded not by lush palm trees and humid air, but by tall, shadow-casting evergreens and shaggy pines. There are several docks in front of it, packed with sailboats and cruisers, and it all seems like a big surprise because you drive and wind your way down a forested road and then there it is, this place so beautiful and strange at the same time.

We order our burgers and have the polite, first-date argument over who will pay. *No really. But I asked you. But that's not fair. Okay, but next time . . .* When we get our food, the bags are stuffed and hot to the touch. We sit down on this bench in front of the hotel and spread out our food. I'm feeling the happiest I've felt in a long time. Henry asks me about San Bernardino, and I ask him who the biggest jerk in his class is. (Zachary Riley, who's a bully.) I ask him what he wants to do after graduation next year, and he asks me who in *my* class I'd take to a deserted island. (Xavier Chung, who is still in the Boy Scouts.) We are joking and talking about our mutual dislike of foreign films, and he is telling me how much he hates movie theater butter squirted on popcorn, and I am about to tell him my popcorn story (don't ask), when my phone buzzes. I decide to ignore it, but then it buzzes again, and I start to imagine that Jenny has fallen on her kitchen floor. She is writhing in pain and has scooted inch by inch over to the phone, where she has just barely managed to kick it off the hook with her one unbroken leg.

"Sorry," I say to Henry.

"No problem."

I fish my phone out of my purse. It's not Jenny at all. It's another text from Dad, a photograph of a pregnant woman sitting on a bench, maybe at a bus stop. There are four children with her. One boy has a toddler on his lap, one kid is under the bench itself, and another is hitting his own head with a drumstick.

Shawntel Believed That One in Five Children Is a Musical Prodigy.

I turn off my phone. "My father."

"Do you need to talk to him?"

"Not *now*. Anyway, he's in Portland. With the creepy-cat-lady version of the baroness in *The Sound of Music*."

"Mine's in the Caribbean. With the ditsy twenty-two-year-old version of the baroness in *The Sound of Music*."

"Hmm. I guess we've got something in common."

We both say it at the same time. "I knew I liked you for some rea—"

We're laughing again. We've been having so much fun that I almost forget how attracted to him I am. I've forgotten all about those sweet eyes, and that swoosh of hair, and that ever, ever so slightly imperfect smile. I'm comfortable with him. That's the shocking thing. It is turning out that Henry is not only gorgeous, but that he could be a great friend. You always hear people say that about the person they're with—*he's my best friend*. But I never felt that way about Dillon. There were basic best-friend requirements he didn't fulfill. He didn't really get me. We didn't make each other laugh. He refused to say *I'd feel the exact same way* if he didn't feel the exact same way.

"Doesn't your friend Elijah work here?" I ask Henry.

"He's a waiter. I was trying to see if I could see him." He looks over his shoulder. The restaurant is inside the hotel, but it also spills out onto the hotel porch. There are a few couples having dinner at tables with white tablecloths and candles that have not yet been lit. "In an hour, this place'll be packed."

"I could never work in a restaurant. The whole balancing-dishes-on-your-arm thing. Have you always worked at the library?"

"There and the bookstore." He gives me that apologetic look again. But there's no need to apologize for loving books. It's one of my favorite things about him.

"I worked at our Parks and Recreation department. I was a helper in this horse class for kids."

"So you like horses," Henry says. "Okay, horses are cool. Did you know they've been around for fifty million years? The first one was as tall as a fox."

"I don't know much about horses at all. I'm not sure I *do* like them. They kind of scare me. All I had to do was walk one around a ring with a kid on its back and, you know, clean stalls."

"Crappy job."

"Ha-ha. Hilarious. Hey, do you always laugh at your own jokes, Mister?"

"I think so. I think I do."

"Wait. I do know something about horses. The whole measuring thing. Each hand stands for four inches. If a horse is sixteen-point-two hands, the point two stands for—"

"Two fingers," Henry says.

I smile. It's possible that Henry and I understand each other. He seems to realize this too. We are both quiet. The sun is beginning to turn to that bittersweet orangey yellow of twilight, and the water is shimmering gold, and the boats are bobbing and sloshing, and it makes this bench a perfect bench for a kiss. At least Henry is looking at me and I am looking at him, and though we barely know each other, there's the sense it's about to happen. I shut my eyes for a moment, ready for him to lean in. But I open them again and find Henry looking out toward the evening sky.

He takes my hand, gives it a little shake. "You're funny," he says. "I like you."

"I like *you*," I say.

And, there, yes, it is happening again. His eyes are on mine, and I am feeling this connection between us. It feels old. Like it's already been, or will be, for a long time. This bench no doubt has seen many kisses; it is likely just all in a day for this bench. But what happens next is not what I expect. Henry leans in and kisses my forehead. It is so tender; it is so *kind* that I almost want to cry.

"Wait," I say. "I almost forgot."

I go reaching for that stupid bag of stupid caramels. And that's when I knock my purse off the bench, spilling everything from travel-sized deodorant to travel-sized shaving cream. At our feet is a Rite Aid for gnomes. Thank God no tampons come rolling out. The perfect kiss moment is ruined as I grasp for the tiny Crest box and the bitty bottle of Scope, the folding-out toothbrush, and the SPF 35 lip balm.

What can I say? I'm an idiot. But right then, I'm the happiest idiot on Parrish Island.

chapter eleven

Solanum aethiopicum: scarlet eggplant. Or mock tomato mini pumpkins. Or Japanese golden eggs, among other names. The seeds of this plant look like tiny pumpkins, the fruit looks like a tomato, and botanists believe it's an eggplant. Some say that slaves snuck this seed onto ships, which carried it to South America, but others disagree. Whatever name you choose, and whatever you decide to believe about it, this one keeps you guessing.

The day after my date with Henry Lark, I returned to the library. Henry and I looked in some books and made a few more Web searches on Pix's behalf, but mostly we just laughed and had fun. And after that, we started spending more time together. To help Pix, I decided to try belief again, lazy, denial-filled belief, which also included a ritual of hopeful watching. Henry Happiness made me feel like everything was going to be okay, including my mother's plant.

But now, ten days after my date with Henry Lark, Pix takes a terrible turn. I feel sick just looking at it. The stem is bare a good three inches from the bottom, and more and more of the clover-shaped leaves are turning yellow. Some have dropped and are sitting on the soil, delicate and wrong.

"Look." I show Jenny.

"Oh no."

"Nothing seems to be making a difference."

"Try to feed it again today," Jenny says. She is frowning. She's getting more comfortable with me, or maybe I am getting more comfortable with her. Her hair is all morning electric-shock therapy. It's sort of Einstein hair, but I'm not one to talk. My hair seems to live it up at night, same I was sure my Barbies did, after I shut the doors of the Dreamhouse.

"Maybe I'm feeding it too *much*. Maybe I should only do it every other day. . . ."

Every solution seems full of possible peril. I remember this feeling. Maybe if I . . . Maybe if I don't . . . There are real options to try at first. There is medical knowledge and there is a treatment plan and there are a million zaps of radiation fighting unseen evil cells. There is soil and light and more water/less water. But then there are the other things you try. Being extra nice to the people around you. Deals with God where you promise eternal good behavior and a lifetime of devotion to the poor. The logic goes downhill from there. Maybe if you eat this grapefruit or don't eat this grapefruit, or think this thought or don't think this thought. If you are positive and optimistic, or see the worst coming, or if you don't jinx the outcome by doing X or Y or Z . . .

"I don't know what to say, Tess. I don't have any answers."

"I've been terrible. I've neglected it. I really only spent those two days trying to find out what's wrong. I haven't tried hard enough, and now look." I'm scared. I'm afraid to even breathe next to Pix. Every time I even accidentally bump the sill, another leaf falls.

"You've been living your life."

"I've been really selfish," I say. I don't know how to explain this, but the thought socks me in the stomach. I wrap my arms around myself. That feeling hurts so bad.

"You've been having fun. That's good."

Fun—it sounds so lame, especially to excuse my irresponsibility. This plant is the last one of its kind, and if it dies, it's gone forever. Pix has been here getting sicker and sicker while Henry and I have been hiking up to the lighthouse at Point Perpetua Park, and walking to the waterfall on Mount Conviction, and picnicking in Crow Valley, where rabbits jumped around us and llamas looked on, blinking their long eyelashes.

I've been thinking only of myself, and I've completely ignored the most important things.

"You've also been seeing a lot of Henry," Jenny says. She runs a finger around the top of her near-empty coffee cup.

"Why do you say it like that? You always sound worried when you say his name."

"I don't 'always' anything." She gets up. Pours herself more coffee. Vito gets to his feet. He's continually convinced that any

human movement means TREAT. He is right maybe 5 percent
of the time. How he lives with those odds is beyond me.

"What are you worried about, anyway?"

"I don't want you to get your heart broken."

"Why would I get my heart broken?" My heart has already
been broken, and I'm still here, aren't I? I pour myself a cup of
coffee too. I've discovered that I like it after all. It's something
new about me. I make it with lots of sugar and milk and sip
it while sitting in Jenny's rocker on the porch. I think about
Henry and smell the early-morning waters of the sound as the
caffeine zips around inside me like a magic carpet.

"A million reasons. You don't live here permanently, for
starters. What am I saying? It's none of my business."

"We don't know what might last or not. How do we ever
know?"

"Well, okay. You got that right."

"Why did I not know you all these years?" I try again. I
keep trying this one.

"Misunderstandings."

"You *always* say misunderstandings."

She sets her mug down on the counter. "Are you okay here,
Tess? Is everything all right with you?"

"Sure."

"I hear you at night. Last night, the night before. Crying."

I don't know what to say. I didn't think she could hear. I usually put the pillow over my head and fold it down. "It's just . . .
night. It's hard. At night, it's just me and me and no one."

"Your dad said a few weeks. A few weeks are almost up."

"Yeah, now that I'm having a good time."

"Do you want to go home?"

"Are you sick of me?"

"God no. I love having you here. It's the happiest I've been since your fool of a father moved out when he was eighteen. I just put myself in your place. You must miss it there. Even if you like it here, that's your *home*."

I try not to think about it. When I ride Jenny's bike down her gravel road, when I turn left at the mailbox and head into the town of Parrish, perched over the waters of the sound, waters known for their healing powers, waters cradling slumbering whales, I do my best not to think about craggy, dry mountains of yellowed grass or the green sign over G street, WELCOME TO SAN BERNARDINO. When I sit once again in Jenny's painting class, with Nathan holding the brush in his teeth, with Margaret telling stories about her beloved Eugene, and with Elijah's painting becoming clearer and more distinct (two figures, two faces), I try not to think about our stucco ranch house or our own street, where some people have rock beds for lawns. I try not to think about my own room with my own pillow and the huge rainforest poster I made in the ninth grade on the back of my door, or my mother's kitchen with the canisters for flour and sugar, or the Snow White cup from Disneyland where we keep our keys.

When Jenny gave me money and I bought some new clothes in town, I tried not to think about my own clothes in my own closet, that orange sundress and my Tall Heels, as Mom used to call them. Or sitting on the floor of Meg's room, doing homework together. Or Meg's stupid cat, Felix, who weighs almost twenty pounds and who lolls around like one of those sea lions on the rocks in Santa Cruz. All of it has gotten mixed up with what I miss most—my mother. My mother's eyes, my mother's voice, my mother's *presence*. Her alive self, just *there*. My mother and our old life together. My father, even. My father *with* my mother. Sure, there was the frustrated way she'd say, *Thom-as!* Or the time she drove off mad, slamming the front door and making the windows rattle. But, too, she'd ruffle his hair. He'd slap her butt as she passed and she'd laugh. I missed him, just him, too. The way he'd yell at those guys on the talk radio stations. How he'd say he was going to make himself a peanut butter and peanut butter sandwich.

One person can hold it all together, and you don't realize that. Not until they're gone and the pin is pulled, and *everything* is gone.

"We could—I could go to California and stay with you for a while," Jenny says.

I can't picture her there. She belongs here, on this strange northwest island of foggy cliffs and odd characters. Vito lies back down by the refrigerator. He groans like an old man. He sounds disgusted. Once again, his TREAT hopes have been dashed. "I want to stay here."

And I do. Because, here, I have that vacation feeling, the

one where you've left your life for a while, and good riddance to it. Here, I am someone new. Here, all that has hurt me is 1,294.6 miles away. And here, there is Henry.

I drop my bag on the counter.

"Henry's not supposed to fraternize at work," Sasha says. "If it's personal, then you wait for personal time."

"Ha," Larry says next to her.

Sasha's got on combat boots and a T-shirt that says I'M PERFECT. YOU ADJUST. She's typing something into the computer. She barely looks at me. I'm assuming the typing has something to do with important library business.

"This isn't personal. I need help."

She looks up. She reads my face. She must see how desperate I'm feeling. "I guess this can wait. Henry's not in until noon."

I sneak a look at her screen.

Abby—I am lost without you. . . .

Larry catches my gaze and rolls his eyes. I roll my eyes back.

"So. What's the big emergency?" Sasha says.

"It's about a plant."

"You still having plant problems?" Larry says. Larry shoves his hands into his jeans pockets. He looks perturbed. "I thought Dr. Lester Frank would do the trick."

"It's not the end of the world when you make a bad book match, Larry," Sasha says.

Larry scratches his sort-of beard. "Man. I can't believe it." He is seriously disappointed in himself.

"It wasn't a bad book match," I console. "Dr. Lester Frank was awesome."

"Kind of a dark dude," Larry says.

"Yeah." He's right about that. "But Dr. Lester Frank said the same thing as Henry. If nothing else works—and nothing else has worked—you need to know exactly who the plant *is*. You need all the information you can get about it. It may have its own *issues*."

"Like Sasha," Larry says. She socks him.

"All right." Sasha grabs a notepad and pen, and both Larry and I follow her over to the two computers. "Name?" I tell her. She types fast. Once again, two atoms split and become a goo that becomes a mass that evolves into our planet before the search results appear. I don't know how they stand it. They seem perfectly okay waiting. I guess if you don't know that things can be better, you aren't bothered when they're not that great.

"This'll just take a minute," Sasha says.

"Ha-ha. Good one," I say, but Sasha's serious. I don't want to tell her that Henry and I already tried this very same search. It seems rude, for starters, but she also seems capable of placing one of those combat boots on your throat when irked. I am standing close to both of them. Larry's denim shirt smells like cigarettes too.

"You guys!" I say. "I thought smoking went out in the seventies."

"It did," Sasha says.

"Being a librarian is a stressful job," Larry says.

It doesn't look stressful. Honestly, there's no one here. Just that same guy reading the newspaper and a mom and her son in the dinosaur section.

"You got your average low-maintenance book lover, sure," Larry says.

"Just here to get their fix," Sasha adds.

"But most everyone else has some problem that you're supposed to cure with—"

"Information."

"And I *believe* in information—" Larry makes his voice sound like a preacher's. "Information solves ninety-nine percent of the world's problems."

"But there's that other one percent that information can't do a damn thing about. Love and loss, baby," Sasha chimes in.

"*How to Make Love Last? Grieving the Loss? Moving on from the Past?* Come on, *A Farewell to Arms?*" Larry argues. "I was talking about acts of God. Tsunamis. Dying plants."

"All right. Here it is. *Pixiebell.*" Sasha shows me the same wrong plant Henry found days ago.

"That's not it."

"That's not it?" She looks shocked.

"Not even close."

Larry takes off. In a flash, he's back. *Photographic Atlas of Botany, Field Guide to Plants, How to Identify Plants in the Wild.* He shoves them at me.

"Region?" Sasha asks.

"Amazon? I think Amazon."

She takes off. In a flash, *she's* back. *Amazonian Beauties. Botanical History of the Tropics. Flora and Fauna of the Rainforest Regions.* I never knew librarians were so competitive.

Larry goes back to the front desk to help a young woman looking for books on making organic baby food. Sasha sits next to me at a table. Her eyes look determined through her round glasses. "Maybe that's not its exact name? It'd help if we knew what it looked like."

"Well, it's kind of . . ." I try to describe. I am using my hands. Sasha slides her notepad over. I've already told you what a great artist I am.

"It's a tree?" Sasha asks.

"No, no."

"That looks like a man in a hat."

"Wait," I say. "I'll be right back."

I dash out, taking the steps fast. I've got Jenny's van, so I pop in and speed the tin can back to her place. Jenny's out front, mowing a small patch of grass with a push mower. She's wearing a sunhat, and Vito is trotting back and forth behind her.

"You should let me do that," I say as I run past her.

"That's a deal," she says. "What are you—"

But I don't stop to answer. I fly up the stairs to my room. I have the last pixiebell on the windowsill, barricaded by three wooden chairs stacked with books, just in case that crafty little mutt learns how to open doors. I don't want to take any chances. If dogs could be cat burglars, Vito would be one.

I get out my phone and take photos of Pix from all angles. I take so many that it should have had its hair and makeup done. I have a film-flash image of Pix romping in a meadow and sitting thoughtfully by a stream and leaning against a fence, like the girls do in their senior pictures. Pix stars in a photomontage sequence in my head. You should have heard the music.

I wish I'd known to take more pictures of my mom. Especially during the last week that I didn't know was our last week. I had no idea that the pictures I had were the only ones I would ever have.

"Don't die," I say to Pix.

I am driving so fast to the library that Jenny's old van is shuddering. But I almost slam on my brakes when I see them. It's Henry, and he's arriving at work. He even has a brown lunch bag in his hand. I would love that about him, that brown lunch bag, but I don't have the chance to love it. I'm taking in what I'm seeing. Of course I recognize that glossy hair—that perfect Millicent hair—and those perfectly quirky Millicent clothes: the crocheted bag, the cotton dress with the embroidered hem. They are arguing. At least that's what it looks like. Henry's arms are folded. She is leaning toward him, and her mouth is curved in an ugly manner. So. Millicent gets ugly when she's mad.

I wish he hadn't seen me, but there's no hiding that van

as I turn into the library parking lot. They wrap up their business quickly. Whatever it is they're discussing, it's obviously private. Millicent strides off toward Main Street. Henry runs his hand through his hair and heads inside to work without waiting for me.

Right then, I know. What I just saw has something to do with that photograph in his room, the one that was placed downward, too painful to look at. Millicent doesn't think Henry is so weird after all.

I rejoin Sasha, who is still sifting through my table of books. Henry is in the back somewhere. I hold up my phone. "Photos," I say.

"Hand over the goods," Sasha says.

I do. She peruses the pictures, cooing and clucking and saying, *Aww*, like the pixiebell's an adorable newborn. I didn't know librarians could be such smart-asses either.

She smacks a book down in front of me. *Botany Through the Ages*. "Get to work, Miss Marple."

And then there he is. "Hey." Henry slides into the chair across from me. My heart starts going crazy. Henry's got that effect on me. The I-want-to-jump-in-his-lap effect. The I-want-to-go-somewhere-together-forever effect.

"Hey," I say.

He doesn't say a word about what I saw outside and what he knows I saw outside. Instead he says this: "I'm going to save that plant if it's the last thing I do."

"Pixiebell or bust!" Sasha's glasses have slid down her nose a little. She's got *Flora and Fauna of the Rainforest Regions* in front of her and is taking notes. She stops to madly scratch her pen in circles, trying to get the ink to flow again.

Who knows what happened between Millicent and Henry. Who cares, really? Because something much more important is happening right now. This is clear: We are now on a mission.

chapter twelve

Ricinus communis: castor bean. The most deadly seed that exists, the castor bean takes many drastic measures to protect itself from harm. First, there's its hard, spiny, spiky outer layer, difficult to crack through even with a pair of pliers. Second, the seeds hidden within have their own hard shells. Finally, intact seeds will do no harm if human or animal swallows them, but poisoning will occur upon biting or chewing. Death will come to your average person after eating only four to eight seeds. Message? Keep out.

First there is the isolated, nearly inaccessible locale—one thousand one hundred kilometers from the North Pole. And then there is the Svalbard archipelago itself, set in the distant and largely unknown Barents Sea. And then the island in the archipelago, a remote island, a barren piece of rock really. And then the mountain. And then the ice, the years and years of ice. Then, of course, the guards, and the polar bears, and the blizzards to fight your way through. The layers of iron are next. And then the secret keys needed to open the dual blast-proof doors with their motion sensors, the two airlocks, the walls of steel-reinforced concrete one meter thick. Finally, the separate rooms. The containers. The specially wrapped packaging. And inside, the seeds.

How many layers does it take to keep something—an object, a person, a memory, a secret—held safe forever?

I don't know how many layers are enough. Maybe there are never enough layers. But I like to think there are. I like to think that there is a place in this world tucked so deeply into the farthest and most barren spot on earth that anything placed inside will always be there, no matter what.

Still—two problems. One: I can't seem to hold on to my mother. She gets farther and farther away every day. This is a horrible admission. I am so sorry. There are those dreams, sure, the ones that seem so real, where she's alive and we're together and I am *so happy*. But when I wake up, she's gone, and the dream fades, and the truth is that it was only a dream. Another day has gone past, and the days just keep adding up, the ones she's not been in.

Two: When it comes to secrets, all those layers only compel them to rise and show themselves. Secrets want to be told. Secrets *need* to be told. Secrets are our worst and hidden failings, buried down, down, down. But they crave the light, and even more than that, forgiveness.

"If I see another picture of another plant, I will scream," I say to Henry.

"My eyes are crossed from all that reading. Are my eyes crossed?" Henry looks at me and crosses his eyes.

"They look the same as always," I say.

We are sitting on the floor in his room, leaning against his bed. This is the thing about Henry and me. It's like we've *been*, for a long time. We have a rhythm together. He's the boy version of me, only I'm not nearly such a genius. Or so talented. Or so attractive. Our *selves*, though—they know each other.

His mom is downstairs, having a glass of wine with a friend of hers. I can hear them laughing, two women talking about men. Every now and then, they do that *Oh my God, I know!* shriek of mutual understanding. My chest aches a little when I hear it. I keep thinking about Mom and Betts, friends since the sixth grade, sitting at our kitchen table eating chips and that horrible bean dip that comes in the can that my mother loves (loved) for some reason.

Henry's mother, Jess, has his brown hair and brown eyes, and she is very quiet and kind, more quiet than my mom, and she made us spaghetti and asked me about school in California. It was all so ordinary. Henry put the dishes in the dishwasher. He hugged his mom and thanked her for dinner. The three of us ate ice cream in chipped bowls in the living room, and then Henry sat down at this piano they have in there.

I thought the piano was decoration. It was old and there were spider plants on top of it, and more books. But then Henry lifted the lid. He placed his hands above the keys. I thought he was joking. I even laughed. I was about to make a crack that he was Beethoven Boy when he started to play. And then nothing was ordinary. The notes were so beautiful and

Henry was so beautiful playing that I held my breath. I'd never heard anything more beautiful in my life.

"*La Campanella*," Henry said when he was finished. "The little bell. Let's say that was for a certain plant."

My heart was in my throat. "God, Henry. Is there anything you can't do?"

"Car mechanics," his mother said, but her voice was soft. The way he played, as if he felt every note—it shifted your soul around.

But now we are sitting in his room, and I notice that the framed picture is no longer on his desk. Henry shuts a book he unearthed from under the bed. It's volume P–R of an old encyclopedia from the early 1900s. I tap his foot with my foot. I am ready for Henry to stop thinking and talking about plants. I'm ready for him to kiss me, although this hasn't happened yet. The unkissed kiss sits between us. I feel it, held back and becoming more and more desired. The absence of it has its own energy. Absence in general does.

"I don't understand why we can't find it anywhere," Henry says. "I can't stand an unsolved puzzle. There *is* an answer. This is driving me *crazy*."

I keep kicking him and poking him. I want him to stop thinking about the pixiebell now. I want him to *see* me. I want him to look all the way in and not see anything else. "*I'm* driving you crazy," I say.

He ignores me, persists. "Okay, you said your grandfather stole the seed."

"Right. From a professor." I tap his toes again. I shove my shoulders against his shoulders to knock him over a little.

But then I picture it. It is Christmas, sometime in the early 1950s. There is a party in a large brick house. There is mistletoe hanging in the doorways and Christmas carols coming from a radio, and the professor's wife has made a spread of food on the banquet table downstairs. Grandfather Leopold excuses himself—

"*How* did they know each other?" Henry asks.

"They were friends, I think." They were friends, so Grandpa Leopold had been to this house before. He knows where the professor keeps his collection: in the long, thin drawers of his study. He knows which drawer holds the professor's biggest prize. He excuses himself after everyone is tipsy, after the professor is distracted with hot rum and tinkling glasses and the cutting of the bûche de Noël—

"Friends?"

"My grandfather once gave a speech at the college where the professor taught. Grandfather Leopold was an inventor. Didn't you think inventors were only in Disney movies? Because he actually discovered some kind of adhesive used in making shoes."

"What did he want with that seed?"

"Well, he was a klepto."

"Oh."

"And the plant was supposed to have some kind of healing powers or something."

"Healing powers?" Henry's eyes light up. "You should have said so before. This is a good lead."

I have stopped poking and tapping Henry. "I forgot all about that part. Until just now."

Yes: Grandfather Leopold sneaks up the stairs and looks both ways before crossing the hall to the professor's study. He tiptoes across the floor. He slides open that drawer. It's as if the seed is being offered to him. It is right there, in a tiny glass box labeled *Pixabellus imponerus.* "Wait," I say. "I know it! I know the Latin name. I've heard it before. My mother said it. When she told me the story. *Pixabellus imponerus? Emponeris?* Something like that. 'Emperor.' I remember thinking it sounded like 'emperor.'"

Henry stares at me. I stare back. I'm excited, but I'm not sure if I'm even right. Something feels like it clicks into place, but the memory is hazy enough that I can't trust my sudden insight. We've been reading Latin words all day. Still, I can hear my mother saying this. I can even see her. She is cleaning out a closet. She tosses me a fedora, and I put it on. I am maybe ten. The hat smells musty. I take it off because I wonder whose head it was on before mine.

That was Grandpa Leopold's. More stolen goods, she says. *My plant in the kitchen? The last pixiebell?* Pixabellus imponerus. *He* stole *it! That's my* father *we're talking about! Well, actually, he stole its seed. A rare seed. From an extinct plant. He snitched it during a Christmas party. My own father! No one ever wanted to have him over. He'd slip your stuff into his overcoat. He'd steal* your *overcoat under* his *overcoat! That man could never stand to follow the rules.*

"*Imponerus?*" Henry repeats.

"Yeah."

He's thinking.

"This is great news, right, Henry? We know how to find it now." I make a bold move to celebrate. I sit on him. I straddle his lap and look right at him. I am happier than I've been in so long.

"That's right," Henry says. The tips of his ears are red. I've embarrassed him, I think, by landing on him like this. But I don't care.

"This is it, Henry. We've got hope now. It just came out of nowhere."

"This plant. It's really important to you," he says.

"Really important."

"Because it was your mother's. And before that, her father's."

"It sounds stupid."

"It's not stupid," he says.

"It's just a stupid plant." I can see her in her sweatsuit, and she is healthy and making blueberry muffins from a box, stopping to fill a coffee cup with water and pouring it gently into Pix's pot. *You old thing,* she says to it. *You keep on keeping on.* My throat tightens. I might cry.

Henry doesn't know what to do with his hands now that I am sitting on him. He uses them to prop himself up, and then he sets them on my arms as if to balance me, and then he gives up the struggle and takes my hands in his. I like this idea best. "Tell me something about her," he says.

"Ah." I look up at the ceiling. So many things. I love it very much that he asks. "Okay," I decide. "She was a pretty peaceful sort of person. I mean, she liked to read, like us. She didn't like big noisy places. My dad loves them. He loves anything big and noisy. But Mom, no. Hated Costco. Hated shopping malls. But she went to Splash Kingdom on my third-grade field trip."

"Water park?"

"Uh-huh."

"Five million screaming kids?"

"Exactly. I wanted her to go *so* bad. She even rode the bus with us. It was, like, an hour and a half of 'Jingle bells, Batman smells, Robin laid an egg.'"

"She really loved you."

"I don't like the past tense yet." Damn it. My voice gets wobbly.

"*Loves.* Loves you."

"And it wasn't like she was some great big hero because she died. People make it sound like that. She was just her. She worked part-time in a dentist's office. She loved Oreos. She got lost whenever she had to drive somewhere new. She was just my mom."

"That's the real loss. Her regular self."

He gets this. And for getting that, I give him *this*. I lean in.

His lips are so soft, and he's not here with me at first because I've surprised him. But then, there. There we both are, and the kiss becomes that kind where you forget you're even in a room in a house in a town. You're just so present and transported that *place* has altogether disappeared, and it's only mouths and mouths and together and together and everything else has vanished, even—*especially*—sadness.

When I pull away finally, Henry's face is blazing.

"Oh wow," he says.

"Finally," I say.

He is shifting around, and things are suddenly awkward. I don't know why, because awkward is usually the last thing I feel with him. I get off his lap. I don't know how to read him.

"We should . . . ," he says.

"Okay. Yeah, I'd better . . ."

Maybe it's *me* being awkward. Maybe I am just thinking about Millicent with her perfect blond hair and icy blue eyes in comparison to my plain brown ones. Or maybe it's him being awkward, thinking the same thing.

Henry walks me to Jenny's van, which I've parked on his street. I lean against the van door, and Henry stands in front of me.

"*La Campanella*," I say. I remember him at that piano. Honestly, I don't know if I'll ever forget it.

"Next time I'll play you the violin," he says.

I open my eyes wide, drop my jaw.

"Kidding. I don't play the violin. Hurts my chin. Makes my neck do this." He lolls his head to one shoulder.

I laugh.

"I like it when you smile," he says. And look. The awkwardness is gone. He kisses the tip of my nose, then gives my mouth a quick sweet kiss too.

"I like it when you do anything with your face," I say.

Jenny is already in bed when I get home, but she's left the porch light on for me and a table lamp. I am shushing Vito because he's jumping around and barking, completely ignorant of the fact that sleeping people require quiet. He's so thrilled to see me, I might as well be roast beef on legs.

"Be quiet, you idiot," I say, and I give him a dog treat from his jar. "Go to bed, squirrelly squirrel."

I sneak up the stairs like I'm guilty of something. Well, I'm guilty of plenty, but not tonight. I haven't exactly been tearing up the town on a rampage of booze and sex. Still, a sense of wrongdoing hangs around me like bad perfume. I smell it even after I've showered. I close my door quietly behind me.

There's a note on my pillow. *Call your DAD!!!*

Oh, Jenny, aren't you one to talk? How many years went by that we never heard from you?

At the word "Dad," though, I see him running around like crazy, hanging a billion Christmas lights and setting up the enormous blow-up snowman, until the big moment when he flips the switch and Mom and I cheer from the lawn. I

158

miss him, but it's a complicated missing. The word "Dad" also doubles the sense of *wrong* that sits just under my skin. We are both guilty. Our mutual wrongdoing is loud between us, and sometimes it just feels better to not hear it. He probably feels the same way about me. Cat-Hair Mary shuts out that particular noise. Well, maybe Henry does too, but never mind.

I don't call. Anyway, it's late. Instead I go over to where the last pixiebell sits on the windowsill. I think of my mother holding one hand to her chest while she tried to breathe, saying, *Sharp*. She gathered her things—her purse, her phone charger—but she was taking her time about it. Dad was getting impatient. I think he was scared. She said she wanted to shower first, but he said, *Anna, for God's sake!* and they argued. She was coughing hard and spitting bad stuff into a Kleenex. *Jesus, Anna! What are you thinking!* I felt the same way he did. She stopped to wipe the kitchen counter! She watered the damn plant! *Mom. Stop it. Everything's fine. Come on!* We both snapped at her. I regret that so much.

"*Pixabellus imponerus*, don't worry," I say to Pix. "Help is on the way."

If this were a movie, Pix would be sitting in a circle of moonlight, and one of its leaves would slowly drop then, turning and falling like one of the rose petals in *Beauty and the Beast*. You'd know that time was running out.

But it isn't a movie, and so the plant just sits there in the dark. I get into bed. I am thinking about Henry. I am being my own selfish self, per usual, closing my eyes and hearing music, remembering mouths, feeling hopeful. You'd have thought I'd have learned something by now. Obviously I haven't, because in all my prancing in the meadow of love, I don't even notice that the pixiebell has changed form. Cells are dividing, its stem is shriveling, and something is beginning to grow at its very top, where the last few leaves remain, as I drift off to dreams of hands on piano keys.

chapter thirteen

Bhut jolokia: ghost pepper. Specifically, the purple ghost pepper. Seeds of the purple ghost pepper are said to be extremely rare and can be purchased only through black markets and shady online sellers. This purple pepper is reported to be the most elusive and hottest pepper on earth. Only one problem: It's a fake. While the traditional *Bhut jolokia* indeed grows one of the hottest peppers, the seeds of the "purple ghost" that are sold are likely from a different plant altogether. No such seeds truly even exist.

He calls me while I am still asleep.

"I need to see you."

"Henry," I say. I look over at the glowing green numbers on the little clock by the bed. "It's four thirty in the morning."

"We have to talk."

"Now?"

"Tomorrow is fine, I guess. I work at two. Do you want to come by the library?"

"You're worrying me," I say. "Why are you up at four thirty in the morning? You sound so awake."

"I have something important to tell you."

"Tell me now." Wait a minute. I don't know if I want to know what he has to say after all. "No. Don't tell me. Is it terrible, Henry?"

"Not terrible. I just don't know what to do."

"It's all right," I say. It's Millicent, I'm sure. That turned-down picture. That scene in the parking lot.

"You seemed so happy tonight. I feel bad."

"I changed my mind again. Tell me." Dread sneaks up wearing his dark cape, pulls me in. How could Henry love me when I'm such a regular girl? I have no amazing talent. I have no elusive, icy charisma. I have no quirky, embroidered shoes. Mom and I usually just went to Payless ShoeSource, for the Buy One–Get One sale.

"There's no such thing as a pixiebell," Henry says.

I've been clutching my pillow, ready for the blow, and I loosen my grip out of sheer surprise. "What?"

"I've been up all night. I'm almost sure of it. The name. *Imponerus*? It means 'impostor.'"

"Wait. You know Latin?"

Silence. I can almost hear him shrug. "I think your professor was having a little fun with old Grandpa Leopold."

"You're kidding."

"Uh-uh. I knew it the minute you said it, but I've been up since, making sure."

"If it's not a pixiebell, what *is* it?" I scrunch my eyes, try to see Pix in the dark.

"No idea."

"Is it even extinct?"

"No clue."

"I don't know what to think about this," I say.

"Think that we are back to square one. Even one-er than square one."

The dark of night is lifting ever so slightly, turning from black to a light purple. Birds get up early here apparently. I hear them chattering out there. I am waking up enough to understand what this call means. "You've been up all night? Really? Why are you doing this for me, Henry?"

"I can't stand a mystery."

"That is such bullshit. You like me, Henry Lark. A *lot*."

It's bold, but I don't mean to be. It's more of a curious realization. A kiss is one thing. Four thirty in the morning is another.

"Of course I like you a lot. How can I not like you a lot? You're so kind."

"I'm not kind! I barely like babies. I'm too critical. I hate people who talk in bookstores. I'm selfish. I don't like to share my French fries. I'm impatient. I make that scoffing noise in the back of my throat whenever I see those pictures girls take of themselves holding out their phones—"

"Tess! Stop. Why do you do this? You are so hard on yourself. People can see your good heart from two miles away, whether you like it or not. I want to help because you need help. Now shut up and help me make a plan."

"It's late, Henry. Or early. Whichever. My brain is still sleeping. I'll come by in the morning with all my great ideas."

"Fine."

"I'm not full of inspiration at"—I look at the clock again—"four fifty-seven."

"Tomorrow," Henry says.

"Tomorrow," I agree.

"Jesus. You're a good person. Stop beating yourself up."

"Henry? Thank you. Ten thousand miles of thank-yous."

Henry and I hang up. I can see Pix's sad, sick outline over by the window. All this time, the last pixiebell has kept its own secrets.

I picture Grandpa Leopold opening that drawer. Downstairs, someone plays the piano. The gathered guests begin to sing. *O come all ye faithful . . .* Grandpa Leopold thinks he looks quite natty in his double-breasted wool suit and Dobbs hat, his silver cigarette lighter in his pocket. He feels so clever as he removes the tiny glass case from the drawer and slips it into his trouser pocket. He is pleased with himself, filled with the glorious buzz of wrongdoing. He rubs his hands together even.

But downstairs, the professor is pleased with himself too. He is downright smug and full of holiday cheer. When he hears the creak of the stairs and the footsteps just above his head where his study would be, the professor smiles. He raises his glass, and he makes a toast to peace on earth and goodwill toward men.

I finally realize that the weeds in the jar that Jenny uses in painting class are fakes.

"They're plastic," I say. I am rubbing a leaf between two fingers.

"Silk," Jenny corrects. She claps her hands together twice, getting everyone to settle in and get to work. She wants this class to be over quickly, she confessed earlier. She's got a new painting she wants to work on.

"All this time, I thought they were real."

Jenny tilts her head just like Dad and gives the weeds a look. "Not what you thought? Still beautiful," she says.

"I guess." I'm having a hard time seeing the beauty through my own disappointment.

"Sorry we're late," Nathan says. Margaret follows behind him, red cheeked and hurrying. "The baby escaped out the dog door and into the garden."

"They thought it was another Lindbergh kidnapping," Margaret says.

I am watching Elijah and Millicent, their blond heads bent together. They are the kind of people who turn your insecurity into one of those out-of-control monsters that invades a city in the movies. Right now my insecurity is raging and stomping and eating parked cars. I am sure they are talking about me.

Cora Lee from the Theosophical Society grabs my wrist. Her hand is a little claw. Her white hair is piled up on her head like a wedding cake. A tiny bride and groom at the top would finish the look.

"Here," she says. She is pressing something into my palm. It's the same way my great-aunt used to try to slip me ten bucks whenever she visited. All that covertness and whispering, you'd think old auntie was giving me a couple of ounces of cocaine.

But Cora Lee has not slipped me spending money. It's a tiny vial, one of those thin glass ones like perfume samples come in, with a teeny-tiny stopper.

"What's this?" I whisper back.

"A tincture. For the ill. Sprinkle a little on the soil."

Word gets around fast on Parrish Island.

"Thank you," I say. Cora Lee winks.

Behind me, Elijah and Millicent laugh. The monster chomps on a building and eats a baby stroller. I'm sure they're laughing at me. I even start to get a little pissed. I run through my options. Spin around with a glare. Make a snotty comment about that little white skirt Millicent is wearing. It's so tiny, you could bake a cupcake in it.

I choose a combo plate—I spin *and* I comment. "Shrunk in the wash, huh?"

It all worked out so beautifully when I imagined it, but they are not following along with the thoughts in my head. They only look at me as if I've begun speaking in tongues. No one says anything. Elijah taps the hard end of his paintbrush against his teeth. He's waiting for something.

"Um," Millicent says. "Excuse me, Tess."

She is looking up and around me dramatically. She is leaning far to the right, sending me a message. I'm standing in front of the fake wildflowers, and she can't see them.

"Sorry," I say.

I want to leave, but I'm too humiliated to go anywhere. I feel shame, but also rushing roils of hatred—partly for them, but mostly for myself. The monster turns inward. He always does. Back to the lair. I return to the chair Jenny has set up for me and paint more brown smears as Margaret hums something sweet and Elijah perfects one of the two noses in profile. I sneak glances at Millicent and count all of the ways we aren't alike.

Four ways, five. I make the crosshatch with brown paint. Six: She does not have a good heart that you can see two miles away. But love isn't always about good hearts or even good reasons. Sometimes it is wild and unaccountable, I know. I can feel that wildness in my own heart when I look at Henry. It is beyond reason. I don't feel the way I do because he is good with small children, or intelligent, or talented. I feel the way I do because he stirs something in me. He could be a bank robber and I'd offer to drive the getaway car.

Margaret is motioning to me. She's making an urgent *Come here!* face and tossing her head in a manner that resembles a slight seizure. All right, okay. Now she crooks her finger so that I lean down.

"Throw that bottle away," she whispers fiercely. "Cora Lee once gave me a 'tincture' and I had gastrointestinal distress for a week."

There is definitely something in the water here.

When I arrive, they are making fun of each other with the library puppets. Sasha's got a princess. It's wearing a pink shiny dress and has gold ringlet hair and a sparkly crown. It's holding a wand, which is mixing metaphors, but oh well. "I'm lying there, asleep!" Sasha says in a squeaky princess voice. "And the jerk comes and kisses me! Slips me some tongue! Do I *know* you? Hands off me, buddy! You're busting my REMs!"

"Do you know I'm one of the most deadly animals around?" Librarian Larry flaps the wide mouth of his hippo, showing off two stuffed teeth.

"Doesn't anyone actually work around here?" I say.

"Watch what you say, lady." Larry points his hippo in my direction. "Just 'cause I wallow, don't think I ain't lethal."

"Henry's working," the princess puppet says. "But royalty is above the lowly masses. Let them eat cake! Or cookies!"

I hear the rustle of little people, and I also hear Henry reading aloud. A second later, he storms over and snatches the puppet off of Larry's hand and then goes for Sasha's. He's got the princess around the neck, and she is squealing as if being strangled until Henry grabs her, and Sasha sighs in defeat.

"Really, people," Henry snaps. "Hey, Tess." He shakes his

head to convey his parental-like frustration, and then hurries back to his audience.

Sasha removes her glasses. She huffs hot air onto one lens and wipes it with the tail of her shirt and then does the same with the other. It's the eyewear equivalent of Clark Kent dressing in the phone booth, because now Sasha turns all business.

"*Imponerus,*" she says. "No wonder we couldn't find it."

"Don't tell me he called you at four thirty too."

"Six," Sasha says.

"So that's why Henry's cranky," Larry says. "Up all night. The kid's obsessed."

"No biggie. I was awake anyway," Sasha says. "I haven't slept in weeks."

"'Heartbreak overlo-oad . . . ,'" Larry sings, then rubs his mangy beard thoughtfully. "You should try yoga. Help you relax."

"Anything called Downward Dog should be done in private." Sasha comes around to my side of the counter. "We have a plan."

"We do?" I ask.

"I'm going to call a doctor."

Not again. "Cora Lee from the Theosophical Society already gave me medicine."

"Not that kind of a doctor. A PhD doctor. A dean I know. We're going to call Dr. Abby Sidhu."

"We are?" Larry says. "You made us promise that if you tried to call her, we'd lock you in the Franciscan Sisters Memorial Reading Room."

"This is business."

Larry makes that scoffing noise in the back of his throat, the one I make whenever I see those pictures girls take of themselves holding out their phones. "She's in the math department!"

"She's *friends* with the guy in Botany and Plant Pathology."

"Fine. But if you end up at my place crying and clutching another box of Twinkies, don't say I didn't tell you so."

"She's been in there a long time," I say to Henry. He is sitting across the table from me. Nathan's little boy, Max, has placed an open copy of *Frog and Toad Are Friends* on Henry's head. Henry is balancing it there with perfect posture, like a debutante.

"Read," Max demands. "Read from your head." He thinks this is hilarious. He starts laughing like it's the best five-year-old joke ever.

Nathan appears now, holding his baby daughter under one arm as if she's a bundle of firewood. He's got a bunch of stuff under the other arm. Man, parents come with a lot of baggage. The sleeve of somebody's jacket drags on the ground. "Max! Come on! We gotta go! Bye, guys. Bye, Tess."

There are people I know here. It feels good. I haven't thought of Meg or my other friends or Dillon or my old house in days.

Henry leans forward, catches *Frog and Toad* in one hand. "Here she comes."

Yep, Sasha is heading our way, all right. She's got her hands jammed in her front pockets. She's beaming.

"We're going on a little trip."

"Who's 'we'?" Henry asks. "You told us to chain you to the book drop if you went anywhere with Abby."

"Us-we. The three-of-us-we."

"We-we?" Henry and I say at the same time. This is pretty hilarious, so insert a couple of minutes of laughing and elbowing each other here.

"We and the plant formerly known as the pixiebell, people. To Seattle. To the University of Washington. You will meet with Professor Harv Johansson. *Dr.* Johansson. *Plant doctor* Johansson. This Friday? Maybe we should take two cars. I might be staying."

She smiles.

"*I* wanna go," Larry whines from somewhere over in Fiction.

"You stay, we leave," she says, too loudly for the library.

"Okay." I shrug. "Why not?"

"Timing couldn't be better," Henry says.

Sasha is positively strutting around. Her chest is out. "Well, well, well," she says, and then says it again.

"Friday," Henry says.

"Friday," I reply.

"At least we'll have an answer," he says. He rubs his face, tired. "Answers are good."

"I should let you get back to work."

"Yeah, look how the place is hopping." He *is* cranky. "Let me walk you out. The boss won't care. I could shelve all the red-covered sex books in YA, and I doubt she'd even notice. Look at her."

It's true. Sasha is acting like she just won a prizefight. She might as well pump her fists in the air.

Outside, Henry gives me a quick kiss and hugs me good-bye. It isn't quite the kiss I'm looking for, but no matter. I walk down Friday steps and into the Friday street and get into Jenny's Friday car. My heart sings Friday joy all the way home.

It is still singing when I turn by the mailbox, but then it stops. It stops abruptly, abruptly enough to qualify as a *screeching halt* because my father's truck is in the driveway, and my father himself is leaning against it.

I park Jenny's van. I sit in there for a while. I don't want to get out. Finally, I do.

"Time to go," he says.

chapter fourteen

Ecballium elaterium: squirting cucumber. The seed-pod of this plant bursts open and shoots its seeds up to twenty-seven feet away from the parent plant. The seeds can zoom off as fast as sixty-two miles per hour in order to get away. Let's just say that some people see the logic in this.

It's where we also begin, every single one of us: a seed. It is our beginning before our beginning. We become an embryo, an immature plant, in our own enclosed case, and we, too, will grow under the right conditions, seeking the sun and light.

Of course, some of us come from a bad seed.

And there is mine, leaning against his truck.

Can we just start with what he's wearing? Because remember when he said he never bought his clothes himself? He's wearing a tie-dyed T-shirt with an ironed-on image of the Road Runner on it. I forgot about that one. Let me make this clear: There is no way in hell my mother would have bought *that*.

I walk past him as if he isn't there and he hasn't just said what he just said.

"Where are you going?" he asks. "Aren't you going to even give me a hug?"

I spin around. I'm furious. I didn't even know how furious I've been. My anger erupts from its own hard case and begins to grow at a manic pace, the beanstalk I will use to climb my way out of here. I just stare at him with narrowed eyes.

"You got shit—" I flick my shirt to indicate he should do the same. Silvery cat hair. He also smells of mildew, the faint odor of old basement. I turn away, stomp up the porch steps.

"If you hurry, we can make the last ferry," he calls out after me. I slam the screen door. He slams the screen door. He's following me. "Tess, *please.*" Oh, look, he's pleading. I rather like how the tables have turned.

Now I slam the door to my room. I lock it. He's jiggling the knob. I sit on the floor with my back against the door. I smell something. What the heck? Baking bread? Jenny did not have her day of painting after all. I am beginning to understand that her cooking is a nervous reaction. She probably makes brownies just to swirl her finger around in the batter when she's having a bad day. It's a miracle she doesn't weigh a thousand pounds. Then again, her life was probably pretty calm before we came along.

"I'm sorry, Tessie Tess! I had myself a little breakdown," my father says through the door. "You know, I'm okay. I got it together. I apologize. We were standing at that canyon, right? And then at the crypt . . ."

I don't want to give him the satisfaction of a response, but I can't help myself. "A pyramid *hotel*. In *Las Vegas*, Dad. Land of all-you-can-eat buffet, Father. Cocktail waitresses with cleavage as deep as the *Colorado River*, Pops."

"Come on, Tess." He tries out a stern approach. "I gotta get back to work. The guys have been great, but their patience is wearing thin."

"*Their* patience? *You've* got to get back? We went on a three-day trip, Dad. It's been a month. I had to buy *clothes*. You *ditched* me."

"I was crazy. I just needed to know who I *am*. Without her." His voice catches. It jabs me. Jabs my heart at that place where truth resides. And I should never have opened my mouth, because all the desperation was bound to spill out. I'm losing the power of my anger. Sometimes when the fury blows through, only a small person is left sitting there. I go silent.

I am eye level with the pixiebell across the room. We've both been through a lot. We lost the main person who cared for us, and we've been left with another who's doing a crappy job in her place. Poor Pix. It looks so pathetic with its few yellow leaves.

Wait. What is *that*? Something's strange with Pix. Oh, no—what *now*? I crawl over toward it on hands and knees, not sure I'm seeing what I think I'm seeing. There's some kind of growth at the top of the stem. I feel awful, because my first sickening thought is that it's a tumor. Is it a *tumor*?

I can't look. Another shameful fact: Even when you love someone more than anything, disease can be so revolting that you want to turn away.

Am I horrible? she asked. A pizza was on the coffee table, and we'd been sitting on the couch together eating it (trying to eat it in her case, trying to eat the tiniest mushed-up tasteless bits of it), and that's when it happened. A chunk of hair dropped out of her head. It landed on the table when she leaned forward. *Horrible,* horridus, *the adjective form of the verb* horrere, *meaning* "hair." *Standing on end,* Henry would tell me much later.

I left her alone in it. It was another wrongdoing. When my face showed that shock and repulsion, when we both looked upon that hair with *horror,* when I answered her question with *No, no, of course not!,* with obvious dishonesty in my voice, I abandoned her. She was in it all by herself.

My father makes a few lame pounds on the door. But then he gives up. I hear him walk down the stairs. I expect that his truck will start up any second, but this doesn't happen. The only thing I hear is Vito sniffing under the door. I hear his hot little breath through his nostrils, in out, in out; in the oldest animal parts of him, he is probably getting the whole sorry story of weakness and defeat.

Taking a stand for any length of time is not easy. I have to pee. I'm starving. But I will not leave this room, at least not until the ferry and/or my father has left. I find one of the old cara-mels I bought a few weeks ago in my purse. I sit on the bed and chew. I find a linty Altoid and eat that too. That'll earn me a few more hours of survival.

A gentle tap. "Tess?" It's Jenny. A paper towel comes inching under the door. Some paper-thin wheat crackers are laid out in a checkerboard on it, sporting slender pieces of cheese. "No liquids will fit under there, Sweetie."

"I've got three to five days without water if the temperature stays below seventy degrees Fahrenheit."

She's quiet, but I know she's still standing there. Finally, she says, "Would you like me to be the mediator? Between the two of you?"

"Are you a good mediator?"

"Not really."

"Okay." I open the door. "But only because you were so convincing."

Jenny sighs. I look at her old face. Her wrinkles are hills and valleys. Her eyes are bright. They've seen a lot of winters and disappointments and new mornings. My mind plays the evil pinball machine game—bam, Jenny's eyes, bam, my mother's eyes, bam, her actual *body* in that urn right this minute, bam, forever *gone*. The realization socks me in the stomach anew. This is how it always goes.

"I don't want to go home."

I realize it's true. At home I can't get away from me, all that's gone wrong and all that I didn't do that I should have done and now can never, ever do. But here I am separated from that girl and that father and that gone-forever mother and every sad thing that happened in that house and that town. Even from that body in that urn in that wall of Sunset Hills Cemetery, 13.5 miles, nineteen minutes, outside of San Bernardino.

"You don't have to go," Jenny says. "My home is yours for as long as you want it to be. But are you running, Tess?"

"Running *away* can also be running *to*."

"Valid point."

It is a short while later. We sit on the couch together, double-teaming Dad, who is in the big cushy chair across from us.

"First things first," I say. "The sixties are over. You should ditch that shirt. No more tie-dye."

"Ouch," he says. "Now that we've got my fashion sense sorted out."

"And no more weed. Not in my house, and not around my granddaughter."

He raises his eyebrows. "Is that right?" he says.

Jenny folds her arms, and I fold mine.

He runs his hand through his hair. "Shit," he says. "I should've known better than to put you two together. You're both the same."

"If you mean intelligent, beautiful, and stubborn, I thank you," Jenny says.

My heart, it just rises.

"I've got some amends to make, I know," my father says.

"I'll be clear with you for the first time in your life and mine. You fucked up big-time," Jenny says.

He looks down at his hands, folded in his lap. I feel a little bad for him, but not bad enough. He starts to talk. His voice cracks again. He is pouring his heart out about his loss and confusion and sadness. But as I said, a Big Moment is not in the cards. We don't clutch each other and weep in mutual grief and newfound understanding. Instead I keep seeing him go off to work when she has her radiation appointments. I see him eating a double cheeseburger when she can barely swallow.

I see him—the captain of our ship—that night in the car. That early morning, actually. That second night, when the hospital called after the *unfortunate series of events* related to *viral pneumonia* and *depressed immune system* and *fluid in lungs* and *aspiration*. I watched his profile as the streetlights flashed light on his face. Nothing was real. He drove like a maniac for no good reason. Just eight hours before, we'd gone home because we were *tired*. Because we were going to *get some rest*. Because we were selfish, terrible people who couldn't even give up our own comfort to be there for someone who'd do anything for us. I was relieved to go home. To be *away*. And now I can barely look at my father and face this, the way we'd left her to die, even if we had no idea it was going to happen. She was *alone*. Horror, *horridus, horreur*—it was inescapable that night. It will always be inescapable.

Dad is crying and making a bunch of snuffling noises and wiping his eyes on his arm, and I watch him like I'm watching a film. Not a great film either. The kind you start talking back to because the logic stops making sense.

Oh, look, he's done. The credits roll. I stare at the floor. There's a small tumbleweed of dog hair down there. I lift it with the tip of my toes. "Check it out. Vito made a hamster," I say.

They are both silent. They meet eyes. I get up and leave them there. I'm not even hungry anymore.

I'm halfway up the stairs when I hear it. "Looks like you're going to have to start being a real father now," Jenny says.

I am sure he's going to leave. But the next morning, he is sleeping on an old couch on Jenny's sunporch. He is too tall for the couch; his feet are hanging over the arm. He's got a crocheted blanket draped across him that someone's grandma must have made. Not mine. My grandma is not the type to sit in a rocking chair with knitting needles.

He is there the next day too. He is weeding Jenny's vegetable garden. He's got a stupid sunhat on, and he's sweating. He's working that hoe like there's no tomorrow.

And he's there on Friday, in the early, early morning as I am stuffing my pack and as Jenny is pouring me a travel mug of coffee. Vito hasn't gotten out of his dog bed yet, the lazy squirrel. His alarm clock hasn't gone off yet. He watches the goings-on with his chin on his paws. Pix is back in my mother's shoe, which is cinched up tight for the long trip. When I see Sasha's headlights turn into the drive, I sling my pack over my arm and hold Pix most carefully in front of me.

He hands me some money, my father does. He kisses my

cheek. "Call me when you get there," he says. "I want to know that you arrived safe."

I don't let him see it. But when he says this, I smile.

"I feel like the damn chauffeur," Sasha says. The sky is only now turning morning pink. I have that leaving-early-on-a trip feeling, where you're tired but excited and you get to see what's going on in the hours when you're usually still asleep. The Jones Farms milk truck heads up our road. A raccoon lumbers across the street like he's had a rough night.

"Home, James," Henry says. He's in the backseat with me. He takes my hand. Pix is on my other side. The shoe is tucked in tight, and I've secured it with books I found on the floor of Sasha's old Volvo.

"Maybe we should've taken two cars. We probably should have taken two cars," Sasha says.

"You made us promise that if you wanted to stay over we'd weigh down your arms and legs with *The International Index to Periodicals* and a couple of *Webster's Unabridged*."

The darkness is lifting, and the sun is showing itself. It's a miracle, when you think about it, that this happens every single day. There are only a few straggly cars in the ferry line.

"Getting up this early should be against the law," Sasha says. But she's hyped up and excited. She's bopping around on the radio, trying out different channels before giving up and shutting it off.

The ferry arrives. A few cars trickle down the ramp. By

the afternoon, the arriving ferries will be packed, dumping tourists by the masses. You start understanding how the people who live there feel. It's a weekend invasion of cars and ice cream eaters and photo takers, and by Monday, it's normal life again. Joe Nevins waves us in. I roll down my window.

"Hey, Joe," I say.

"Morning, Tess. Have a nice ride," he says. My insides squeeze with happiness. I love belonging.

"You're getting to be a regular regular," Henry says.

Sasha sets the brake and turns off the engine. We're way at the tip of the boat, where the chain runs across the front and where you can't help but have a flash image of cars rolling forward and tumbling in. "You kids go ahead," Sasha says. "I'm going to have a little snooze."

I want to race up the stairs to the upper deck, I'm so excited. The ferry is practically empty, so it feels like it's all ours. Henry follows along, putting up with me. This ferry stuff is old news to him, but it's only my second time. The huge windows and the outdoor decks that nearly hang over the water are thrilling to me. The ferry engine rumbles, complains, and then lumbers forward anyway. I stand at the very farthest point on the front deck. The wind kicks up. My hair's going to look fabulous, but oh well. Out there, the sound is all mine, and Parrish gets smaller and smaller behind us.

"Damn it, Henry, put your arms around me."

"Are you cold?" he asks. My sweatshirt sleeves are flapping in the wind.

"Yes, I'm freezing. But you're putting your arms around me because it's romantic, you idiot." I am learning this about Henry. Sometimes his mind is on ideas and concepts and beliefs, and he forgets about the sentimental stuff. Like Meg used to say about her last boyfriend, Kyle, some boys just need reminding.

Henry puts his arms around me from behind, and I lean my head back against him. Even with his thin frame, I feel him there for me.

"Have you ever had your heart broken, Henry?" It's time I asked this. I am feeling fearless with all that wide water in front of me.

"I suppose most people have at least once by now," he says into my hair.

"My mother broke my heart. My father did. But not a boy."

"Hmm," he says, but that's all. I turn around and give him a good look, but his face reveals nothing. There are just those sweet eyes looking at mine.

"Your face is becoming familiar to me," I say.

"I know what you mean." He pulls my hair into a ponytail, lets it drop. "You are really very beautiful."

I know you're supposed to just say thank you when you get a compliment, but I haven't perfected that technique yet. "Ha," I say.

"You are. I don't understand why you don't see your value."

"'Value' sounds like buying tires. And who really sees their value, anyway? Does anyone?"

"Yeah! Absolutely. Some see it too much. What about Elijah? I've known him and Mill forever, but sometimes the whole superiority thing just really gets under my skin."

"That's too bad," I say. Hey, I'm no dummy. It's fine for him to say that about his friend, but I'm not supposed to agree. "So, have all three of you been in the same class since preschool? Is that how it works?"

"Basically. Look." Henry points. My attempt to get more information falls flat. He obviously has no interest in discussing Millicent or Elijah, and I can't say I mind. "I want to live there. Posey Island, one acre."

"Cutest island ever." It is. I picture Henry and me washing ashore there after the shipwreck. We're in amazingly stylish island clothes for all the rough seas we've just swum through. My hair looks great too. Henry is hacking tree branches into a fabulous home. Not sure how that grocery store got there, but I like it.

Henry breathes in deeply. "Take it all in," he says, which just becomes another thing to love him for.

When the ferry lands, we drive through a small seaside town and then through miles of farmland. Finally, we're on the freeway. It all looks so different from San Bernardino. There are high, forested hills, and even the farms look lush from rain, surrounded by clumps of green trees everywhere.

"TacoTime, next exit." For the last twenty minutes, Henry has been pointing out all of the fast-food possibilities. This is pissing off Sasha, which gives him more incentive to do it. "Arby's, next exit."

"Henry, put a sock in it," she snaps.

"I'm huuungry, Mom," he whines.

"We just ate!"

It's true. The backseat is littered with garbage-filled bags marked with the glorious red *M*. The car is filled with the sad smell of empty hash brown wrappers and flattened syrup packets. Henry is turning out to have a pretty good appetite, which I'm thinking is a sign of character. Anyway, I've lost count of his fine qualities. For once in my life, numbers are eluding me.

I hunt around in my purse. There are no more caramels or fuzzy Altoids, but I find what might be a cough drop. I hold it out to Henry, and he gives me a scared look, like I've just pulled out a knife.

"Read the damn map, people, if you're bored back there."

Good idea. I want to know how much longer we have to go. I can't keep my eyes off of Henry, and so I keep missing the freeway signs. He must want to know too, because he's fishing around down by my feet, where the map has dropped. He holds it up like it's the winning lottery ticket, but then he does a double take. His floor scrounging put him eye level with Pix.

"What is that?" he asks.

"What is what?" Sasha is looking back and trying to drive at the same time. "Don't tell me there's a cop."

Henry ignores her. "Did you see that?" he asks me.

"I noticed it a few days ago."

"Why didn't you say something?"

There are a million reasons, but no real good one.

"Say what about what?" Sasha asks. She's still trying to see what's going on, causing the car to swerve alarmingly.

"It's a bud," Henry says. "On the plant."

"A bud? I thought the plant was dying." Sasha catches my eye in the rearview mirror.

"It's not a bud," I say.

"Let me see." Henry holds out his hands and wiggles his fingers, directing me to pass him my mother's shoe.

I shake my head. "Too much bumping around."

"Fine." He leans across my lap, jams his elbows right on my legs, and studies Pix where it sits. "It's a bud, Tess."

Sasha looks over the seat, squinching her eyes, and I have a near-death experience when that semi next to us honks loud and long. "It's a bud," she says.

But they're wrong. I know it.

"Tumor," I whisper. All morning, I've been so happy, but now I think I might cry. I'm feeling all choked up. I try to concentrate on Henry's shoulder blades and his swath of black hair as he leans on my lap, but even Henry Magic isn't working.

"Tess, it's not a tumor. It's a bud. I'm telling you."

"Pix has never flowered in its life. Never."

"Well, it's about to flower now."

"Ow," I say, as Henry raises himself up with the help of my cushy legs. I don't want to do it, but I give Pix another look. I don't see a bud, honestly. I have a feeling that Henry just sees beauty where beauty really isn't.

"I don't think so," I say.

We are quiet. No one says anything. Sasha concentrates on the road, and Henry watches as all the small towns whip past, and I watch Henry watching. I've ruined the mood, but then we move from awkward silence to just plain silence. We pass outlet malls and big casinos advertising concerts by old guys from the seventies. Sasha can't help but pipe in then.

"Alice Cooper!" She chuckles. "Did you see that? I've gotta call Will!" When her brother, Will, was seven, she tells us, he saw Alice Cooper on a record album of their dad's. Will thought Alice Cooper was a bad clown, and he used their mother's makeup to dress like him. Then he scared her by jumping out of the coat closet. "You'd have thought that kid would have ended up in prison, but he's in library science too."

I smile. Not just at bad clowns, but at "library science." I like that name. It makes a library sound as vast and mysterious as the universe or the ocean, requiring specific study to be understood.

As we get closer to the city, the traffic slows, and the red brake lights of cars stack against each other. Sasha is jazzed. She pounds the steering wheel with her fist and says, "Hurry up, Car." She gives helpful instructions to the drivers we pass, including, "Use your signal, asshole," and, "If you want to change lanes, have some bleeping balls, Datsun!"

Henry pops his head over the seat. "Why did you and Abby break up again?"

"Too bossy," she says.

"*Who* was too bossy?" he prompts.

"Me."

"And you're crazy about Abby and want to make this work, correct?"

"I will be so, so not bossy."

"Perhaps now is a good time to practice," Henry says. "We're almost there."

"If I might make a *suggestion*, Honda, MOVE THE FUCK UP!" she snarls.

"Poor Abby," I say to Henry.

"What are you going to do," Henry says.

"Love has the power to transform," Sasha says.

Henry snorts. "*Transformation* has the power to transform."

chapter fifteen

Quercus: oak tree. The oak takes an extraordinarily long time to produce seeds. While some plants and trees do so within days or weeks, the oak can take up to fifty years to mature enough before it's ready for offspring. The same can be said for certain people who shall remain nameless.

"It's a bud," Dr. Harv Johansson, head of the University of Washington Department of Botany and Plant Pathology and director of the Shaw Mountain Field Station (he gave me his card), says. He is bent over Pix, studying it through his reading glasses.

"Really?" I say. I know he's the expert, but I still have a hard time believing him. You can be so sure you know something, and you can be so wrong. People always tell you to listen to yourself. But *how* can you, or, rather, why *should* you, when You are speaking to You from your own place of bad experience and misinformation?

"What did you think it was?"

Dr. Harv Johansson has short gray hair, a gray beard, and a nose as round as a tulip bulb. His eyes are kind. He smells good, like earth and oak, or a cellar of wine barrels. He's wearing a red sweatshirt and jeans, and his reading glasses are smudged, and this gives me some sort of hope that he has no time to clean them because he is too busy saving the lives of plants. Those kind eyes twinkle at me a little as he asks the question.

I'm embarrassed to answer. Henry sets his hand on my back. Dr. Johansson's office is pretty much a big mess. There are rectangular plastic tubs full of dirt and plant samples covering various surfaces, and there's an old Mr. Coffee, with a pot so brown tinged you might think twice if the good doctor offered you a cup. And there are books everywhere—books on his desk, on shelves, and stacked on the floor. His desk also sports a softbound volume called *The Seeds Inc. Yearbook*. I imagine individual seeds posed in class photo images, *Most Likely to Suc-seed*, ha-ha. I am so hilarious in my own head.

Dr. Johansson is still waiting for me to answer. He's as patient as an elm.

"Tumor," Henry says.

Dr. Johansson does not laugh as I feared he would. He only makes a *hmm* sound. Obviously, Sasha has told Abby my story, and Abby has told Dr. Johansson, or else he's used to the idea of similarities between plants and people.

"I see," he says, and nods. Sasha is minding her manners. She's standing next to Abby Sidhu, doctor of mathematics, who we met after making our way across the campus of Gothic libraries and red brick buildings. Abby is tiny and has delicate features and a smile that's bright against her dark skin. She seems as soft-spoken as Sasha is loud, but in the back of the room, they stand together, shoulders slightly touching.

"It's never bloomed *before*," I say. I want to let Dr. Johansson know that my tumor idea has not just come from some misguided grief response. I have my reasons.

"You said you didn't know what kind of plant it is, right? That it's been growing for more than fifty years since your grandfather planted the stolen seed?"

"Right."

"Well, it's most likely a type of plant with a reproductive strategy called 'monocarpic.' That is, they flower and produce fruit only once in their lifetime, and then they die. Some live ninety years before this point arrives."

"So it *is* dying."

"I believe so."

"What can we do?" There is something about hearing this news spoken so directly—a wave of imminent loss hits. My voice is rising. I feel desperate. I know it's crazy to feel this strongly about a plant, but this is Pix we're talking about. "What if we stop it from flowering? What if we, I don't know, *cut it off*. That bud." This sounds oddly gruesome, but I'll try anything if it keeps Pix alive. I don't want this flower or fruit or whatever Pix will leave behind. I want Pix, my mother's plant, which lived in her college dorm room and then in that house she shared with her girlfriends and then in that apartment my parents had when they first married and then on the windowsill in our kitchen.

"That won't work, I'm afraid. The plant is just completing its natural life cycle."

"There's *got* to be a way. I need to keep it *here*."

The doctor's face is grave. "I'm sorry." He sounds like those other doctors, and well, for a second I almost hate him.

"Flowering, fruit . . . ," Henry says. "What kind of fruit?"

"I have my suspicions," Dr. Johansson says. "But I need to do a little research."

"A rare fruit?" I try.

"Not exactly. This may be the most usual of unusual plants."

He's probably just trying to make me feel better. I think of the most common, mundane fruits I can, whether they grow on plants or trees. Apples, oranges, bananas, pears . . .

"I think it's a strawberry," Dr. Johansson says.

Great. Forgot that one.

"A *strawberry*?" Even Henry can't believe it.

"The leaves, see? They're a miniature version of the notched leaves of a strawberry, but gathered together in a clover shape."

"It's tall, though. Strawberries are low to the ground." Leave it to Sasha to argue with the head of the University of

Washington Department of Botany and Plant Pathology.

"Tall *and* monocarpic. If it's what I think . . . This may be a great research specimen. May I keep it?"

He is so friendly in his red sweatshirt, and I like this warm office with all these books. But I am quite clear on this.

"No," I say. "It stays with me."

"Can I get a leaf sample?"

"There aren't many left."

"Photographs, then."

Photographs I can do. "Okay."

He opens his office door and calls out. "Alex!"

"Yo!" a voice from the hall replies. And then there is Alex himself. He's a younger version of Dr. Johansson. He's got a beard and short hair, but his hair is brown. He's wearing a sweatshirt too. Either this is the way botanists look, or Alex is taking on Dr. Johansson's qualities, same as people start looking like their pets.

"A monocarpic *Fragaria*," Dr. Johansson says, as if he's handing Alex a surprise gift.

"Cool."

"Let's get some images."

"Usual but unusual," Sasha says.

"Regular *and* one of a kind," Abby Sidhu says, and elbows Sasha with private meaning.

Henry takes my hand and squeezes. Alex is taking photos and Pix is having its ten minutes of fame on the scientific celebrity red carpet. If it didn't look so sickly, I'd be happy for it. But I've got a really important question for Dr. Johansson.

"The dying. It wasn't because of too much water or from being moved or from not being taken care of in the right way, was it?"

Dr. Johansson stops the media madness and straightens up. He looks me firmly in the eyes. "This was going to happen. No matter what you did or didn't do. It was just plain *going to happen.*"

My stupid eyes start to water. I could practically drop to the floor and cry like a big baby. My chest aches with grief. Something terrible and cruel is squeezing and squeezing my heart.

Dr. Harv Johansson, head of the University of Washington Department of Botany and Plant Pathology and director of the Shaw Mountain Field Station, does something unexpected then. He puts his arms right around me and gives me a hug. I am smooshed right up against that wet wood smell of his red sweatshirt. It's not the smell of a cellar, I realize. It's the smell of a forest after a hard rain.

And that's when Henry says it. "Wow. *Wow.*"

Dr. Johansson lets me out of his big bear grip, and we stand apart again. We both look at Henry, who is staring, transfixed, at a framed photo on Dr. Johansson's wall. Now I am staring too. It's a photo of a building, a narrow wedge of a green glowing triangle set deep into ice. All around it is the eerie blue-black of a polar sky. The image gives me the shivers.

The building looks like a half-buried sci-fi mystery, something dropped from space.

"Svalbard," Dr. Johansson says.

We stay to have dinner with Abby at the Northlake Tavern, a pizza place with slices piled so high with sausage and cheese and pepperoni and mushrooms that you can barely get your big fat mouth around it. That's what Henry says to Sasha, anyway.

"You can barely get your big, fat mouth around it, Sash."

"Sha wup, Hewy," she answers with stuffed cheeks.

We give Abby and Sasha some time alone. Henry and I take a walk in this weird park across the street from the pizza place. Set next to a lake, the park also has a huge, rusting industrial plant on it. It sounds awful, but it's kind of beautiful. People are flying kites on a high hill, and children are rolling down it. I remember how much I used to love doing that, and so it makes me happy to watch. There are all kinds of boats out on the water. Little chubby boats chug around, and sailboats slip by gracefully, and kayaks cut through the waves. There are people standing on paddleboards, rowing with long oars, like they're off on a voyage to Polynesia.

Henry and I sit on the grass next to each other. Around us, couples are stretched out or entwined on blankets, having picnic dinners, drinking wine out of plastic cups, kissing.

"Tess?" Henry says. "I'm really sorry. I feel bad. I know how much you need the pixiebell to be okay."

A seaplane lands like a dragonfly on a leaf. I don't want to talk about this now. It hurts my heart to think of Pix in my mother's shoe back in Sasha's car. "Kiss me, Henry," I say.

And so he does.

We drive home. At the ferry terminal, Henry's fingertips touch mine in the backseat. It's dark. The ferry is lit up like a grand ship from the olden days. Looking at it from afar, you picture an orchestra and ladies in ball gowns dancing with men in tuxedos. Inside, though, there are only vinyl bench seats and slumped travelers and tired hot dogs spinning under heat lamps. The trip back over the sound is a different one at night. You know those lumps of islands are out there somewhere, but you can only see blackness and more blackness and your own reflection looking back from the windows.

Driving home, we're quiet. We're all tired. I watch Henry's profile light up in flashes as we pass street lamps. When we see the mailbox at Jenny's driveway, Sasha finally speaks.

"My butt hurts," she says.

"Home again," Henry says.

Stupid, emotional me. I'm exhausted and it's been a long day, and nighttime always splays me open and lays my feelings bare.

"You know, I can't believe you guys made this trip." My voice wobbles. "Thanks so much. For caring about Pix."

Sasha is looking over the seat. "Silly girl," she says. She gives my knee a squeeze. "We care about *you*."

Henry gives me a quick kiss good-bye, and I gather up my bag and my mother's shoe with Pix inside. It is not difficult to make this particular calculation. Pix has lost three more leaves on this expedition to Seattle. There are only six more sad leaves left.

I can hardly believe my eyes when I haul my stuff back inside Jenny's house. The lights are off, and there is only the soft glow and low hum of the television in the living room. Popcorn was popped earlier. The smell is still hanging around, like a guest who doesn't realize that the party is over. Jenny rarely watches television, so it's one of those chunky old TVs that weigh a billion pounds. My father—he's got his feet up on the coffee table, and a newspaper is folded over his stomach like some 1950s dad. He's in some gray sweatsuit I've never seen before; it's new—the fold lines are visible. There is a cup of *tea* on the table. I can see the string with the little tag hanging over the edge of the cup. Vito is curled up next to him, and . . . wait. Are those *slippers* on his feet?

"Oh hi, honey," he says. He actually says *Oh hi, honey,* just like a television dad.

"What have you people done with my father?" I ask.

"What?"

"Never mind," I say. "Did you *wait up* for me?"

He sets the newspaper aside, sits up. "I wanted to make sure you got back okay. How was it?"

"Vito's not allowed on the couch," I say. Vito and my father look at each other. I swear, Vito shrugs. "Are those slippers? Where'd you get slippers?"

"I got 'em at Island Madness. I got you some too and some

other things you might need. Snazzy, eh?" He holds one foot in the air and swivels it. Now that I've dropped my stuff and I'm a little closer, I see that the slipper is shaped like an orca and that the orca is smiling a large ironed-on smile. I'm relieved. That man actually is my father.

"You waited up." I still can't believe it. Only Mom waited up.

"Well," he says. He doesn't know how to explain it himself.

"And you bought me slippers."

He gives the orca a good look and then gives another to me. "Thomas Believed in the Healing Power of Marine Life Footwear," he says.

chapter sixteen

Prunus persica: peach. While the fruit of this plant is juicy and sweet, the seed—like the seeds of cherries, apples, plums, and apricots—is full of poison. Yes, that pit you throw out is a little woody ball packed with cyanide. The Seed Moral of this story? Be careful of what's at the center—yours or anyone else's.

"Svalbard," Henry says. He slides the book across the library table for me to see. There it is, the same image from the photo in Dr. Johansson's office: that wedge jutting from permafrost, that narrow rectangular window in the outermost nowhere. It is otherworldly. That it exists at all makes other unearthly things seem possible.

"How could I not have known about this? Listen: Two and a quarter billion seeds from the planet's most important crops will be stored there. It's a huge seed library. This is *monumental*. This is how we restart civilization if we ever needed to."

"Wow."

"There are only four keys." His beautiful brown eyes shine.

Four keys, and guards, not to mention the polar bears. Every person on Svalbard is required to own a gun and be trained in its use, for protection from them. In Svalbard, it's common to see people walking around with rifles slung over their shoulders. But I am not at that part of the story yet. I am at the part where I am sitting across from Henry at the Parrish Island Library, listening to him say "There are only four keys," and then answering: "Incredible."

It is incredible. But I don't realize what Henry is really trying to tell me. I don't catch on that Henry has a *plan*.

"The seeds of these plants will last for centuries. Maybe even for thousands of years. And, Tess—once you deposit a seed, it's still yours. You own it always."

I am running out of superlatives, so I just shake my head in appreciative wonder. He leans forward and takes my hands. Why Henry is so nice to me, I'll never know.

"Hey, I've got something to show you." I open my phone. I find the picture I took this morning, just before I left.

"It's flowering," he says.

It's a delicate-looking flower, the one Pix has made. White and lovely, with four thin petals and a yellow center. "It's so sad, Henry."

"It's beautiful."

"It's dying."

"You should show Sash."

I look around. "She here?" I don't see her. There's only Larry, helping a little boy fill out a library card application.

His mother watches proudly, as if he's just been let through the gates of the city, which in a way, he has.

"Sasha's *always* here. You should see her apartment. There's nothing in it. Books and a bed. Fridge with old take-out containers and bottles of Snapple. Her fridge is a single woman cliché. Come on." I follow him. He heads to the desk. "Joseph, my man," Henry says to the little boy, and gives him a high five. "Larry's the only sucker here actually doing anything today." Larry swats Henry as we pass, and then he swats me, too.

"Hey!" I protest. "I'm a customer." Oh, the dear sweet pleasure of belonging. I love it more and more and more.

In the back room, Sasha is sitting on a pair of unopened cartons, leaning against the wall, talking on the phone and laughing. She makes big, annoyed eyes and waves us away, but Henry ignores her. "You gotta see this," he says.

"Just a sec," she says into the phone. And then to us: "All right. Hand it over." She examines the photo, holding it up near her nose. "Oh, Tess. I don't know what to say. It's blooming." She looks sincerely stricken. A tiny cartoon clown voice comes from the phone. "Abby gives her condolences."

"We should send that picture to Dr. Johansson," Henry says.

The tiny clown is talking again. "Abby says she just saw him. He's got some news for you."

What astounds me, what I just can't seem to believe, is that all these good people are helping me. I don't understand it. And in a way, it makes me feel bad. They look at me and see a girl who's lost one of the most important people a girl could lose. But it makes me want to hand them back their gifts. They don't know the truest thing, which is that I don't deserve this. Their kindness—I want it so much. It is almost a forgiveness. But it makes me feel ashamed.

"Did you hear that, Tess? He's got news!" Henry gives me a second look. "Are you okay?"

"Yeah. I'm fine."

But I am trying not to see it, my father and me there that night, in my mother's room. My father yawns. I gather up our coats. It is the last time, but we don't know it is the last time.

Here is the bad, bad thing: I wanted out of there. Desperately. It was sad and scary in that place. When I walked down the hall, I was afraid I might accidentally see something I didn't want to see. I was tired of sitting on that metal air conditioner over by the window while Dad perched in the green vinyl chair, all of us watching *Wheel of Fortune* on the TV up high on the wall, when we never ever watched *Wheel of Fortune* before.

The neighbor lady on the other side of the sliding curtain scared me too. She moaned every once in a while in her sleep. My mother breathed wheezy breaths. Her hand was all bruised at the top where the IV went in. That blue gown tied in the back smelled like some kind of antiseptic bleach, and it accidentally revealed parts of my mother's body that seemed pale and vulnerable. I was *glad* to be in the car with my father. We *escaped*.

I was so ungenerous. I was such a coward.

If I'd been giving and brave, the least my mother deserved, I might be able to accept Henry and Sasha's compassion. If I hadn't been *guilty*. But this—this is like a nice couple picking up an injured hitchhiker, not knowing he was stabbed by his own knife while he attempted to rob a bank. If my father and I had stayed, we might have seen it happen. *Aspiration*. We might have saved her. My chest caves in with regret each time I run it over again in my mind. All night long, I play it. My coat stays where it is. I sit in the green vinyl chair. I hold her hand. I am listening. I am there.

"As I suspected, it's a *Fragaria singularis*," Dr. Johansson says. Henry and I are hunched over the phone so we both can hear. "Singular strawberry." I make wide eyes to Henry, and he nods his head back as if he suspected Pix of greatness all along. "It is not extinct, and not even particularly rare, but it is remarkable."

Oh, Pix. "Remarkable how?" I ask.

"You've seen what look like seeds on the outside of a strawberry . . . ?"

"Yes."

"Each apparent 'seed' on the outside of the fruit is actually one of the ovaries of the plant, with a seed inside it. A seed within a seed. But *singularis*—it has hundreds and hundreds of these seeds on the one fruit it bears. And given that it lives for so many years, it's believed to be particularly resistant to disease. Botanists have attempted to breed *singularis* with *ananassa*, the garden strawberry, with no luck so far. Imagine the abundance if a disease-resistant plant that bears millions of seeds is crossed with a plant that bears more than one fruit! But that hasn't happened yet. *Singularis* just goes on stubbornly being itself, a plant that lives a long life and bears one extraordinary progeny."

Henry walks me out after we hang up with Dr. Johansson.

"Plant ovaries." I snicker.

"Creepy plant ovaries." Henry snickers back.

"We're childish."

"We're ovaryish."

This cracks us entirely up.

I have Jenny's bike. I show Henry the brown lunch sack in the basket.

"He packed me a lunch. He even wrote my name on it."

"If he included the four food groups, I'm giving him double Dad Points."

I hadn't thought to look inside yet. Okay: A small bag of Tostitos. An orange. A couple of Jenny's chocolate chip cookies wrapped in foil. I show Henry.

"An A for effort. The only thing my father packed was a suitcase for Aruba."

"You've got to come over and meet him."

"I want to come over and meet him."

I hand Henry the cookies. And then the chips. And then the orange. I want him to have every good thing there is. I'd give him my sweatshirt, and my shoes, and this very bike, and the band in my hair. I'd give him words of love and gratitude.

"No." Henry laughs. "These are for you." He tries to hand back all the food.

"Just the orange."

He hands me the orange. "I have an idea," Henry says, as he unwraps the foil package and takes a bite of cookie. "Damn, that's good."

"Even better with milk. What idea?"

"It's going to sound crazy."

"Lay it on me," I say. *And then lay yourself on me,* I don't say.

"At first I thought, Let's just plant the pixiebell's seeds."

"But that doesn't *save* it."

"That's the same conclusion I came to." He pauses. "Tess?"

"What?"

"There's no getting around the fact that it's going to die, right?"

"I know." I do.

"But we can keep it forever anyway."

"Press it in some book?"

Henry groans. *"Forever."*

"Nothing is forever."

I know I'm being slow here, but I find Henry so distracting. Those lips, for one. Besides that, I didn't eat breakfast, and my mind's dragging. They know what they're talking about when they say you've got to start the day off right. I peel that orange. I hold it to Henry's nose. "Smell," I command.

"Mmm."

"One of the best smells in the world."

"Tess, you aren't listening."

"Forever," I say, to prove him wrong.

"Svalbard," he says. "We're going to get the pixiebell's seeds into the Svalbard vault."

"I knew you were going to say that, Henry." Okay, I'm not *that* slow. I'm just not that keen on walking willingly toward disappointment. "But that's impossible. You told me yourself. You said that only three US organizations have gotten seeds into that place."

"I love having a mission," Henry says. He polishes off that cookie.

"I love having a mission with *you*," I say.

"You want to keep your mother's plant forever? Well, Tess, Svalbard is the last forever on earth."

I get chills when he says it. And suddenly I want that. I want that so bad. The vital part of Pix, in the most protected and permanent place that exists. "The last forever," I say.

Henry is excited. He puts his arms around me and lifts me off the ground. That's when we both hear the whistle. One of those high-pitched ones that people make by putting two fingers in their mouth. I always wanted to know how to do that.

Henry sets me down, looks around. I see him walking up the street, carrying a bag from Quill, the stationery store. Elijah.

The mood goes awkward. Once again, I don't know if things feel weird because I feel weird, or if I feel weird because things feel weird. Let me just say this: If you're even thinking, *Is it just me?* It isn't. Trust me.

"Hey, stranger," Elijah says.

"Hey, 'Lij," Henry says.

Elijah grabs Henry's wrist, bends it behind his back. It's one of those playful gestures that actually kind of hurt. "I'm surprised you even remember my name."

Henry wrenches free. "Come on. Don't." He sounds weary, as if they're continuing a private disagreement that's been going on for a while now. One I obviously don't know anything about.

"And, look, it's the damsel in distress," Elijah says.

I can't stand that guy, I really can't. Him and his iceberg sister with their perfect blond hair and their perfect noses and their perfect eyes. Elijah's wearing white shorts and a bright green shirt and plaid sneakers. People who dress like they're in a perfume ad shouldn't be trusted, in my opinion. They're disingenuous with floral overtones.

"What's that supposed to mean?" I say.

"Henry loves to save the day. Especially for a female."

"Shut up, Elijah," Henry says.

"Reminds him of his mother."

"Elijah's parents are both psychiatrists," Henry tells me. "He forgets he didn't get the degree himself."

"I know Oedipal issues when I see them."

"You're an ass," Henry says.

"One of the finest around. Hey, aren't you supposed to be working?" Elijah asks.

"Slow day."

"It's always a slow day." Elijah lifts his bag, gives it a shake for Henry to see. "New ink pens."

I don't even want to say another word to the guy, but standing there with my mouth clamped shut is making me feel small. "Are those for the piece you're doing in Jenny's class?"

"Using a lot of black," he says. "This one's dark. A dark tale of love and war."

No one speaks. Henry is looking down at his shoes. I don't know what's happening here, only that it feels bad. I realize that Elijah is waiting for me to leave. I should stand my ground or something, but Elijah's presence is shrinking me by the second. This is a contest of some kind, and I'm coming in second place. No, I'm not coming in at all. I'm the marathon runner still slogging along the day after the race.

"Well, hey, guys. I'm going to head out," I say. I don't even kiss Henry good-bye, and he doesn't kiss me. I kind of slink off on my bike, which is even more awkward than it sounds, especially when you have to pedal uphill with your butt halfway in the air.

Elijah's eyes—they're not perfect after all.

He's got the eyes of a pickpocket.

chapter seventeen

Cannabis sativa: marijuana. When male plants are eliminated in a crop, it is possible to generate "feminized" marijuana seeds. Essentially, the female plants grow "balls" and reproduce by themselves when no males are around. Growers sometimes ditch the male plants purposefully, as the seeds from the females are more potent and supposedly grow a far superior product. Enough said.

Once I get up that damn hill, I'm pissed at Henry. Damsel in distress? I'll show him damsel in distress. I know Henry wasn't the one who said it, but he could have done more to defend me. Wait. Does that make me even more of a damsel in distress? What did Elijah mean, anyway? Obviously, Henry was Millicent's big shoulder to cry on, which is a little like the rabbit helping the viper, if you ask me.

I make it home, ditch Jenny's bike on the lawn, and try to ignore Vito's excessive display of joy at my return a mere three hours after I last saw him. "Jesus, Vito," I say. Either he has the shortest memory in the world, or his watch is broken. His devotion is more annoying than usual, probably because he's me in dog form, jumping all over Henry with slavish adoration and bad hair. Vito isn't the least bit discriminating. I could have just stolen a baby from a carriage and he'd still jump on me with all the love in his tiny heart.

I might've slammed that door a little.

"Easy," Jenny calls down from the stairs.

I'm pissed *and* hungry, which means that two crooked fingers are beckoning to my inner monster. I head straight to the kitchen. I notice my father in the living room, but I don't see the important thing. I don't see that he's stuffing things into his backpack.

"Hey, Mogli," he calls to me.

"Baloo," I say. They're our old, old names for each other, from when I was maybe five.

I do one of those kitchen who-are-you-kiddings—I eat half a cookie, knowing full well I'll come right back for the other half. That's when he leans his head into the doorway.

This time I do see it. Right away. Great. Just great. "What's that?" I nod toward the backpack over his shoulder.

"I wanted to tell you—"

"You're leaving again."

"Only for two days, Tess. I promise."

"Oh, right. You promise. Got it."

"Tess, I've just got to go look in on things. Get the mail. Talk to my boss. There's still *food* in our fridge."

"It wasn't my idea to run away from home."

"Do you want to come with—"

"No!"

I don't want to go back home or even *think* about home. It would be hot and stuffy in the house now, all these weeks without an open window. My mother had bought some of that food in the fridge—the ketchup, the mustard no one uses, a jar of pickles that has been in there forever. Her coats are hanging in the closet. Her clothes and her shoes and her scarves and her bathing suits and sunhats, her robe, and those flannel pj's with the moons on them are all there too. So many objects, too meaningful and not meaningful enough—her address book, her calendar, those stupid protein shakes, that lamp with the beads hanging down—nothing *alive*, though. Not like Pix. Just things that have lost their magic and that are now only sad.

Our house, my room, my friends. It was a life that belonged to a different me from a different time, someone I remembered fondly but who was fading fast. When I thought about Meg and Caitlin and Dillon and Nate and Michelle (Michelle— wait. Remember Michelle? I guess not. I've known her since sixth grade and haven't thought about her once in all the time I've been gone), or my middle school journal still hidden in my underwear drawer, or my box of earrings, or that pillow I tried to make one day because I was bored, *all* of it seemed like a best friend from elementary school, the one who moves away, the one you're sure is so important, but who you stop writing

211

to after the first few weeks. *I* moved away. I ran from the scene of the crime, and with each passing day, the idea of going back only fills me with more and more guilt.

"Two days, I promise. I've got a ticket. . . ." My father pats the pocket of his jeans. "Okay, goddamn it, where'd you go?"

We are having a moment where everything comes full circle, I am sure of it. I flash on the image of that lost lighter with the dolphins on it, the one that went missing the day before we left for the Grand Canyon. My father's black-gray hair is pulled back into one of my bands, and he is patting his shirt where the pockets would be if he had pockets. This feels like the end of something.

"Thomas!" Here is Jenny now. I had been the one to find the dolphin lighter in the silverware drawer, and now she has found the missing ticket. "Don't forget this."

"Thanks for telling me, guys. What, you were just going to take off and it was going to be one big surprise?"

"I just bought the ticket, Tess. An hour ago. I got it cheap because it's a red-eye. I've got to pick up my paycheck, babe. There is some old *fruit* in the fridge. There was that meat loaf you made. That stuff's gonna be scary. That stuff could be another Nagasaki."

Half a cup of oatmeal. One quarter cup of ketchup. One pound of ground beef. One half of an onion, chopped in quarter-inch cubes. I can't think about that life. In my mind, I see the girl who slipped on those rocks at the Grand Canyon, and maybe, just maybe, I have fallen ten thousand miles and am now, finally, climbing slowly back up.

"It's just for two days, honey," Jenny says.

I don't know how she can believe in him again and again and again. I imagine Dad arriving home in San Bernardino. He opens the windows. He turns on the TV. He sits in the rocking chair and watches his favorite old shows. Neighbor ladies arrive with casseroles. They all have long black hair like Mary, and under the dish lids, the casseroles all look like cat food. He's getting comfy back at home, and wait—the ladies are wearing my mother's clothes. Neighbor Mary takes a spin in my mother's red plaid robe, like it's a ball gown. This film version is revolting.

"What happened to 'Mary'?" I ask.

"I told you. Mary's an old friend. That's all. I needed a friend."

"Is Mary the Old Friend meeting you at our house?"

Jenny sighs.

"No one's meeting me at our house. Maybe Rob, to bring my check." Rob's a guy my father works with. Rob's hands are always dark brown from the black walnut stain they use on the furniture.

"Thomas, you don't want to miss the ferry," Jenny says.

"Two days." He kisses my cheek. I give him the coldest, unfriendliest cheek I can. It'll turn friendly again when he's proven himself. I sniff his shirt when he gives my cold, unfriendly shoulders a hug. I don't smell any weed, that accidental plant rolled up in those Zig-Zag papers. No, he actually smells like Old Spice, the Television Dad soap I give him every year for Christmas, hoping it might transform him.

From the front window, I watch him walk out to his truck. He must feel my eyes, because he turns and waves. He blows me a kiss. He holds up two fingers and shakes them at me. His lips purse dramatically. *Two.*

But I know an ending when I feel one.

Jenny puts her arms around me from behind. She holds me close to her. We both watch him.

"He'll be back," she says.

"Why do you have so much faith in him?" I ask.

"That's my own son."

"Still."

"It's the way a parent loves a child. That love is the most steadfast thing I know of."

"Even if that child does wrong? Even if he does *really* wrong?"

It's my worst thought—how I've disappointed her. Even if she's dead, she's disappointed. Out there, wherever she is, the feeling I've left her with, the very *last* feeling, is how much I've let her down.

"You love your child so much, your heart could break with it. Nothing can change that. No-thing."

My throat gets tight with tears. I want to believe her. My father beeps his horn twice. Two long beeps, sending a message: two days.

"You're probably going to have to go home too at some point, my girl."

I shake my head.

"Yes."

"I don't see why."

"Roots," is all Jenny says.

I hear that old, loud engine before I see the arc of lights through the curtains in my room in Jenny's house. Vito loses it at the sound of a strange car in the driveway. Yeah, he's twelve pounds of pure terror. Anyone who's on his way to murder Jenny and me in our beds will turn and flee at the sight of Vito's tiny, barred teeth. He's as scary as a gerbil in a bad mood.

Jenny taps at my door. "I believe you have company," she says. She has a book under one arm, and she's wearing a night-gown and reading glasses, and it's as close to a granny look as she'll ever get. We just need a big bad wolf, and we'll be in business.

Well, of course I knew I had company. As soon as I heard that gravel crunching under car tires, I peeked out the curtains and started throwing on clothes. I'm sure Millicent never goes to bed this early.

"Tess?" Jenny says.

"What?" I don't have time for a big discussion right now. I've got exactly one minute to get amazing.

"I worry. I mean, look at you racing around here—"

"We had this discussion once already," I say, shoving past Jenny.

"You're right. I'm sorry. It's just . . . You've got your heart on the line. I see it."

"It's called living in the moment," I yell down the hall. "It's called throwing caution to the wind. It's called trusting that sometimes things work out okay!" I am in the bathroom, but I can still hear her.

"It's called love," she says.

I practically break the sound barrier, flying around at the speed of light as I attempt to brush my teeth and throw on some makeup before Henry rings the doorbell. My aim is to do all those things and then be casually watching some informative documentary on TV, but that's stretching it, as I can never figure out how to work that remote. Every time I use it, the TV gets subtitles.

"Well, Henry Lark," Jenny says, answering the door. She's got Vito tucked under one arm. He's gone from fierce protector to ardent lover, trying to squirm his way to Henry so he can shower him with affection and sniff his pant legs.

"Sorry to come over so late," Henry says.

"It's fine," Jenny says. Poor Jenny. I've ruined life as she knows it.

I'm out of breath due to all of my panicked efforts to be casually together. "Oh hi, Henry," I say. I'm pointing the damn remote at the TV, which is now displaying a Tuna Helper ad you can read along with.

"I'll leave you alone," Jenny says. But her voice has edges. I'm not sure who she's actually miffed at, so for the sake of simplicity, I assume it's me. This is my general life policy.

"You're mad," Henry says when we're alone. At least, it's just the two of us and Vito, who's watching Henry and me like we're an episode of his favorite show.

"What gives you that idea?" I ask, my voice giving him that idea.

Henry rolls his eyes. It's another thing to love about him, really. The way he'll always be someone to call me on my bullshit. "Why haven't you been answering your phone?"

"Oh, have you been calling?"

"Are you mad at what Elijah said? Because you might want to remember that *he* said it. I didn't."

"I'm not a damsel in distress." I give up on the remote control.

"I know that."

"I don't need your help."

"I know that. I *want* to help."

"Because you go around helping girls who are sad. That's your thing." Oh, I am being childish. Even my words are pouting. I hate myself for it.

"Millicent used to call me a lot when she was having trouble with her mom. That's what he meant. Their mom—she's always on them, you know, Mill especially, to be more of this or better at that. So much so that Mill can barely try anything new without feeling like she'll fail. Sometimes she'd call when we were in the middle of something, and he'd get pissed. But she doesn't have a lot of people to talk to."

Yeah, I wonder why. Poor "Mill." I feel terrible for her. My heart is so not breaking.

"Elijah—he's . . . He forgets there are other people in the world besides him."

"I don't know why you're friends with him, then." I'm on dangerous territory. He's only known these people his whole life.

"It's not like San Bernardino here. Someone gets under your skin, you can't just forget they're there. Elijah and me, I don't know. He knows me better than practically anyone." Great. Terrific. This means Elijah is a permanent fixture, like it or not.

"He was being an idiot," Henry says. I say nothing. He tries my trick. He knocks my shoulder with his. "Hey," he says.

"Hey," I say back. It's a Hey of Almost Forgiveness.

"I've got something I want to show you. Will you come somewhere with me?"

Oh, all right. As long as it's anywhere.

"Okay."

Henry takes my hand and pulls me up. I call up to Jenny and let her know I'm going out. Outside, it's dark. Really dark. Way more dark than San Bernardino, and the stars are brighter, seemingly closer, close enough to touch, close enough to hold one in your hand. Crickets are making a racket. You think night is quiet, but it's as noisy as day if you really listen.

"What's that?" I ask. I freeze, with my hand on the door. It's a shivery howl.

"Coyotes," Henry says. "We've got a lot of rabbits here, so, you know, coyotes are happy with the menu."

"Oh my God."

"Come on, damsel. That's what I'm going to start calling you."

"I'm going to start calling you smart-ass."

Henry drives like an old man out toward Deception Loop. "You drive like an old man," I tell him.

"You backseat drive like an old woman," he tells me.

Henry's profile is so sweet in the dark car that my heart lifts. He's got the windows rolled down, and summer falls in; it's all night meadow smells—dry grass and fruit ripening. "I really like you, Henry."

"I really like *you*. Do you recognize where we are?"

"Not a clue."

Henry was distracting me again, and I forgot to watch where we were going, but it's also so dark out there that you can't quite make out this dark from that dark. But then we turn into the desolate parking lot of Point Perpetua Park.

"Now?" he asks.

"Yes." It's the whale-watching park, though I doubt he's going to try to show me whales. Those beasts are hard enough to spot in the daylight. Whales mind their own business. I have no idea why we're here. "Man, I hope you can find a parking space," I say.

"Parking gods be with me." Henry shakes his crossed fingers in the air. Of course, there's not a soul in sight. Wait, no. There's a Volkswagen Beetle with a big kid in a puffy coat sitting on the hood. Parrish Island must be where all the old VWs in the world go to die.

"I'm blind at night," I say, and Henry takes my hand again. We walk down the forested path toward the beach. The trees loom, their branch arms outstretched. It's dark and shadowy, one of those places where you try not to think about bad guys and evil fairy tale beasts and wild animals leaping out, but of course you think of those things. "This is spooky."

"Wooo-hoo . . ." Henry wiggles his fingers in a ghostly fashion.

There's a lighthouse on the beach, and its high, intense beam swivels slowly around until we are momentarily blinded. Henry leads us in the other direction. We pick our way over the rocks. The moon is barely out, but its sliver of light colors the breaking waves a yellow-white against the endless black. The beam of the lighthouse swoops across the sky. I take off my shoes when we reach the sand, and so does Henry. This night and this place are both eerie and romantic. I am aware of how alone we are and what that might mean. If it were Dillon, well, Dillon liked to make out anywhere—under the bright fluorescent lights in the school hallway, dark movie theaters, the empty school bleachers after practice, and once, in a car in the Mario's Pizza parking lot.

But Henry has other things on his mind. He is heading us toward a curve of the beach, a cove, a pitch-black cove, where the beam of the lighthouse falls away. As soon as we are in the cove's generous half circle, I can see why Henry has brought me here.

I can't speak because it's so beautiful. The beach—it is glowing with endless blue dots, a spilled curve of them, along the water's edge. They're in the water too. It's magic. It's a glow-in-the-dark painting, not possibly real. I close my eyes and open them again, and it's all still there before me—a cast spell, blue-glowing fairy dust.

"What is this?"

"Plankton, basically," Henry says. "A plant. A bioluminescent plankton called dinoflagellates."

Oh, Henry. He's so romantic.

"Did you know that eighty percent of all creatures known to produce their own light live in the ocean?" he asks. "And did you ever stop to think that all along this part of the sea, this muddy ground we call beach, it's all planted with *seeds*?"

"Kiss me, Henry." I want to be in the moment of beautiful, glowing blue. There's science, and then there's the wonder of science. Henry has things to teach me, but maybe I have a thing or two to teach him.

He leans in. It's a distracted kiss. When we stop, he says, "Seeds. Everywhere. They can lie dormant for years. And then, with the right set of circumstances, a seed rises from the ground and floats into the ocean. It can germinate and reproduce and from there it can drift and drift until it plants itself into new, far-off waters."

"Sit," I say, and pull him down beside me. This is a nice, big flat rock I've found. I lean my head on Henry's narrow shoulder. He puts his arm around me. The waves crash and sigh, crash and sigh. The sheer number of things I don't know sets me awe-struck. Life is large, large, large. Knowledge is so comforting, but so is mystery.

"Seeds," Henry says.

"Henry, enough about seeds."

I didn't know Henry well enough yet to know how fixed he can get on a topic and how determined. Don't even try to budge him, is my advice.

"I've been trying to call you all day to tell you something important. About Svalbard. And about our very own Dr. Harv Johansson," he says.

The sky is all white sparkles above us, and below, on the sand, are those glowing speckles of blue. The night smells briny and deep, and a lone seagull makes his way across the sand as if contemplating where it all went wrong.

"Okay, I give up," I say.

"Dr. Harv Johansson is a"—here, Henry crooks his fingers to make quote marks in the night air—"*Notable adviser* to Seeds Inc. And what, you may ask, is Seeds Inc.? It's an orga-nization that preserves heirloom plant varieties. They regener-ate them and then distribute them. Their aim is to preserve all these diverse and endangered plants for future generations.

They have their own seed bank, but more important? They were one of the three."

"Three."

"The Svalbard Three."

"Sounds like a band of criminals."

"Listen." Henry whacks my leg. "Only three groups from the United States have deposited seeds into Svalbard, right? Well, Seeds Inc. was the only citizen-led group. They put five hundred varieties in there when it first opened. And now? They're planning to contribute another nine thousand varieties this winter."

"Wow."

"And old Dr. Harv is a 'notable adviser.' And his wife is an agriculturist and plant conservationist, also a 'notable adviser.'"

"Wait. I remember. He had this book on his desk. *The Seeds Inc. Yearbook*. I thought it was kind of funny."

"Tess," Henry says. He sets those brown eyes on mine. He holds me there with them. "It's more than funny. It's fate."

"Fate."

"*Fate*. We're going to get the pixiebell seeds in that vault."

"How are we going to do that?"

"I have no idea. We have to get them accepted, from what I know so far. And after that, we're going to bring them there."

I laugh. I mean, I saw the pictures. It is the most far-off place in the world. I am a regular girl, in a real place, with a regular (sort of regular) boy.

"Ouch," he says. "Why'd you pinch me?"

"I was thinking about you being real and regular." Henry pinches me back. "Ouch! It's the Arctic, Henry. Come on. We don't go places like that," I say.

"We do."

"We do?"

"Yes."

And as I sit on that real and regular rock, looking at that unreal and mystical glowing blue, I almost think it's possible.

chapter eighteen

Beta vulgaris: beet. The seeds of this plant are impossibly hard and inflexible. They resemble a knucklebone, and to even get one to germinate, it's advised that you soften it up first, soaking it in water for hours or even days. The seed obstinately grows in the most hostile environments, and has a history that dates back to the second millennium BC. Remains of the plant itself have been excavated in the Third Dynasty Saqqara pyramid at Thebes, Egypt. But don't plant different varieties too close together. The seeds need at least a quarter of a mile between each other, lest they intermingle and try and take each other over. In other words, the beet seed is wildly stubborn.

"I told you he wouldn't be back in two days," I say to Jenny.

"I can't concentrate when you keep talking." Jenny's back is to me. She is facing a large canvas, now tacked up on the far wall of her studio. She has a brush in her hand, and the tip is glossy with an orangey brown paint.

"Naples Yellow Deep. Raw Sienna." I read the tubes. I like the names of paint colors. "One *week*."

"And you know why, Tess. He told you. He told me. He is settling some financial matters of your mother's. Several accounts she had . . ."

"She probably hid her own inheritance money so he wouldn't buy a bunch of pot plants and start a business. I can't blame her."

Jenny lowers her eyebrows at me in warning.

"Is this why you and my mother didn't get along? You defend him no matter what? Two days, my butt."

"Okay, fine." Jenny sets her brush down with a snap. Little bits of Naples Yellow Deep and Raw Sienna fleck the table. She scoots a stool over, one her students use in art class, and it screeches against the floor in protest. She straddles it, sets her fists on her hips. "Go for it. Let it out. Sock it to me."

Now that I've been given permission to say whatever I want, I suddenly have no inclination to speak.

"Your mother and I are both stubborn people." I love Jenny for using the present tense, even though she's scowling at me. "Do you know how your parents met?"

"Of course I know how my parents met. Chamber music concert their first year of college. Held in a room in the music building. A whole six people in the audience. Love at first sight."

"I never understood why Thomas went to that concert. He was a rock 'n' roll boy. Never met a cello he didn't dislike. That's a double negative for you."

"He saw her shiny hair across the quad. Followed her in."

"Ah. I never heard that part."

I feel a little superior about having more information about my parents than she does. I also feel sort of superior about my mother's beautiful hair, which had the power to draw the rock 'n' roll boy into a whole damn room of cellos.

"He told me they were getting married after only three months."

"A year," I say.

"*Three months.* I was there, remember?" My superiority vanishes. "Three months, and I told them both that I thought it was a hasty decision. Well, neither of them liked that. I told Anna that I thought Thomas had some growing up to do. She disputed this fiercely. Of course, his playful, free spirit is what she loved best about him, and whatever you love best in a person is what'll likely drive you craziest later. Naturally, they got married anyway."

"And then you wrote them out of the will," I said.

"Ha. No. But your mother never forgave me for my disapproval, and I never forgave her for not forgiving me. And then, for many years to come, we proceeded to love and defend the same person, your father. They brought you to visit once. You were maybe two. Toddling around. He took you to the beach. Let you climb rocks. You fell and cut your chin." Jenny motions to her own, rubs two fingers there. "Old Dr. Marshall Fey had to give you stitches. Your mother was furious with him. Your dad, not Dr. Fey. She was furious with *me*. Probably in part because, by this time, she saw I was right about some things.

But she also thought I never held him accountable when he was younger, and therefore . . . Well. He was a boy with two hardheaded mothers fighting over him. He stayed with me once, when he ran away from home for a weekend. Five or six years ago, maybe. Do you remember? Some argument over . . . I don't even know. Money, perhaps."

I don't remember him ever leaving, except for that camping trip he took with his old friends from high school, Johnny Frank and Matt Pattowski. So this was the camping trip? His mother's house on Parrish? Mom and I ate pizza in bed and watched movies. We had a mass cleaning that even involved the fluff and stuff under our beds. It was the weekend she let me get my ears pierced.

"Mostly, though, I think your mother and I were just a lot alike. Too alike."

"That's it?"

"That's it. What were you expecting?"

"I don't know. Something more, at least. Some big, dramatic story. Some buried secret that makes it all make sense."

"That's part of what's so damn sad. It was pettiness. Mere pettiness. The shameful secret was how little it all mattered. Your mother and I—we made a fatal error—we let hurt feelings get in the way of love. And I made another one. The first one. I didn't keep my big damn mouth shut."

"You're right. It *is* sad," I say.

"We thought we had all the time in the world. And now,

well . . . You do things that you can't undo, and that's just a rotten fact about life."

I look at Jenny in her big denim shirt with the sleeves rolled up and her wrinkly tan face and her blue, blue eyes. If she and my mother were alike, then I am also like both of them. The three of us are all stubborn and loving and petty; we're guilty and easily hurt and big-hearted. And we all love the equally mixed bag that is our own Thomas Quincy Sedgewick.

"Why do you always paint trees, Jenny?" I can see them now in that canvas in front of me, more clearly than I did when I first saw the large painting in her living room. There are three trees, in Naples Yellow Deep and Raw Sienna and Cadmium Lemon and Gold Ochre. They are set against a sky of Davy's Gray and Titanium and Silver Number Two.

"I guess I like how calm they are. The way they *do* keep their big damn mouths shut. And they are settled to their fate, right? To the story? They rise from the ground. They spend their life growing and giving, and then they die. Such a simple story. But such a majestic one."

"Hey, I'm going to go write a poem now," I joke.

"You asked."

"I did. And I love your trees."

"And I"—Jenny stands, swings the stool out of the way to get back to work—"love *you*."

A paperback *Roget's Thesaurus* props open the front door. Henry Lark is worried he might not hear me knock because he is playing the piano. The music filling that room is dramatic and sad, and I watch Henry's narrow shoulders play passionately. His fingers fly until he somehow realizes I am there, and then he stops.

"Don't stop," I say.

"You're here." He pushes the bench back and stands to greet me.

"What was that?"

"Schubert. *Winterreise*. It's a series of poems, actually. That one's called 'Rückblick.' 'Retrospect.' Usually there's a singer."

"La-laaaa." I try my best opera.

"Hmm. Or something," Henry says.

"Is your mom home?"

"Nah. She's at work. We're alone." But he doesn't say it like a lot of boys would, like Dillon would have. There's no eyebrow-raising opportunism in it. Too bad. He's just stating a fact, without expectations. One thing about Henry Lark, he's a gentleman.

"I came right over."

"Good. You're going to love this."

Henry is taking the stairs two at a time with those long legs of his. I follow. "Is he back yet?" he asks.

We know enough about each other now that our conversation unrolls with its own shorthand.

"No. Legal stuff of my mom's is taking a while, supposedly. It doesn't even hurt me anymore. He and Cat-Hair Mary are probably in Hawaii."

Henry Frisbees a postcard to me, and I catch it like a pro. Pretty good for someone who can't bounce a basketball and walk at the same time. The postcard is a photo of a beach with the word "Mexico" in playful letters above it, festooned with a cartoony Mexican flag and a pair of maracas with googly eyes. I read the back. *Miss you, kid.* "Glad I got the mail before my mom."

"I don't picture you with a father like that."

"He doesn't picture himself with a kid like me." Henry sifts through the mess on his desk. Somewhere in there is that framed picture, and I imagine myself opening the desk drawer, lifting it out, turning it over. He and Millicent will have their arms around each other under a ridiculously blue sky. Her cheeks will be flushed pink, and his eyes will be dancing. I want to ask Henry about his broken heart, but I don't want to ask him. I'm not sure I want to know. The past is a good place for the past. And there's something about Henry. . . . I don't even want to admit it, but there are pieces of him that feel very far away. So far away that maybe he himself can't reach them. Those pieces scare me.

"Now, in *good* postal news . . . ," Henry says. "The reason I've asked you here."

He hands me an envelope. This is not thrown my way, but given over most gently. In the corner it says UNIVERSITY OF WASHINGTON, DEPARTMENT OF BOTANY AND PLANT PATHOLOGY, HITCHCOCK HALL. "It's fat," I say.

"I should've given him your address, but I didn't know it."

"I thought we were just going to get a letter. A yes or no about Pix." I squeeze the package. "Squishy," I say. "Something plastic."

"Are you the type who always tries to guess what's in your present?"

"No." Yes. I open the envelope. It's a letter, but there's also a sheet of instructions printed on green paper and several shiny Mylar sleeves that appear to seal shut.

Henry snitches the letter. He scans it quickly. Of course, Henry is the fastest reader alive. "Tess, listen. This is fantastic. "'Dear Tess and Henry—'"

"I like it already."

"'Thank you for your interest in Seeds Inc.'s next Svalbard deposit. I think it's a wonderful idea. There is no formal application process for inclusion. We choose seeds from our own seed bank. Our aim is diversity. The goal of Svalbard is to secure all the world's food crop varieties, so we would most certainly be interested in including Tess's *Fragaria singularis* both in our bank and in our next shipment to Svalbard. *Of course*. Instructions for seed preservation and shipment to us are included. . . .'"

Henry hands me the letter. He beams. "Did you see that, Tess? '*Of course*.'"

I see that. I see Henry's and my names next to each other. I see Dr. Harv Johansson's small, neat signature in blue ink. I see the padded envelope with the return address, postage already included. And all at once, my chest begins to ache. It's

232

a deep, bottomless ache, an unfixable yearning. There's no way I can put Pix's seeds in that envelope and drop them in some mailbox after Pix dies.

"We're not going to just drop them in some mailbox," Henry says, reading my mind. His kindness threatens to tip me over. My throat squeezes shut and my eyes get hot with tears. He grabs that postage-paid envelope out of my hands and then he leans down and shoves it into an already overflowing garbage can. The bold move snatches me from the gravelly ledge, the ten-thousand-mile fall. Sweet Henry looks so fierce shoving it in there, I almost laugh.

"You should take the stamp off anyway, so you don't waste it," I say.

"Fuck the stamp."

Henry doesn't talk like this, so this cracks us both up.

"Do you think if I had a sibling, I wouldn't be so attached to Pix? There'd be, I don't know, someone *else* of her?"

"Maybe," Henry says. "Do you think if I had a sibling I wouldn't be so attached to books?"

"Maybe," I say. "You'd be playing board games and tossing a football and fighting over who got the last doughnut, or whatever siblings do."

"They fight in the backseat of a car, I think. Which one Mom likes best and all that."

"And tell on each other too."

"God, Tess, you're so cute."

"Thank you," I say primly.

"We got the pixiebell seeds into Svalbard. Now we've got to get *you* there."

"I've been looking stuff up, Henry. Reading all about it. Presidents go to Svalbard. Dignitaries. Scientists. Not girls from San Bernardino."

"We haven't tried yet." Henry folds his arms. He pushes his glasses up with one finger, and it looks so nerdy and adorable I can barely stand it.

"It's in the Arctic! I've never even been to Florida." Even the film version seems too crazy to imagine.

Henry pulls me down onto the bed. Now we're talking. He's a gentleman, and I'm ready for him to be less of one. But nothing too juicy happens. He only takes my hands and looks into my eyes. Still, it makes me shiver.

"I need to ask you something," he says.

"Yes," I say.

"I'm serious. I want to know if this is something you really want. To bring the seeds of your mother's plant to Svalbard."

"Yes, but how much would that even co—"

"No buts. No nothing. Just, is this something you really *want*?"

I haven't yet told Henry that my mother's ashes are in a small copper urn in a cubby of a wall in Denver, next to her parents. I don't know anything about Denver. I've been there only once, when that urn was placed there. It's warmer than you'd think. Flat for miles, surrounded by shortish mountains off in the distance. I never even knew my mother's parents, in that adjacent cubby. It's like we've left her all alone there. And that urn has a rose etched onto it. She never even liked roses. She wasn't a rose-type person at all.

"More than anything," I say. "More than *anything*. I've been reading, looking at those pictures. . . . It's so beautiful there. It *is* the last forever, Henry. The only thing is, I want it so much, I have to pretend I don't want it at all. That's how much I want it."

"Okay."

"I'm worried to even *dream* it. I mean, the *disappointment* . . ."

"Not if we make it happen."

It is 3,185.1 miles from here to Oslo, four hundred miles from Oslo to the Longyearbyen airport. One kilometer from Longyearbyen Airport to the vault by snowmobile. Average temperature in winter is minus-eighteen degrees.

"Impossible."

"Stop saying that. Especially when we have so much work to do."

I toss off my sandals, stand on Henry's bed in front of the huge map hanging there on the wall. I am hunting around for the tiny word, my finger swirling around in the general vicinity. "It is on an *island* in the *Arctic Ocean*, for God's sake."

Henry stops my finger right on Svalbard. Then he grabs me around the waist and gives me a shove, and we tumble to the bed, causing a few books to fall off. We are on our backs, staring up at the map. "You gotta remember," Henry says. "The *whole thing* belongs to us. The whole wide world is ours."

The flower—it's turning into a fruit now, there's no doubt about that. The petals have fallen away. I have gathered each one. I have lifted the plastic sheet of the last page of the photo album I brought, and I've set them on the sticky page. I've placed them in a circle, under a photograph of my mother and me that my father took. It was the summer before we learned she was sick; after that, we stopped taking pictures. Don't stop taking pictures if your loved one is sick. Just don't. You'll be so sorry later.

In the photo, her hair is up in a ponytail, and so is mine. Our cheeks are together, posing, chins out. We are both squinting because it's bright. I was heading out to go with Meg's family for the weekend, to her aunt's cabin on Silverwood Lake. We were supposed to learn how to water ski, but I never could get up on those skis. I felt like I was a giraffe under water. But that day, Mom was driving me over to Meg's, and Dad caught us before we got in the car. I was bugged at him for messing around when I was already late. But you can't tell in the picture. I look happy.

Every day, the tiny green nub of fruit grows wider and thicker. It's strange to watch something that closely, to notice change like that every day. There's so much you don't notice. I think about the lemon tree we had in the backyard in San Bernardino, how it always seemed like one day there weren't lemons and then the next day there were. That tree smelled so good, though, and my mother made lemon bread with the fruit, squeezing the juice into one of our green bowls, plucking out an escaping seed with the tip of her finger. I might miss that tree, just a little.

There are no more leaves on Pix at all. It's bald and thin and its color is wrong. Of course, I can't help but think about the people in that waiting room. I think of that radiation symbol on the door, and of the end of the world, and the only thing that will be left, a vault in the Arctic.

I've fallen asleep right there on the floor in front of Pix. I have trouble sleeping at night in my own bed. Jenny is gently shaking my shoulder.

"Dinner," she says, and when I wake up, there is Pix and Jenny and the open photo album and the flood of remembering about where I am and why. I was lying when I said it didn't hurt anymore that my father is gone. She is gone, and he is gone, and we have lost so much.

chapter nineteen

Taraxacum officinale: dandelion. The one round, white poof of a dandelion that comes after the yellow flower is actually hundreds of tiny seeds gathered together, all with little white parachutes, all waiting to be released. When the time is right, the seeds fly off into the air in various directions like a dandelion army. They drop from their parachutes onto land, ready to infiltrate.

"What is *this*?"

The sheet is taped to the checkout counter of the Parrish Island Library. I can hardly believe what I'm seeing. It's a picture of me. And it's an awful picture—

"We took it while you were sleeping," Sasha says.

An awful picture of me *sleeping*, slumped over in the Leave Me Alone chair. My eyes are shut. My chin is resting in my palm. I'm too shocked to take in the words underneath the image, something about Pix and me and Svalbard. There are blank lines for signatures. Sasha's name is on there already, and then Henry has signed underneath, and then Larry, and then Kenny Travis.

"Kenny Travis?" I ask.

"He stole the pen, but at least he signed," Sasha says. I remember. Kenny Travis, the eight-year-old thief of dogs, bikes, and yard sale signs.

"What are you guys doing?" I feel slightly panicked. I should perhaps rip this page right off, leaving only the tape and a small, clinging bit of paper.

"Getting you to Svalbard."

"By signature?" Okay, they're not exactly getting very far, but still.

"Never underestimate a determined librarian," Henry says.

"Petitions! Power to the People!" Larry says, and raises a fist in the air.

Sasha slides a different page across the counter to me. It is a printed list. I don't understand at first, and then I do.

Back-country ski boots. Insulated overboots. Expedition-weight base layers. Down suit. Breathable wind pants. Fleece pants and jacket. Synthetic mittens. Wind-resistant mittens. Balaclava. This goes on for two pages.

"Baklava?" I say. "A little Greek pastry for the trip?"

"*Balaclava*," Sasha corrects.

"Bank robber hat," Larry explains. He mimes pulling on a ski mask. "Where only the eyes peek out. When you come back from Svalbard, you can hold up a convenience store."

"There's a 'two' next to everything," I say.

Henry shrugs.

"You're coming along?"

"Protect you from polar bears," he says. He grins at me, that shy, knee-weakening grin. Oh, if only.

"Guys," I try again. "Thank you, really. But I've done my homework. The vault administrators have been flooded with requests from people who want to visit. They only open it maybe twice a year to deposit new seeds. They don't exactly give tours. Invitation only."

"Switch your RSVP to Ready Mode," Larry says. He swivels his hips a little, which is something he shouldn't do. He's obviously had too much coffee.

This is nuts. There's not that much to do here on Parrish, obviously. I get it. That's the conclusion I come to, anyway. I guess they can't do much harm, though, can they? I mean, there's not a soul in sight at the library right now, and it's generally not exactly busy.

I protest on vanity grounds. "This is a terrible, terrible picture."

"You look like an angel," Larry says.

"I wouldn't go that far," Sasha says.

"I Photoshopped out the drool," Henry says. I look at him, alarmed, but he's chuckling.

"Very funny. You're a riot."

"Tess, my darling," Sasha says. "Can you do something for us? We've been up all night. Can you run down to Java Java Java and get us some lattes?"

"You've been up *all night*?" Oh no.

"Just go," Henry says.

Well, of course I go. And the minute I do, I understand why they're sending me into town. I don't know whether to groan or run away or laugh. There I am, my stupid sleeping face, the plea for Pix and me, on the telephone pole outside Randall and Stein Booksellers. And there I am, on the door of Sweet Violet's Chocolates. And when I go way, way down, *blocks* away, to Java Java Java to get the coffee, there I am, on the counter by the cash register.

"Hey, aren't you the . . ." The barista, who's got a beard like Larry's and a hemp bracelet, squints at me, taps the petition.

"You must be"—I read the first and only signature—"Nick Talbott."

"Call me Nicky," he says, and pushes the cardboard tray of cups to me. "I'll call you Cool."

I laugh. The bells jingle against the door when I leave. I keep walking. Now I see my face at the Front Street Market, on the wall by the shopping carts. I see it at Eugene's Gas and Garage. My closed eyes are on the window of Bud's Tavern.

I carry the coffees back, balancing their cardboard holder carefully. I open the library door with one hand and a foot. Henry has started story time, and in that half hour, many more signatures have appeared on the sheet. I see Nathan's and Max's, the big loopy print of a boy just learning cursive. I see names I don't even know, probably those mothers with overflowing strollers and diaper bags. Several toddlers have apparently done the deed. The name BEN is written in extra-large print. A name I can't make out has a backward *R*.

"Lattes," I say to Sasha, who's looking mighty pleased with herself. "Do you have reason to think the Norwegian government will care about a petition from Parrish Island, USA?"

"Do you have reason to think they *won't*?"

I stop to read the words there, really read them. It's a plea. It's practically on its knees with folded hands raised—*Help poor, pathetic Tess Sedgewick get the seeds of her dead mother's plant into Svalbard*. It doesn't exactly use those words, but it's pretty clear, and I'm just not okay being some petition version of those starving-children/abused-dog commercials with the sad music that make you end up hating starving children and abused dogs.

"It's a pity plea," I say. "I shouldn't get special treatment because my mother died. People's mothers die. Their fathers die. Every day. I don't deserve something special because of that. I don't want to win some dead parent lottery."

"That's such bullshit," Sasha says. "It's not about pity! It's about having a mission. And besides, Abby says people aren't even reading the paragraph."

"Abby? You've got these petitions in Seattle?" My voice is rising. You might even call it a shriek.

"Well, Dr. Johansson has some in his lab and over at the Shaw Mountain Field Station. Oh, and his assistant may have posted them at his synagogue. Abby put them up around campus. Probably, there are a few around the city. She and Dr. Harv have way more signatures than us already, which *sucks*, since this was my idea! But Abby said the university students see the picture and just sign. They love it. They think it's hilarious, you with your eyes closed like that, chin on your hand, *How to Keep Almost Any Plant Alive* by Dr. Lester Frank open on your lap. It's adorable. Look how sweet you look."

I look like me, only asleep. I don't get it. I could fight this. I could explain how stupid the picture is, or complain about people feeling sorry for me, or convince Sasha and Henry and Larry of the futility of this huge gesture. But I decide to do something else instead. I decide to take what they are offering me. Jenny said that sometimes the simplest things are the most majestic. And this kindness, this love? Well, it is offered over plainly, but really, it is so large and so splendid and so beautiful that my astonished self can barely take it in.

I cruise around the island a bit before heading home, driving Deception Loop halfway before turning around. This time I am not gazing out toward the twinkly waters of the sound, viewed through the lacy boughs of evergreens. No, I'm on an odd Easter egg hunt, the eggs being my own photograph on an eight-by-twelve sheet, lined paper attached with a staple. Yes, there I am—a petition in the window of the real estate office, next to the houses for sale, and one on the creepy cabin-y bathroom at Point Perpetua Park. There is one on the old water tank, next to a HAPPY 60TH, HANK! ROCK 'N' ROLL

NEVER DIES, OLD GEEZER! sign. There is one on a tree stump in Crowe Valley. It is tacked there with way too many pushpins, my face bent around the curve of bark.

And, oh, I am riding such a high, full wave of love that I *have* to fall. Of course I have to. Of course, because life and love is joy and pain, fullness and emptiness, highs and lows, tide in, tide out. I will have to fall hard from that high wave, smack right down on my sorry face, but we are not at that part of the story yet. No, we are at the part where my heart is soaring in Jenny's VW bus, and where my own picture keeps surprising me, on a telephone pole and on an abandoned truck in a field and on the front door of the Rufaro School of Marimba.

I am driving too fast. I have Happy Accelerator Foot. All of my delight is pressing right down on that pedal. Happy Accelerator Foot is dangerous, and so is Mad Accelerator Foot. Emotions need to be kept in the head and heart where they belong. Your poor old extremities get a hit of high emotion and they go a little wild, like a hyperactive boy given too much candy at the classroom Halloween party. But I want to hurry home and tell Jenny about this. And then maybe I will plant a garden or paint the whole house or move a mountain.

Tilting mailbox by gravel road. I once made this turn in a car with my mother and father when I was very young. I know that now. My mother would have worn that grim face she got, a pre-pissed face, when she was anticipating her own anger. A preemptive strike against her enemies—tight mouth, expressionless eyes.

She wore that face when we went to a meeting with Mrs. Confrites, my ninth-grade algebra teacher who gave me a D. I told my mother that I was failing because Mrs. Confrites never took the time to explain things well, and that she was always yelling, and I didn't tell the part about *why* she was always yelling—how Kyra Thomas, who'd never even so much as looked at me before then, in all the years I'd known her, liked to talk and laugh with me in class. I didn't tell the part about how giving up that attention from Kyra Thomas was just plain asking too much, and that getting yelled at by Mrs. Confrites (*You! Out!*) was completely worth it, and a little bit thrilling, too.

The thing is, my mother *still* wore that face even as the meeting went on, and all I could do in the midst of all that unwarranted loyalty was look down and scrape some dried glue off the desk with my fingernail. My mother was a warm person, a person who wanted to feed you and take care of you, who bought you a brand-new box of Kleenex when you were sick and lemon candies rolled in dusty sugar to help your throat, but she could believe in things, in people, in us, against all evidence. You didn't want to cross her when it came to her loved ones.

The driveway is smashed full of cars, and so I ditch the van near the back of the line, hop out, and jog a little toward the studio. I forgot it was lesson day. But joy needs company, more company than Vito the dog, who *always* greets you like you've both just won the lottery. I need someone who can discriminate between general joy and this wonderful, specific, fabulous event.

I open the white, rough-hewn door of the studio. My eyes go directly to him. I'm shocked. I guess this is what you get when you stop listening to your phone messages. I didn't even see the truck out there. But, sure enough, here is my father, sitting on a stool in front of an easel, and it is quite clear that I've inherited my abundant artistic talent from him. His vase of wildflowers looks like it's had a run-in with a terrorist flinging an acrylic bomb.

I am standing over his shoulder; I take on the posture of Teacher, one even Jenny doesn't wear. "You've stolen my technique, Pops. Of course, I stole it from every kindergartener with a paintbrush."

"Shh. I'm concentrating," he says. He sounds just like Jenny.

"You got your sleeve in the paint."

He looks. Sees that I am right. "Shit," he says. His cuff is dragging around, making a trail not only on his canvas but on his favorite jeans.

"I think you've got a gift. A God-given *gift*. You need to paint a ceiling or something."

"Thomas Believed There Was a Statue in Every Piece of Stone."

"Welcome home, Dad."

"Home?" He raises his eyebrows. It's a question. It's an *option*.

Perhaps I don't know an ending when I see one after all.

I sniff his shirt. It smells only of clean cotton and maybe a little of that man soap I gave him.

"I know what you're doing. And I promised. I keep my promises."

"Ha. What about the two days? You promised *that*."

"If you would have listened to my messages and called me back, you would have known what happened. It was unavoidable. I had to take care of some of your mother's last business, and ours. You don't just ditch a life."

"Listen to you," I say. "'Let's just do it,' a wise man said. 'Let's just f-ing do it.'"

"I suggested going. You suggested staying gone."

"After you ditched me and left me no choice!"

"Children," Jenny reprimands. We have been whispering, and it's true, the whispers have been getting louder and more intense.

"Don't stop on our account," Millicent says. "I feel like I'm watching reality TV." Millicent is in all pink today. She is wearing some retroish pink romper, with pink shiny shoes and two braids tied with pink ribbon. Ha, it's a fashion misstep. She looks like a bottle of Pepto-Bismol.

My father snaps his head in her direction. There he is with his black-gray hair pulled into a ponytail and his big nose and his flashing eyes. I missed that big nose. He doesn't get that protective hard face Mom would have gotten. No, he only looks at Millicent with a flippant smirk. "Honey, I think your braids are too tight."

"Let's all mind our own business." Jenny's voice shuts down any possibility of more nonsense. It's the voice she probably should have used on my father years ago.

Margaret has been concentrating on a poppy, the bright orange of its small, closed purse. She doesn't look away from it when she speaks. Her chin is still tilted up in concentration. "How is the plant, dear? I signed something for you at the pharmacy. I couldn't read the words, as I didn't have my glasses. But I saw your picture."

"We put them up on all the ferries," Joe Nevins says, and chuckles.

"Now Max wants to go to the Arctic too," Nathan says. "He's walking around with a stick from the yard, saying he's an iceberg explorer."

"The magnetic force of the poles has healing properties," Cora Lee whispers. "I signed the petition at the post office."

"You were holding that book by that plant doctor," Margaret interrupts. "I recognized that cover even without my glasses. We had Dr. Lester Frank speak to our Garden Society. He was quite the contrarian. He complained that we did not have decaf and that the cookies were too sweet."

"Arctic?" my father asks.

"I'll explain later," I say.

"Are we here to work, people, or have a social circle?"

"Social circle," Elijah says, and Millicent elbows him.

"You," Jenny says to me. "Out."

I am reminded of Mrs. Confrites and ninth-grade algebra

all over again. Here is another message my mother *would* send, in lieu of rainbows and butterflies. *Very funny,* I say to her in my head, just in case.

I have to be content to share my fine day with Vito after all. I let him out of the house and into the yard, where he runs in circles, speediest dog in the West. He crosses the finish line near my feet, and I pick him up. I feel his little heart beating like mad and he's panting.

"The winner!" I say to him. And then I lift him high in the air against the blue, blue sky. We both celebrate, and we are both grateful for all the triumphs the day has brought.

He startles me. I am lying on an old lounge chair I found in Jenny's garage, and I'm in my bathing suit. I've dragged that chair way, way over into a corner of the grassy field in front of the house, where no painting class member could ever see me. I've gathered the essential elements for a perfect summer afternoon: chair, book, towel, cold drink (that I've sloshed across the lawn, losing an ice cube on the way), and companion (panting dog who recovers the ice cube and crunches vigorously before circling down in a spot of shade). Once settled, I promptly fall asleep. It seems I can sleep anywhere but my own bed.

I am dreaming, and so when he says my name, I jump. Terrific. I must look just great, with the bumpy towel marks on my face and the lines from the rubber strands of the chair on my calves where the towel didn't reach. My face is flushed and my hair is damp with sweat. It got hot out there, in that patch of grassy meadow. Even Vito has gone back to the house, I see.

"Elijah," I say.

"Sorry if I woke you."

"That's all right." I sit up. This sounds simpler than it actually is. I am scooting my bathing suit around and clutching my towel and peering down at various spots on my body, making sure everything is covered up. Elijah makes me feel exposed.

"I'm having a surprise party for Henry next week. For his birthday. Maybe you'd like to come?" He tosses his hair. I don't imagine this. He actually does it. He flings it back so that I can admire its glossy sheen.

But an arrow of, I don't know, regret, disappointment, jealousy, is shooting toward my heart. It hits its mark, takes the sad, beating beast down. I didn't know Henry was having a birthday. We've never even *talked* about birthdays. He hasn't mentioned a thing about it.

"Our house? Next Saturday night. Let's say eight."

"Sure. Great. Where?" The question is a lie. I know exactly where their house is. Henry pointed it out one day, when we were headed to Point Perpetua with a pizza from Sneaky Jake's. Actually, that's a lie, too. I knew where the house was even before that. I looked it up, in the narrow Parrish Island Directory in the library. And then I drove past that huge Victorian with the perfect paint and the wide lawn and I imagined Henry and Millicent running across it holding hands, Millicent's perfect hair flowing behind her. Henry tackling her under the perfect lilac, kissing her passionately. Millicent lifting herself up from the lawn afterward with the nastiest, most disgusting case of poison ivy ever. You should have seen her. Ugh.

He gives me the kind of directions that involve landmarks of various kinds. Just past Asher House B and B, turn by that big tree, et cetera, et cetera. My mother loved those kinds of directions. She'd always ask people on the phone, "What's it near?" Give her a 76 Station or an Albertson's and she'd be set.

"Exactly how far past Asher House is this tree?" I ask.

He looks—pardon the pun—stumped. "Um. Half mile? Mile?"

It is exactly .33 miles, but I'm not at that part of the story yet. I'm at the part where I'm clutching my towel to my chest and saying, "I'm sure I can find it."

"Great," he says, but it doesn't seem great to him, not really. The *Great* doesn't convey enthusiasm. No. The *Great* is high pitched and self-satisfied. It says only one thing: that Elijah has finally put an end to one very nasty piece of business.

chapter twenty

Verbascum blattaria: moth mullein. In the longest-known ongoing scientific experiment, Dr. William James Beal, a professor of botany, buried twenty bottles of twenty-one different seeds (including *Verbascum blattaria*) in a sandy knoll in 1879. The purpose of the experiment was to determine how long the seeds could be buried in the soil and still germinate when planted. The crazy old coot dug up one bottle every five years. He died twenty-five years after he started the experiment, so he was able to dig up only five time capsules. Another scientist kept the experiment going. For the next fifteen years, *he* dug up a capsule every five years. The last time capsule was unearthed in April of 2000, by yet *another* scientist. The seeds inside had been buried for 120 years, and some of them, most notably *V. blattaria*, could still germinate, proving that life (and a life's work) goes on, even after death.

This is what I imagine now: Grandfather Leopold, walking home in his overcoat after that party, his breath puffing clouds into the cold night air, his leather-gloved hands in his pockets, one finger tapping the seed case now deep in the satin lining of his pocket. He is whistling. His mustache is white with frost. Snow begins to fall, landing on his wide shoulders and the brim of his hat. That night, he can barely sleep, and in the morning he rises and putters with his coffee and scrambled eggs, prolonging the excitement of what is going to happen next. The seed sits on his bureau like a jewel in a box. The snow, which has blanketed the city, is no obstacle to what he has in mind today. Because his kitchen windowsill is warm. It is near his large stove and the curved, accordion iron of the room's radiator.

He washes his cup and plate and fork and lays them out to dry on a kitchen towel. He can't bear the anticipation any longer. He climbs the stairs and carries the case with the seed back to the kitchen. He has already placed a pot in the sink, filled with scoops of the good soil from the large palm in the living room. He holds the seed between his thumb and forefinger. *One and only,* he thinks. Rare.

These seeds—the ones I am now gazing at on the outside of this singular strawberry that Pix has grown, are the progeny of that one tiny speck that Grandfather Leopold gently placed in the soil of that blue terra-cotta pot. There are hundreds of seeds on this fruit. The way life goes on, it seems like a miracle, even if a devastating one.

We have been waiting for it to ripen, and now that it has, Henry and I have debated when it should be picked. After it is picked, Pix will die. Henry has been saying, *Now,* and I have been saying, *Not now,* but I know it's time. We can't wait too long. Jenny has suggested that we celebrate the night we pick the berry. It sounds corny, like one of those things people do—a Celebration of Life when someone dies: doves set free, sappy music, bad poems, and school project-ish posters with sad photos of happy times set on easels.

Still. What is there to do in the face of it?

I call Henry. "Now," I say.

Pix is in the center of Jenny's dining room table, which I've told you before is made out of a huge old door. The door of some barn, my father has told me. Pix looks like the guest at the party, the honoree, the Plant of the Hour. Jenny has cut flowers from the garden and placed them around the house, which is perhaps a wrong way to honor a plant, akin to eating bacon at a pig party. My father has put on some music. Jenny still has records and a record player. He plays Jenny's old hippie stuff—Blood, Sweat & Tears; Three Dog Night; Simon & Garfunkel—shouting out the names of each just before it plays. He is dancing to "Cecilia," a song about this guy finding his girlfriend in bed with another guy. Dad knows the words and is singing along. I don't care how old you are; watching your parent dance makes you cringe inside a little. Or, after that pelvis swivel he just did, *a lot*.

"Jesus, Dad," I say.

"What?"

I show a great deal of restraint and keep my mouth shut and my eyes averted. Jenny is making chicken and dumplings and I leave to help her in the kitchen. But then the doorbell rings, and Vito, well, you know what Vito does when the doorbell rings, and Dad rushes to get it before me. He's ridiculously excited when Henry comes over—Dad, not Vito, though Vito is too. Dad loves Henry. Maybe he even loves him more than I do. Now that Dad is not stoned half the time, I realize he's enthusiastic about practically everything. Not just old TV shows and politics and mammoth craters made in the earth a jillion years ago, but about ancient composers and Roman philosophers. Planetary orbits and hieroglyphics. The northern lights of Longyearbyen, Svalbard, and seed formation. He and Henry are a match made in heaven. I am beginning to understand what my mother saw in him when they first met. The world opens up with someone like that.

My father actually flings the door wide. There is a great deal of back patting. My father finally releases Henry from his manly grasp, and Henry kisses my cheek. He is holding a present. It is a box with a red bow. My father gestures him inside and shows him where to set it—on the coffee table in front of the big white couch with the enormous painting of trees behind it. On it is something I hadn't seen yet. Another box. A smaller one, another bow. You wouldn't think someone was dying here. The party atmosphere feels wrong.

"Almost like it's my birthday," I say. I've been dropping birthday references to Henry ever since Elijah told me about the surprise party a few days ago. I pointed out cakes at the Front Street Market when we went in to get a soda. I told him

I had the same birthday as President Kennedy and Mother Teresa, which isn't even true. I asked him if he ever read his horoscope.

"Horrorscope," he replied, but didn't say more. Coming out and asking might give away the surprise of the party, but I was getting more and more annoyed. Most likely, knowing Henry, he just didn't want to draw attention to himself. But I *know* him. I wouldn't go buy some *Happy 18th, Henry Lark* message to play on the JumboTron during a Mariners' game. He should *trust* me.

"Pix party!" my father says. He likes the sound of this, apparently, because he's said it about five times now.

"Homage," Henry says, giving me reason number infinity to love him.

"Henry Lark," Jenny says, coming out of the kitchen. She kisses him on the cheek, which is the warmest she's been to him yet. Whatever grudge she held against him seems to be fading. He probably picked some apples from her tree when he was six.

"You married your mother," I say to Dad, but no one is following along with my thoughts again, and so the comment floats away amid shoulder shrugs of incomprehension and *Oh wells*.

"You guys can set the table," Jenny says. The music stops suddenly, and Dad leaves to turn the record over. There are songs on both sides of those things, set down in thin, lined ridges, which seems even more incredible than music playing on computers.

"Too bad there's no piano," I say to Henry.

He thinks. "Tchaikovsky. Symphony no. 6. *Pathétique.* Requiem; impending death. Plus he lost his mother when he was fourteen. Plus—"

My father interrupts. He's listening in. "Rock 'n' roll's got us covered." There is the scratchy sound of needle hitting vinyl. And then, "Let It Be," by the Beatles.

Stupid song. I hate that song. I could be at the happiest carnival, riding the happiest elephant ride and eating the happiest, tallest pink cotton candy, and one note of that song could choke me up.

"Silverware, people," Jenny commands. But I catch her. She is wiping her eyes with the corner of a paper towel.

Henry sets his napkin by his plate. I push my own away. I'm stuffed. I can barely move.

"Gifts," my father announces. He's got a biscuit crumb by his mouth.

"Dad," I say. "Biscuit mouth."

He brushes it away distractedly, practically tips his chair hurrying to retrieve his box. When he returns, I notice that his eyes are gleaming.

Uh-oh.

I take it from him; I slowly undo the bow. Under the lid, there is tissue paper that I carefully unfold. I take out the item, made of blue wool. I don't understand.

"It's a baklava!" he says excitedly.

"Balaclava," Jenny says.

"You don't want to freeze your face off when you and Henry go to Svalbard," my father says.

"That's really sweet, Dad. But we want to be realistic here, right?" These big dreamers, they can really be a pain. Big dreamers come with a stubborn streak. They are a dog with a knotted sock. They just don't let go. "Um, money? Plane tickets." I count off obstacles on my fingers.

"We covered that," Henry and my dad say at the same time. My mother's estate had money, apparently. Quite a lot of it from her own parents, which she'd kept for my education. Dad says there's more than enough, and Henry says Cancún Pops has a pen in hand ready to pay away his guilt.

"We haven't exactly been invited."

Now it's Henry who pushes his chair back. He's more careful. His eyes, though, they are gleaming too when he hands me his box.

"It's not an invitation," he says as I untie this bow and lift this lid. "Not yet." It is not an invitation, but what's in this box leaves me speechless. A large stack of paper. Pages, pages, pages, and more pages of signatures. Signatures in black ink and blue and green, narrow loops and fat ones, tiny ones and large, statement-making ones. There's a Robert and a Janine and two Elizabeths and a Che; there's a Yankovitch and a Vazqueze and a Brown and a Navaro. Some of the pages are crinkled, as if they'd been in the rain. Some have coffee cup rings. On one of my photos, someone has drawn a party hat and a mustache. It makes me look both evil and festive as I sleep there with *How to Keep Almost Any Plant Alive* open on my chest.

"This is only one box. We've got at least twenty of them."

I don't even know if I heard him correctly. It is . . . *astonishing.*

"You'll have to give it back. Sasha wants to mail them all to the consulate with her letter."

I imagine this now too. A beefy Norwegian with his white hair and thick hands, sitting behind his desk, which is piled with an unusual arrival in the mail. Box after box after box from Parrish Island, Washington, USA. And a letter from the same. He opens it and reads. He smiles.

It is not an invitation, but for the first time, this crazy idea, the idea that was set in motion that first day I walked into the Parrish Island Library, searching for Pix's identity, seems maybe, possibly, actually, within reach.

"You guys," I say. Well, there are no words.

"Try on the baklava," my father says.

I do. "Stick 'em up," I say.

He takes a picture of me with his phone. I pull off the hat, and my hair rises in a static standing ovation.

Tink, tink, tink. Jenny taps her knife against the globe of her wineglass. "I think it's time for a speech."

We wait. She is looking at Pix, that now thin, yellowing stalk with its single berry. We *all* look. I am thinking she's got a plan here, some big emotional speech that puts meaning to this unusual, unspeakably sad situation. We wait some more.

But apparently this speech was an impulsive, unplanned idea, now suddenly proved impossible, or else the words she carefully chose earlier are somehow in the moment all wrong.

"To . . ." Her voice is cracking. I swallow hard. This good-bye mirrors another good-bye. This thank-you does.

Henry takes my hand under the table, holds it tight.

"To life," she says.

And then it's time, and so I stand up. My chest caves in. My heart squeezes. I am crying. I want to do this in some dignified way, but I am crying hard. I set my fingers around that perfect berry, and I pull. It's a beautiful berry. It's a singular plant. Now it looks so bare, just its thin, empty stalk. Just a simple collection of cells and flesh, which has completed its life's work.

Tears roll down my face. I'm a big mess. Jenny's eyes are wet, and so are Henry's, and my dad honks a loud nose blow into his napkin.

I hold out the berry in my palm for us all to admire. A million seeds, or even a single one—we continue.

Henry and I follow the instructions. We take the ripe fruit and crush it in a glass mixing bowl. We add water to the bowl, and the seeds sink, and the skin and pulp float. We separate seed from skin and wash the tiny, tiny seeds in a piece of cheesecloth. We will dry the seeds before putting them inside the Mylar envelope. And I will choose one to plant, just as Grandfather Leopold did. I will place it in Pix's pot. I will keep that plant with me wherever I go, dorm room to apartment to house, and I will put it on my own kitchen windowsill one day, as my mother had.

Henry is about to leave. My father hears the sounds of a departure and he comes bolting out of the living room, practically accosting Henry. There is more back slapping. He even says "You're a good boy," which sounds like he's talking to the dog. It's all rather embarrassing. I'm surprised he doesn't jump up and lick his face. Actually, I'm surprised he doesn't follow us to Henry's car when I walk him out.

But no. We're alone. The moon is full and low and large. I smell the cool deepness of night and the insistent drift of salt water. Henry is leaning against his car, and I am leaning against Henry.

"You okay?" he asks.

"I'm okay," I say.

"Did you know that in Longyearbyen, the sun sets each year for the very last time on October twenty-fifth, and that it will not rise above the horizon again for four months?" His eyes look soft in the light of the moon. They look a little sleepy now too. It's been a big night.

"It officially returns on March eighth, when it is finally high enough above the horizon to shine down on the steps of the old hospital, where the entire town gathers to await its arrival."

"Tess." He smiles. "You know, I really love you."

Oh, beautiful words. Oh, joy and pain, fullness and emptiness, highs and lows, tide in, tide out. Right then, our future together and all its unknowns sit like a fragile puff of a dande-lion, waiting for a wish. I close my eyes and blow. "I really love you too, Henry."

When his car is all the way down the drive, when it has turned at the tilting mailbox, I go in. My father scares the crap out of me. He's got that ski mask on. Of course he couldn't resist. He's probably been wanting to try it out all night.

"Thomas Has Always Harbored a Secret Desire to Wear Baklava on His Head," I say, when my heart stops beating wildly in fear.

"How late is the bank open?" he says. He chuckles in a sinister manner.

"Take that off and give me a hug good night," I say.

He does. And then I look at him, and he looks at me.

As I said, there will be no momentous, earth-shattering, father-daughter talk in this story, no big crying scene and sob-bing reunion. Right then, we do not have some revealing, cli-mactic conversation about that night we left her alone in the hospital to die.

Instead, tonight, we have simply shared a meaningful event. And next we share this: a look between us that says we've gone from here to there, from shame to a shaky, mutual forgiveness; from a time when our lives felt like a to-scale model, three feet equaling one and a quarter inches, to now, where the whole wide world is ours.

chapter twenty-one

Datura: angel's-trumpet/devil's-trumpet. Though nobody can seem to agree what to call it, there is no argument about the danger of ingesting any part of this plant, most especially its seeds. The seedpod is a menacing ball covered in sharp spines, and the flower, which possesses a strange, seductive beauty, blooms only at dusk. Datura was well known as an essential ingredient of love potions and witches' brews, causing delirious states and death. Some believe that eating the seeds of *Datura* was what caused the erratic behavior of the young "witches" in Salem. And, in 1676, British soldiers ingested *Datura stramonium* in a boiled salad and remained in a stupor for eleven days. If this is a love potion, no thank you.

I need to choose a gift for Henry. I want it to be just right, something that speaks to our mission, how we tried to save Pix, how we sort of failed but sort of triumphed, too. I think along the lines of plants and seeds; I even consider using one of Pix's seeds to grow Henry his own pixiebell. But it's too much my mother and me and not Henry and me, and so I go to Old Sh**—that's what it's called, with the asterisks and everything.

It's an antiques shop in town. Out front, there's a mannequin dressed in an ancient diving suit, with a beautiful brass helmet on its head, and in the window there's a creepy stuffed cougar, a Civil War flag, a line of tin flasks, and rusty lunch boxes with the Lone Ranger on them.

The big-bearded man behind the counter doesn't waste any time. "Hey, aren't you—"

I close my eyes as if I'm sleeping and rest my chin on my palm. "Her?"

He chuckles. "It was right here." He taps the counter with his knuckles. "Mine was the first name on it."

"Well, thank you," I say. He goes back to breaking open rolls of coins into the register while I look around. I make several slow loops around the entire store before I spot it. It's on a table with the sort of glass dishes you see at carnivals and a magnifying glass like Sherlock Holmes's: a compass. A brass compass, the brass so worn that it's almost black. It has a lid that opens and closes, and inside, the compass rose is an intricate black-and-white. This is not about our quest to find Pix's identity—this is about what happens next.

The bearded man wraps the compass in tissue paper. "For your trip?" he asks.

"If it happens. I hope so."

"True north," he says.

A few days ago, Henry told me he'd be busy Saturday night, that Elijah wanted help with some project. I have not spilled the secret yet, which has taken some doing, especially since I'm confused and mad that Henry still has not mentioned his birthday. But I love Henry, and I trust him, and so I keep telling myself there will be an explanation.

And, oh yes, there will be one, all right.

I'm nervous. This will be the first time I'm with Henry and all his friends, people who've known each other forever, and me, the interloper, the tourist, the maybe transplant. So of course I change my clothes a bunch of times and screw up my hair and have to wet it again, which makes it look worse. I do everything I can to make the situation a crisis, accidentally poking myself in the eye with my mascara wand, touching the hot part of the hair blower against my neck, spilling some I'd-better-eat-something yogurt on the shirt I finally decide on. Between bad hair and mean people and junior high, your poor old self-confidence gets so many bullets shot at it, you're lucky if it stays alive.

I shout out a good-bye as I leave, because I'm too anxious to have any kind of annoying *Have a great night!* chats with either Jenny or Dad. I've written down instructions to Elijah and Millicent's house, even though I know exactly where it is. This knowledge is sure to evaporate as soon as I'm down the driveway (see Mascara Wand in Eye, above). And so I smooth out the piece of paper on my leg and turn the key again after the car is already on, which causes the engine to scream as if I've just accosted it on a dark night.

So far so good.

Past Asher House (.33 miles), there is the massive oak, looming minion of Middle Earth, arms stretched in a warning I don't heed. I turn. After that (.14 miles) is the street, Parrish Point. *Perish*, I think, because there it is, that Victorian, the kind of house that looks so gingerbread friendly in the day and so haunted house at night. This night, though, all the lights are blazing in its ornate windows, and I can feel the bass beat of loud music in my own body before I even find a place to park. My mind goes parental, the way it tends to do when things feel out of control. I wonder where Elijah and Millicent's parents are. I wonder what the neighbors will think.

I have a sudden longing for Meg and my own friends, who I've so carelessly tossed aside. You can ignore a person's calls only so long before they give up on you. I haven't heard from Meg in weeks. I feel all wrong here. Meg and Caitlin and Hannah and me, we're not really party people. We're friends-in-small-groups people. I don't even have much party experience, except for some band get-togethers of Meg's that I went along to. A track team party with Dillon at Matthew Harris's house. My skirt feels prissy, and so does my little present in the same box and with the same reused bow from Dad's gift. All I need is a pair of patent-leather shoes, and I'd be the same me I was in the third grade, when I went to Ivy McLellan's birthday party, but only because her mother insisted she invite every girl in the class.

The lawn is huge. It's beyond huge; it's parklike. Nearly an estate. I hike across it, not seeing the paved walkway a few yards away. The front door is open. People are spilling out onto the porch. A lot of people. I'm surprised. I didn't think there were that many people our age here, unless Elijah also invited everyone in the class. There are the glowing orange tips of cigarettes, beer in cups. *Alcohol and minors!* my parental mind screams. And, now, too, all the power talk I'd given myself while getting ready—*You can do it! You look great!*—is hightailing it out of here. It's running for its life. Straitlaced vibes are shooting out in every direction from my body, and I don't know how to hide them.

I walk up the steps. I smile at the two guys and two girls on the porch. I attempt to hold my little present casually. I attempt to walk into the house in my little heels casually too. They are people-pleaser heels. Newly grass-stained people-pleaser heels. My skirt is shouting *Like me!* to the various tossed-on jeans and shorts. This is not one of those surprise parties where people jump out from furniture. Everyone is here already.

I look around for Henry. I am desperate to see his familiar face among these other ones. I see Millicent on a couch with her arms slung around two guys. This seems insensitive at Henry's birthday party, if you ask me. She's laughing it up, and the guys have swoopy hair like Elijah, and one is wearing an argyle vest (or gargoyle vest as Dad calls them) that no one would be caught dead wearing in San Bernardino. He has his hand on her leg.

The music is so loud that my eardrums are thrumming. People are actually standing right next to the speakers! Do they want to be deaf in their later years? And do I smell the familiar grassy scent of pot? I try to loosen up. I even give my shoulders a shake, which causes my purse to fall on the floor. I am scrambling down there to get it, and some girl bumps me with her rear end. I've been worrying that everyone will stare at me, but the opposite is true. No one seems to even notice I'm here.

I wind my way around bodies and large, dark pieces of furniture. It's a serious house. There are Oriental rugs. There are chandeliers. I try to find the kitchen. I assume it will be the friendliest place, as kitchens often are, and so maybe that's where I'll find Henry.

Okay. I see Elijah. He's over by the fancy stainless refrigerator, leaning a shoulder on it. He's talking to an older man, who is wearing a bow tie and black-framed retro scientist glasses. Nerd-hip, gotcha. Elijah is laughing, and then he reaches up to straighten the man's tie. The gesture surprises me. It's almost flirtatious.

And then, thank God! There is Henry! He is by a long table, dunking a chip into a bowl of dip, eyeing Elijah. He doesn't see me. His face—I don't know. He looks pissed. I don't know if I've ever seen Henry angry before. His cheeks are flushed red. His eyes are narrowed almost meanly.

I edge my way toward him, scooting around the edge of the room so that I can take him by surprise. I grab a pinch of his white sleeve and tug.

"Hey," I say. "Happy birthday."

He spins around. He looks shocked to see me. "Tess!" he says. "I guess this was Elijah's big mystery project. I didn't know he invited you."

"And I didn't know it was your birthday," I say.

"Oh!" He laughs a little. His face goes from flushed to pale. "No. It's not. My birthday is in February. This is"—he gestures up to the black balloons that say HAPPY 50TH—"an attempt at irony. A surprise on me, ha-ha. Elijah's idea of a . . ."

Self-centered bid for attention, if you ask me.

"Joke," Henry says. "You brought a present."

He seems sad about that. The present itself seems sad. I feel suddenly sad, sad and a little humiliated at my earnest gift, as if maybe Henry and I have a relationship that's not meant for his real life. "I'm sorry," I say. It's the wrong response, but the one I most feel.

"Oh, don't be sorry! He should have told you." I don't know what to do with the gift now. It's wrong here. It's too sincere.

I hand it to him anyway. I try to remember that Henry loves me. "You can open it later. Maybe at home or something."

He takes it, and we're awkward together again. I try to smooth over the moment. I try not to be as sad and disappointed and out of place as I feel. I shout, and he leans in. I make my voice jovial. "You know all these people?"

"Not all," he shouts back. "Some are Elijah's friends. Him." He nods toward the man.

"Bow tie man."

"Right."

Someone jostles Henry. "Empty cup, birthday boy!" a tall, lean guy says, and snatches Henry's cup off a nearby table.

"This is some place," I shout again. This is the degree to which Henry and I are not being Henry and I. I am saying things like *This is some place.*

"The parents are both . . ."

"Psychiatrists. You told me."

The lean guy comes back with two cups—one for me and one for Henry. They are filled with ice and some kind of brown—

"Home brew," the guy says. "Hey, I'm Jackie Jack." He holds out his hand. I don't know if this is his actual first and last name, or an adorable nickname he calls himself. Still, he's the only halfway friendly person here, so I'll take it. I take the cup, too, have a swallow. It's a blazing fire rocketing through my body. My lips turn instantly to rubber and my knees weak.

"Jackie Jack Jack," I say. And then the bow tie man is cruising around the food table with a little plate, and Elijah is next to us.

"Having fun, birthday boy?" He shoves his hands in his pockets, rocks on his heels. "Hey, Tess. You made it. Look here, we're all together in one place. All in the very same *room.*"

"Are your parents out of town, or something?" I ask.

"They're at a hotel. They're guilt ridden over their deep-seated lack of interest in us, so they give us anything we want."

"As I tell my mother, you weren't exactly *available.* . . ."

Millicent has ditched her boys, and now she's here, nibbling a carrot stick. "No wonder I'm depressed half the time."

"Kids of head doctors are well versed in parental blame," the bow tie man says. He is piling on pieces of cheese and something that looks like bean dip.

"They think it's a sign of our mental health," Elijah says.

I think it's a sign they're spoiled brats, but I don't say this.

"I think it's a sign you're spoiled brats," Henry says.

Did I mention how much I love him? I chuckle. My knees are weak, and my heart is on fire, but it's a good kind of fire. I take another sip.

"Are you mad at *me*, Lark?" Elijah asks.

"Not at all." The tips of Henry's ears are red.

"Sulky, jealous boys," Millicent says. She's yanking my arm and pulling me away from Henry. "You should meet Drew." I give Henry a Save Me look, but he's busy glaring at Elijah. I want to go home. I don't understand what's going on here, but I feel like I'm in a game, and I don't know what the game is, let alone what the rules are.

"Drew, Tess. Jenny Sedgewick's granddaughter, but she has no artistic talent." Millicent laughs a twinkly laugh.

"Neither do I," Drew says. Drew is a rumpled-looking guy with a brown-blond head of curls. He seems uncomfortable in his shirt—at least, he keeps squirming around in it and readjusting. I know how he feels. Drew tells me he's an ocean-ography student at the University of Washington's Parrish Island lab. For the next twenty minutes he tells me various facts about ocean mammals, while I ask polite questions and look for Henry out of the corner of my eye. Drew is actually very nice, with a nervous laugh and one untied shoe, but I finally excuse myself to use the restroom.

I want to find Henry, but Drew points upstairs to where the nearest bathroom is, and since he's watching, I now have to go there whether I need to or not. It's pretty quiet upstairs. At least, the thrumming and the thumping are muted, and no one seems to be up here. The rugs are thick. There's a grandfather clock at the end of one hall and a writing desk at the end of another, with a quill pen on it and a silver paperweight in the shape of a leaf.

I am suddenly filled with the spirit of Grandfather Leopold. I tip open one of the doors—Millicent's room, obviously, and then Elijah's. He makes his bed like he's in the military, and she makes her bed like she's in a hurry. There are matching bookshelves in each room and matching desks. I am taking inventory. Elijah has a hockey stick and a military jacket on a hook, and . . . A girl laughs; her footsteps are on the stairs. I hurry out of there. Before I go back downstairs, I actually think about pocketing that silver paperweight. Maybe it's rare and extraordinarily valuable, and I will take it from them and keep it for generations. More likely, it's not even silver at all.

The music has changed. It is some kind of Spanish tango, probably snitched from Mom and Dad's music collection. Elijah is leading the older guy around by his bow tie. Millicent is sitting on the lap of the boy with the argyle vest. He twirls a lock of her hair around one finger. He kisses the corner of her mouth.

There is Henry, finally.

He scans the room. He looks disgusted. "Let's get out of here."

"And leave before you blow out the candles?"

"I'm finished with this." He seems angry again, maybe even furious.

He takes my hand. He is pulling me, actually. People are starting to dance, and he is yanking me through the door. He shoves past a couple kissing on the porch. I am flying behind him. I am glad to see he has his present from me under one arm; it's as if we've just rescued the kidnap victim and are now making our escape. Outside, it's the pure bliss of liberation.

"Thank God!" I shout. We are running. But we are not running in the direction of my car. Maybe toward his? I don't know. I don't care. We are running across the parklike lawn, the huge width of it.

"Where—" I ask.

"Here."

It is an enormous lilac tree, the tree I imagined Henry and Millicent beneath, and the lilacs are in bloom, stark white against the dark sky, and the tree smells delicious and potent, capable of inducing the dreams of Oz. Henry is kissing me. He is kissing me hard, like I've always wanted him to kiss me. It's passionate in a way Henry hasn't been, a way I've waited for. There's moonlight and the sounds of the party in the distance and the smell of lilacs.

Henry pulls me down, or I pull him, or we both go together. We are falling ten thousand miles, and I want to fall. For me, there is such relief that Henry is back again, but there is also the oddness of the night and the driving need to prove myself with mouth and hands and tongue, to verify my importance in his life, to remind him that he belongs to me, not Millicent, not Elijah or these other people, *me*.

Henry is pressing himself against my body, and above me, his sweet eyes are squinched shut. His cheekbones have new angles in the shadows of the moon. My hands are under his shirt, on his smooth skin, his very own ribs, his chest. My skirt is shoved up, and I've lost a shoe, and he will know I am his, and I will *be* his, and no one will take that away, and the thought of it all fills me with such desire that I fumble with the button of his jeans and the buttons, buttons, buttons of his white shirt.

We aren't us, but we are us. We are more than us. He is pressing, pressing, and this new Henry wants me so bad, and it feels so good.

But then he stops. "Wait," he says. He is reaching for his pants. His wallet. "My father gave me this when I was fifteen." His voice, these actual words, break some lilac spell, and I look around, and I'm aware that people are not that far off but far off enough. A car engine starts, and someone shouts and people laugh. I am gauging this, people, distance, and then he says, "Do they have an expiration date?"

And, of course, I don't know if they do or not, but this

makes us both laugh, and it's as if he actually sees me, Tess, down below him, and he's trying to open the darn thing with his teeth, and then trying to figure it out, and it all gets ridiculous, much more the real Henry and me than this fiery passionate couple on this lawn who I don't even recognize, this Henry who *needs* me.

It breaks some spell, and he is fumbling and I am fumbling, and neither of us knows anything about this, and so it becomes, now that we are here, something to be completed, only it isn't really completed. It is sort of completed, I think. I can't really tell. You will wonder how that is so, and I can only say it *is* so. I don't know and I can't exactly ask. I only know that the minute he opened his eyes and spoke moments ago, we became halfhearted and awkward, and whatever lit between us on this strange night is now over. We are on Elijah and Millicent's lawn and he is reaching for his pants and I am pulling down my skirt and I don't know exactly what has happened or hasn't happened, only that it has been significant. It has changed me and us, probably forever.

That's when I hear him. Elijah. He's not far off; he's close enough for me to see his face quite clearly. And all the smart remarks and witty jabs and sarcasm are gone from it. Every bit of his cockiness has left, and he stands there only plain-faced and scared.

"Henry?" he says. It is so plaintive. It is the quietest agony. I think he might cry. And then he turns and runs, and I know in that instant everything I need to know. I know who's really in that turned-down photo in Henry's room. And I know who it is in that photo I thought I saw on the bookshelf in Elijah's room when I heard that girl laugh. I know whose two faces are in Elijah's painting. I know what is likely written in the journal stuffed down in the seat of Henry's car and the reason his heart was broken.

"Lij!" Henry calls. His thin legs are so white under that moon. And now, with Henry's own plaintive cry, it is my turn to run.

chapter twenty-two

Pinus banksiana: jack pine. Although most people consider a forest fire to be a destructive force, fire can actually be the mechanism that allows a forest to regenerate itself. The jack pine, for example, relies on fire to spread its seeds. Its cone is actually sealed shut with resin, but during a forest fire, heat from the fire will melt the resin and release the seeds. The seeds *need* fire. Without it, they will be forever locked inside. What looks like destruction can lead to renewal.

"You knew," I cry. I am gutted. My chest aches, my stomach, every bit of me is grief and more grief; the loss of this hope, Henry hope, is every loss all over again. It's the loss of progress and new life and, God, the loss of love. Real love. True love. Last-forever love.

Jenny has her arms around me. My father has been kicked out of my room. It's a time you need another woman. It's a time you need your mother.

"I didn't know," Jenny says. "I mean, I knew he and Elijah . . .

I was worried you'd be hurt. But, honey, only Henry *knows*. And, obviously, it's complicated for *him*."

I don't want her arms around me anymore. She kept something from me, something that would have prevented me from being shattered like this. I wrap my arms around my own self. My shirt is wet from tears and I'm still wearing that stupid skirt, and I am in shock. I am in such shock, I simply can't believe this night happened. I go over it again in my head. I was getting dressed. I drove over. I held that present. I was in that house. Henry and I were on the grass and then confusion and then . . . My stomach feels so sick.

"Why didn't you tell me anyway? Why didn't you *say* something?"

"Oh, honey, I'd done that before! Intervened, got involved in things that weren't my business . . . I tried to say what was what when I didn't know what was what. And I lost your dad and your mom and you. I didn't want to lose you again."

"I feel like such a fool." I feel like such a fool, and I feel betrayed, and I feel confused. Henry's body was next to mine only a few hours ago. And now, this whole universe of Henry I never knew existed. I didn't even see it. "He said he *loved* me."

"Oh, sweetheart," Jenny says. She puts her arms back around me even though my own are not open to her. She doesn't care. About this she will be stubborn. "I'm sure he *does* love you."

"How could he let me love him like that?" I cry. "How, how, how?"

"He didn't mean to hurt you. Even I can see that. He's a human being, sweetie. Us human beings, sometimes it takes a while to understand ourselves." Jenny rocks me. "Sometimes it takes a long while." I let her rock me like a baby. I am crying so hard.

"We left her alone," I sob. I don't know why I'm telling her this terrible secret now. My grief is all mixed up, or else it's just a night to be done with secrets. "No one was there. We left her alone and she died."

Jenny doesn't seem shocked at my confession, or even surprised at this grief mixed with grief. She doesn't let go of me, the horrible person I am. I am breaking in half. I am breaking open, and it hurts and my chest is crushing in on my heart. "You didn't know. You were doing the best you could. Henry too. That's all we can ever do."

I cry and cry until I feel too empty to cry anymore. My phone rings and rings again until I turn it off. If he thinks I ever want to talk to him again, he's crazy.

I am devastated. I am scorched earth inside. "I think I want to be alone now," I say.

"All right," Jenny says. Her own face looks old and sad and defeated. When she opens the door, my father actually falls inside, just like in the movies, when someone is listening in with a hand cupped around one ear.

"I was just . . . passing by," he lies.

I don't even care. Nothing really matters. All that we've built here seems gone. Jenny and me, Dad and me, this place and everyone in it. It all feels different now.

This is how Pix dies. Over the next several days, its stalk narrows and shrivels. It turns black. It is a wretched, limp black, and then it falls. I don't want to wait for it to dry up. It feels obscene to watch. It feels private.

I am empty inside and Pix has left me. It feels *gone*; it has felt gone ever since that night with Jenny and my father and Henry and the berry and the seeds. I don't want to think about plants and seeds and icy lands. I don't want to think about the good people of this town, all those signatures, or a faraway place with the most important possibility of all—forever. Forever isn't possible, and so I ignore Sasha's calls too. I turn off my phone, and then I let the battery go dead, and then I finally do it. I pull Pix from the soil, pull it up by its roots. I lay it on a paper towel, and I press until what little moisture was left is no longer there. I place it where it now belongs, in between the pages of the photo album.

Grandfather Leopold's blue-glazed terra-cotta pot has only dirt in it now. Just dirt. No seed, no plant.

It's over.

By this time, I know Henry's schedule at the Parrish Island Library. I know he won't be here, but I still check for his car anyway. But no. There's only Larry's Toyota and some big old RV with a license plate that reads CAPTAIN ED and a worn bumper sticker on the back that says HOME OF THE BIG REDWOODS. I see movement near the Dumpster, a flash of red. Sasha, in a crimson T-shirt.

"I thought you quit," I said.

She tosses the stub to the ground. Puts it out with the toe of her Converse. "Damn," she says.

"Did you and Abby break up again?"

"No. You and Henry did."

"I came to say good-bye."

"I was afraid of that. Well, come on. Larry's inside."

She stomps up the steps, opens the big library doors. I am remembering a pounding sheet of rain, and running up these same stairs, and my first view of these large windows and this warm wood, and this domed ceiling with the sky painted on it.

And once again, that high, domed sky makes me feel a wide vista of emotion, and once again I could weep at an overturned chair or a torn page, or today, Larry's scruffy beard and the ink on his fingers that I can see from here.

"Don't say it," he says. He's a big softie, that Larry. "Don't say you're leaving."

Once again, I am translucent. I could break against rocks. I am ten thousand miles down and ten thousand miles across and around and it's too far and too long and too deep, but there is no black-haired boy with wide, soft brown eyes looking into mine and seeing exactly who I am.

"I came to say good-bye."

Larry steps away from the counter. He puts his arms around me. He slaps my back. I am trying not to break down and weep against his READ RESPONSIBLY T-shirt.

Sasha clears her throat. She's a big softie too, but don't tell her that.

"We sent it all off. The letter and the boxes. We're going to get you to that vault. Whether you're here or not."

"Say it like it is, sister," Larry says.

I can barely speak. "Thank you so much." My voice is a whisper. It will crack if it's any louder than this. "For all you did." Svalbard, though—it doesn't matter anymore.

They hear what I'm not saying. All that defeat.

"That seed," Larry says. "It's the chance for something *big*. For you, for everyone."

"Cue the music," Sasha says. She rolls her eyes at me, but I can see that this is only to match my state of mind. She agrees with Larry. They both understand the largeness of Svalbard and the seed. But I have no energy for largeness or greatness or even for motion at all.

"Wait," Larry says. "Before you go." He hurries off between 570—Life Sciences and 580—Plants. Well, of course, he brings me *How to Keep Almost Any Plant Alive* by Dr. Lester Frank. He hands it over.

"You're giving me library property?" I ask.

"I'm just checking it out to you," he says. "You have to bring it back."

"And you should see our overdue fines," Sasha says.

We have accumulated some extra stuff. There are two pairs of orca whale slippers and new clothes. There's a quilt Jenny is giving me that I especially like and piles of food that won't fit into the cooler we'd brought. I am carrying things out. Dad and Jenny are hunting around for an old suitcase she's sure she has around somewhere and a Styrofoam cooler my father used for camping trips while he was in high school.

I don't need to be that careful with the blue terra-cotta pot anymore now that Pix is gone. But I return it to my mother's shoe anyway. I sling one of our bags over my shoulder and carry the shoe out to the truck. Dad spent the day before this one changing the oil and filling the tank with gas. He slapped the side of the truck when he was done. *Ready, old girl?* he said, as if it were a horse he was particularly fond of.

Ready.

I tuck the shoe snug between a bag of pears from Jenny's tree and a rolled-up jacket of my father's. I am arranging this when I hear the shotgun blast. Okay, not a shotgun blast, but Henry's stupid car backfiring. Really, he ought to get that thing fixed.

I know it's Henry without turning around, given that there are no hunters in plaid jackets to be seen anywhere. My heart starts thumping wildly. I want to flee. I don't want to see Henry. That night—it's still so painful, I can barely revisit it in the privacy of my own mind, let alone out here, with him. I feel ashamed of it, my own offering. The confusing, humiliating failure of it.

I sort of crouch down. I have the ridiculous momentary thought that he won't see me, but the truck door is open, and I am hunched there in plain sight. The tires crunch on the gravel and stop. The engine shuts off. My stomach is twisting and I want to cry, and then the car door opens and shuts and he calls my name.

I feel stuck in that humiliating posture. I do not want to stand and face him.

"Tess," he says. "Please."

I hear him walk toward me. If he kneels beside me, it will be too much tenderness and my heart will crack and I will cry and he will hold me, and I don't want his arms around me. That is the last thing I want.

So I stand up. I look at him. And the weird and crazy thing is that it's still Henry there. Regular but far, far from regular Henry, with those goddamn gentle eyes and that swoop of hair and those cheekbones. Those thin, vulnerable shoulders, and whether I want it or not, my heart cracks. I love Henry Lark.

"Sasha said you were leaving. You *are* leaving."

I don't say anything. I don't think I can speak. It is one of those moments where there is so much to say that there is nothing to say, no adequate words, anyway, to speak it all.

"Tess, I want to explain."

This, thank God, makes me angry. The anger saves me. "Ah. There's an explanation," I say. "Well. Terrific. Would've been good to hear ahead of time, but you take what you can get."

"I am so sorry. I am so, so sorry. I never meant to hurt you, Tess. That's the last thing I would have wanted. We met . . . Well, you came into my life at a very weird time for me."

"I'll say."

"Please."

I fold my arms. I stare off at the big tree in the meadow. I look at the lacy pattern of light between the leaves. Like Jenny says, a tree is settled to its fate. To the story.

"I saw you—we met, and I don't know. I just—you. I love being with you. If I could spend time with anyone, *anyone*, I would pick you. You're so funny, and sweet, and we just . . . Well, you know. You were there. We just . . . We're the same in so many ways. . . ."

"You're describing a friend, Henry."

"I love you, Tess. I love being around you."

"A really good friend. A *sister*."

"I don't know who I am." I look at him now. Sweet eyes, sad ones. He looks like he's about to cry. Damn it. He is hurting too. "Or else, I do know, and I'm not sure I'm ready to know."

"I don't think this is a conflict I can help you with, Henry. Given that, you know, you pretty much broke my heart."

"I'm so sorry," he says again. He clears his throat. He's trying to hold it together. "I just want you to know that I do love you. I do. That's *real*."

"Henry, just go," I say. He's making this worse.

"Wait. I almost forgot." He trots back to the car. Henry's got a funny run. I never mentioned that before. If you were a mile away, you'd know it was him.

He's got the box. The one that held the balaclava and then the "birthday gift." I can't even look at that box. It brings a drowning wave of humiliation.

"I don't want it," I say. "You don't have to give it back."

"I'm not giving it back. I'm lending it to you."

What is with these people and lending? "Throw it away."

"I will not throw it away." He steps around me, toward the truck. "I want it back after you take it to the vault."

And what is with these people and their refusal to see when a dream is dying?

"Whatever, Henry."

He moves to set the box on the seat. But then he sees Pix's pot tucked into its spot on the floor, and he makes a space in the nest I've created. His eyes are wet now. He sets the box there, and before I can alter this plan of his, before I know it, he kisses my cheek and dashes back to his car. "I want it back," he calls over his shoulder.

And I know, I have no doubt, that he is not just referring to that compass.

But what has happened here is over, and I can't watch that car back out onto that road. I just can't. I turn away. I head into the house as Henry Lark drives out of my life.

"Roots," Jenny says. She is squeezing me hard. I am crying. She is. And Vito is watching us with worried eyes.

"Roots," I say.

I kiss Vito's stupid, furry face good-bye.

chapter twenty-three

Rhizophora mangle: red mangrove. The red mangrove grows in the tropics, in brackish water and swampy salt marshes. Because of the harsh environment they live in, these mangroves have evolved a special mechanism to help their offspring survive. Unlike most plants, whose seeds germinate in soil, the mangrove seeds germinate while still attached to the parent tree. The seeds become fully mature plants with the help of their parent before dropping off of the tree and into their own ground. In tough times, even seeds need their parents.

The waters of the sound are wide and shimmering, and I now know that they are rumored to have healing powers. I know that whales slumber beneath them. I know that on the shore, in the dead of night, in a cove not far from a lighthouse, the sands and water glow a mystical blue.

Joe Nevins, in his orange vest, is gesturing the row of cars up the ferry ramp with one ever-circling arm. But he stops our truck with an upraised hand. He's got a tattoo I've never noticed before—a heart with wings. My father rolls down the window, and Joe ducks his head to meet my eyes. "Take your sketch pad to the vault."

"Very funny," I say. His eyes are twinkling at his own joke. He's well aware of my artistic talent.

"Camera would probably be better." His arm goes back to circling. I've barely gotten to know Joe, or Margaret, or the others, but now I'm leaving them behind. We *ba-bamp* our way up the ferry ramp and settle in our own tight space between cars. I will not cry when that ferry pushes off from the dock and begins to make its slow journey to the mainland. Instead, I keep my eyes on the map. It is a twenty-seven-mile ferry ride to Anacortes. It is 80.2 miles from Anacortes to Seattle. And it is 1,188.2 miles from Seattle to San Bernardino.

"Want to stop and see Mary in Portland?" my father asks. We have been driving a long while, long enough that my legs are stiff and the wind through the windows has gone from cool to warm to hot and back to cool again. I roll mine up, hunt around in the back for my sweatshirt jacket.

"I find you less than humorous," I say.

"I'm sorry I got crazy. I didn't know what to do with myself. I was lost. I just loved your mother so fucking much."

"I know," I say. I do know.

The signs to Portland pass us by. My finger, which follows along the red route of I-5, indicates we are approaching McMinnville.

"We need to eat," my father says.

"Again?" Jenny has packed us enough food and snacks for a month-long expedition.

"Not just Red Vines and tuna salad. Something involving beef. Or bacon. A sit-down eat. With menus."

"With *bathrooms.*"

"Right."

He pulls off the next freeway exit. It is getting dark. We spot our kind of place. The Walk Inn. Plastic-covered menus. Breakfast anytime.

We, well, walk in. We wait behind the sign that says PLEASE WAIT TO BE SEATED. There is a bar off to our right. It's dim and small, and maybe that's why it's called the Vault.

"Thomas Knows a Sign When He Sees One," my father says.

"Don't," I say. "Don't even."

He scratches his chin. His whiskers are already growing a road-trip forest. "No?"

"No."

We stay overnight at the Riverside Motel, somewhere just after Salem. We get up early and head out, Jenny's scones and bad motel coffee for breakfast. I sleep and stare out the window and complain about it being hot. It's the middle of August. I haven't been home in almost two and a half months.

After driving all day, things begin to look familiar—the terrain of California, bad traffic, the dry brown hills and new, packed-together condos along the freeway advertising their low, low prices on big banners. The smog, the palm trees. Dread begins to inch in. No. Dread isn't one of those subtle emotions. It moves in and takes over, and then it drips and hangs, like Spanish moss.

We're almost there. I don't say it: home. Home shouldn't make you feel like this. The sky turns dusky. We begin to pass the outlying cities around our town, the places we had to drive to for games during my one unsuccessful year of volleyball, or when the movie we wanted to see wasn't playing anywhere closer. My father begins to whistle. He has one arm out the window, and this might all seem to be a casual display of homecoming happiness, but my father whistles only when he's nervous. It's a habit he pulls out of the arsenal during awkward moments or while attempting to do something he actually knows nothing about, like changing the oil in his truck. You can hear him under there, lying beneath the car and whistling away, surrounded by tools he barely can name.

"It's freezing in here," I say.

"You cold?"

"It's practically *dark*."

Dad rolls up the window. He sighs. "Well." That's all he says.

"Do you even have a job anymore?" I ask.

"The guys have been very understanding."

And then there is the Santa Ana River and the massive white wedding cake building that is the old Arrowhead Resort. Dad takes the exit before downtown, and soon we pass my

school, and then we are nearing the streets named for trees—
Elm, Alder, Orange—and then our own street, definitely dark
now. The streetlights are on, illuminating circles of asphalt
and bits of driveways. The *tick-tock*, *tick-tock* of Dad's turn signal says we've arrived. I know this place and don't know it. It
seems like somewhere I had been a hundred years ago.

"Let's just get what we need for tonight out of the truck.
I'll unpack tomorrow. My fucking eyes are ready to fall out of
my head." Dad jams the gearshift lever to park, sets the brake.

I feel almost sick. That house, walking through that door,
it seems like a wall to climb over. A mountain. An icy, treacherous, mountain *range*. But Dad is already hauling his bag out
of the back. There's nothing to do but follow him.

It's oddly the same in there. Our leather couch, the Navajo
blanket on the wall, the rocking chair, the green glass lamp
my mother loved. Her *Better Homes and Gardens* magazines
are still in the basket under the coffee table, and the lemon
tree's shadowy self is right out there in the back window. Even
the smell inside is the same—some mix of coffee and vanilla.
It feels preserved; I am trying to have a connection with this
place as mine, my own home, where I belong. Instead, it has
become the place where Mom once was.

I dream of trees, and Henry, and paint splashed on large canvases. I dream I can play the piano. I dream of my mother, and
it is one of those horrible dreams I keep having, where we were
wrong about her dying. She is alive after all, and she's been

trying to reach us and wondering where we've been. We are so happy to see her, it's like the actual *her*, and we're so relieved she's not dead after all, and then I wake up. I have a moment where I don't know where I am. I'm actually disoriented in my own room. It scares me. My ceiling feels lower (than Jenny's), the table by my bed is farther away (than Jenny's), the window smaller (than Jenny's), and it feels like I'm in an entirely foreign place.

In the morning, I call Meg. She's still miffed at me, but gets over it after I apologize a thousand times for not calling. It's been above a hundred degrees here all week, she says, so Meg and Caitlin and Adam and this new girl, Kelsey, who just moved into a house on Meg's street, are all going to Lake Gregory, which is this lake in the mountains that's only fourteen miles away. You can swim there. You can get a little boat, or ride down a couple of water slides. Mostly, it's cooler there than in the city.

They pick me up, and soon we are all stretched out on beach towels on the one bit of sand that's free of other bodies. The place is packed. Screaming kids are running around with goggles on their heads, people are floating on air mattresses, guys are rubbing lotion onto the shoulders of already tan girlfriends. Meg's hair is different. She's wearing it in two braids, and she got a little carried away with the spray-on lightener when I was gone.

"You look so different," I keep saying.

"*You* look so different," Meg says.

"I do?"

"I don't know what it is."

Caitlin is standing by the edge of the water. She slips one finger under the elastic leg of her swimsuit bottom and tugs, maximizing coverage. Adam is standing over us, wet after his swim. He shakes like a dog, sprinkling us.

"That actually feels good," Kelsey, the new girl, says. She's got long, flat shiny hair that reminds me of Millicent, but she has none of Millicent's icy confidence. She's hanging on Meg like Meg's the last bottle of water on a deserted island, capable of saving her life, or at least her social life. She's doing that thing girls do sometimes, competing in a little triangle of rivalry. She keeps bringing up all of the fun and hilarious and amazing things they've done together since I've been gone. She's used the phrase *Remember when we* . . . so many times, I think it's time for their wedding album, or at least a scrapbook.

"I can't believe your dad just let you skip out on school like that for a road trip," Kelsey says.

"Oh, so you heard."

"Where'd you go again?"

"Mostly the San Juans," I say.

"I looove Puerto Rico," she says.

From the water, Caitlin squeals. She's up to her belly button in the lake, and her shoulders are scrunched up, bracing against the cold.

"*I* looove being with four ladies," Adam says. "You're my

harem, right?" He clicks his thumbs and forefingers together like he's wearing little cymbals.

"Wrong," I say.

Meg glares at him. "Quit being a creep," she says.

"Remember that creep we saw at La Plaza?" Kelsey pokes Meg's leg.

A lumpy woman in a bathing suit walks past us fast, spitting sand from her heels, yanking a crying girl by the arm. Another kid is standing on the beach holding the crotch of his shorts like he has to pee. Caitlin finally dunks her head. Kelsey holds her bottle of lotion out to Adam and says, "Would you?"

Meg says, "I can't believe how different you look."

It's the longest day of my life.

"I think you're depressed," Dad says through my shut door.

"What gives you that idea?" I say. I can barely hear him through the covers over my head.

"You can't just lie in there all day."

"Leave me alone."

"C'mon, Tess . . ."

After a while, he gives up. I hear the truck leave. In three hours and forty-two minutes he will phone. We will chat for approximately two and a half minutes, or one hundred and fifty seconds, enough for him to be reassured that I haven't stuck my head in the oven since he's been gone. Four hours and forty minutes after that, he will arrive back home. Every hour feels like it's a million o'clock. I miss Henry. I miss Jenny.

I miss Sasha and Larry. And, dear God, I miss my mother. It is a permanent ache, a low-grade fever that never leaves. I even miss Pix.

Henry would understand why it feels so strange here. I would tell him how odd it is to see the contents of my dresser sitting all together: the balaclava, which is next to Pix's pot, which is next to the piggy bank I've had since I was six, which is next to a dish of rings I've had since junior high. He would know why these things don't go together.

It has been above one hundred and five degrees every day that we've been back. We are having some kind of heat wave. You can't even breathe outside. I crank the air conditioner. I don't leave the house. I'm too sad to move. Thanks to my Frigidaire Energy Star five-speed machine, it's like the Arctic in here.

My father is making Thai chicken salad. At least, this is what he tells me, shouting from the kitchen. He is expanding his horizons beyond Thomas's Famous Meatballs. I have been watching entirely too much television. I watch *The B&B Gourmet*, where Willa Hapstead creates egg soufflés and apple fritters and French country omelets for the guests at Red Gate Inn. I watch *I Dream of Jeannie* reruns. I watch the news. Sometimes I put on Bob Marley and eat way too much mocha-chip ice cream. If I had my way, Dad would serve me dinner on a tray in the living room, as if I were a sick person.

"Bring it to me," I shout back.

"No way, Jose. Get your ass in here."

It smells good, but I'm not that hungry. Dragging myself in there will be like pulling a railroad car with my teeth. I groan. I get off the couch. My pj's are made of lead, and my feet seem to be too, and I apparently am also carrying lead weights on my back. That's what it feels like to walk.

When I arrive at the kitchen chair, the lead becomes a cheap, wet washcloth. I flop down. I can barely keep my head up.

"Don't tell me you wore those all day again," my father says. "You even got—" He gestures to his chest so that I examine mine.

"Chocolate," I say. "Some old chocolate chips from the back of the cupboard."

"You look like hell," he says. My father actually looks pretty good himself. He's got his shorts on and a super-loose T-shirt. His hair is in a ponytail, but it's his face that looks, I don't know, *healthy*.

"Thanks. Appreciate that self-esteem builder."

Dad tosses spices around and chops things like he's a pro. He's been watching the Food Network at night. He narrates his actions, as if he's the star of his own cooking show.

"Never cut the lettuce," he says primly. "Gently *tear* it." He tears it high up in the air, lets the leaves fall onto the plates like large, green snowflakes. "Now. The dressing. Made from one hundred percent pure peanut butter." He opens the lid, sticks a spoon in, and has a taste. "De-licious. It has the crunchy, ripe flavor of peanuts."

"Ripe flavor?" Even my sarcasm feels effortful.

But my father—he's energetic, I realize. His eyes dance now that he's not stoned anymore. He's *here*.

"Any questions from the audience? Yes, you in the pajamas."

Of course I haven't raised my hand. That would require lifting five thousand pounds of dead weight.

"Phone," my father announces.

"Nooooo," I say. It's ringing somewhere in my room, which is hundreds of miles away. I don't care. Whoever it is, or whatever it is, I don't care.

"Phone!" he insists.

I sit there. I rest my head on my arms. I don't even see that he's left the room. I only hear him answer my phone as he heads back to the kitchen: "Tess's House of Hell," he says cheerfully. "What? Can you say that again? I can't hear you with all that noise." I lift my head. He makes his eyes large for my benefit. He drops his jaw dramatically. He's acting like it's the California Lottery calling to tell me I've won the Triple Million. "Let me get her." He hands me the phone. "You gotta hear this, I promise."

Uhh. Damn him. "Hello?"

I don't know what to expect. I have no idea who it is. Certainly I don't expect *this*. It's Sasha. It's Sasha, and she's shouting. She's talking a million miles an hour. I can barely hear what she's saying, though, because there's all this noise in the background. A party, music.

"Where are you, Sash?" I ask. "Jeez, it sounds crazy."

"Bud's. We're all at Bud's. The whole damn island is here. Wait! Nathan is waving! He says hi! Oh my God. Margaret is drinking a beer the size of a toddler!"

"Margaret?"

"I told you, the whole town is here. We did it, Tess! We did it! Wait. Larry wants to say something."

Here is Larry now. "Mission Impossible is Mission Possible!" Larry screams. "Whoo-hoo!" He sounds a little tipsy. Actually, a lot tipsy. Now Sasha's back.

"We got the letter, Tess. You're invited! We did it! The Norwegian government! The letter even has a seal on it! It's silver! You, child, are bringing your seeds to that vault!"

"Sasha . . ." I don't know what to say. My father is standing really close to me, breathing his peanut butter breath on me, trying to listen in.

"Nicky says hi," Sasha says. "He's flashing me two thumbs-up!"

"Nicky?"

"Talbott. Java Java Java? He says he knows you!"

"Right! Of course."

"You should see how happy everyone is here, Tess. And drunk. Okay, that too. But happy! This is incredible! I got the letter right here. I faxed it to Dr. Harv and Abby—"

She hasn't mentioned him. Not a single word. "Henry?" I ask. None of this would have been possible without him.

"Of course he's here. He's actually standing right next to me, trying hard not to say a word."

"Sash!" It's Henry all right. My heart goes thumping around. It's going to have to stop that.

"You probably don't want to talk to him."

Yes. No. I don't respond.

"Okay. Just for a second, then," Sasha says.

And then there he is. "It's yours, Tess." His voice is sad and thrilled and triumphant and a little broken. Full and empty, high and low, tide in, tide out. "It's all yours."

"So? What do you think?" My father asks. We are sitting at the kitchen table. We haven't eaten a meal in the living room even once since we got back. We are in our old spots, me in my chair, him in his, my mother's empty chair across from us. My father's Thai chicken salad is arranged artfully on the plate. Points for presentation.

"I think it's surprisingly delicious."

"Not about *that*, you monkey butt."

I just shake my head. I mean, the whole idea is crazy.

"You and me," he says.

"Me and you?" The only thing crazier than me going to Svalbard is me and my father going to Svalbard. I mean, he'd have to really pile on the old concert T-shirts to stay warm.

"You don't say no to something like this." He's shoveling in his dinner. Someone—Jenny—should have taught him not to talk with his mouth full.

"You don't?"

"Hell no!"

I shake my head. Maybe I grin ever so slightly. Just picturing it.

"Right now, the difference between going and not going is *going*."

"Very philosophical, Father."

"Fucking awesome road trip?" He wiggles his eyebrows up and down, in a How Could You Resist manner.

There are things I've learned by then about Longyearbyen, the tiny, remote capital of Svalbard, that settlement built on stilts on permafrost, the town nearest to the vault. Polar bears wander into its streets, hungry and curious. You must wear a rifle outdoors. Reindeer wander through too. Transportation is by snow scooter. It is home to the northernmost church, the northernmost post office, and the northernmost airport.

"Did you know they've got a gourmet restaurant there?" my father says. "It's true. And one of the best wine cellars in the world."

He's been reading up. I can tell by his eyes and his goofy smile that he's caught vault fever, same as the rest of them.

I am clearly outnumbered.

I smile just a little.

My father lets out a whoop. He shoves his chair back. He trots down the hall, ponytail bopping up and down. "Where is it?" he yells.

"What?"

"Never mind. I found it!"

He returns, and of course he's wearing that balaclava. He's a deranged Arctic burglar.

"Get that thing off. You look scary."

Henry is right. This—the seeds, Svalbard, this triumph—it is mine. Mine and my mother's. But it is also Henry's. And it is also my father's, and it is Grandfather Leopold's and Jenny's. It is Sasha's and Larry's, Dr. Harv Johansson's, and Dr. Abby Sidhu's. It is Margaret's and Nathan's and Cora Lee's; it is Joe Nevins's and Nicky the coffee guy's. It is Bud's, from the tavern. It belongs to every one of us who makes this trip from here to there. Every one of us who can use some reminding that even after the worst disasters, down deep, the truest things endure.

chapter twenty-four

Salix arctica: arctic willow. This plant has evolved to survive its unique and extreme Arctic conditions and now can live as long as 264 years. Its roots have developed to withstand permafrost; its leaves have grown fuzzy hairs like its own sweater, and the plant itself has created its own pesticide against insects like the Arctic woolly bear. But the seeds . . . They have changed over time to become sticky, so that when they are dispersed in high winds, they don't travel too far; they have evolved to stay on the island where they belong.

We take a Lufthansa jet out of San Francisco, 5,871 miles to Munich, eleven hours and twelve minutes, and then Munich to Oslo, 979.6 miles, five hours and fifteen minutes—

"Stop that," my father says. "No more counting. Just . . . live it."

He rolls up his coat to use as a pillow and gets his big legs up on the airplane seat. After so many hours in an enclosed space high above (I won't say how high) the earth, my head feels full of explosives. I watch movies on the little screen that is on the back of the seat in front of me. I like when the other passengers laugh at the same spots in the film where I laugh, all of us with our headsets sharing a good joke in the otherwise silence of the plane.

We board our SAS flight to Tromsø, a town that sits at the northern tip of Norway. It is a clear day, and outside my window, I can see the fjords in the sea, icy humped lands, which resemble the surfacing back of a San Juan whale. The white fjords, the blue-green sea surrounded by snowy mountains, it doesn't seem real, except that my father is leaning over me to see too, and he's squashing me.

Back home, kids are slamming lockers and studying *The Rime of the Ancient Mariner* in AP English and buying roses for the stupid student body Valentine's Day fundraiser. And I am here, getting closer and closer to the vault, landing in Tromsø, in a small blue airport out in what feels like the middle of nowhere, a modern airport of glass and tall, exposed architectural rafters.

This trip, this mission, has brought us through our first Christmas without my mom, which we spent eating a big Indian dinner my father made while we watched *Orion's Belt*, a Norwegian film set in Svalbard, and then *The Golden Compass*, because the armored bears in it are from there too. We spent the anniversary of her death, ten days before we leave, in REI. My father buys a small GORE-TEX bag for the seeds and two pairs of wool socks.

That day, there is a postcard from Henry Lark in the mail. On the front is an antique drawing of a strawberry plant, with its various parts labeled in Latin. On the back, *Thoughts and love* in the small and geometrically perfect letters I recognize.

In the airport, we take our bags into the bathrooms and do what everyone is doing here, shedding our travel clothes and changing into our carefully planned gear. I am finished before Dad, and I wait out in the lobby in front of the men's room. I crack up when I see him in his boots and snowsuit. He's got his largest parka over one arm, but he still looks like he's about to jet off to the moon.

I point and laugh. "You're stuffed," I say.

"If we have to go to the bathroom, we're screwed," he says.

We wait for our plane on blue chairs. I shove my hand down into my bag again to check for the seeds, which I've done about a hundred times since we've left. It's actually pretty crowded in the airport. You wouldn't think it'd be anyone but us, but Svalbard is a destination for adventure travel, and so there's actually a couple on their honeymoon and a group of guys in jackets with patches that say ANTARCTIC SURVEY 1996, and even a couple of old ladies in fur-lined GORE-TEX parkas.

My father eats a packet of peanuts in his astronaut suit. He strikes up a conversation with two students who are heading to Svalbard to see polar bears and the northern lights. I've gone past exhaustion and am heading back where I began what seems like days ago now when we left home—excited anticipation. Nylon rubs on nylon whenever we move. It means we're almost there.

The plane lands in winds and snow, and we hang on tight, because outside, there's only white and gray and snow and haze and it looks like we're headed for the climactic scene in the disaster movie. But the pilot sets the plane down fast and neat. The cold—you feel it as soon as they open the cabin door. We climb down the stairwell to the tarmac and then we are hit with the full force of it. But we are here; there's the low black building of the airport with SVALBARD on it in silver letters.

Once he's on the icy ground, my father turns to me and shakes a victorious fist in the air, and I shake one back at him. It's too cold to talk. The air is so piercing, my lungs burn with the freezing temperatures. I am in another world. It looks like a different planet, even here at the airport. On the ground, beneath those blizzard clouds, the late-afternoon light is blue. Everything is blue—eerie blue snow and blue mountains and blue sky. It's beautiful and otherworldly. My father stops to try to take a picture of me for everyone back home. This takes some doing, taking off a glove with his teeth, fumbling with the camera; me hopping from foot to foot, the snap, and then camera away and glove on again. I wish I could send it to Henry. I wouldn't even care how stupid I look. Henry is with me on this trip, of course he is. I've got our compass in my pocket.

Dad and I retrieve our bags and take the local bus into Longyearbyen. On the ride, he elbows me and points. He stares up at something out his window, up on a mountainside.

"Is that it?" I ask.

"I think so."

Yes. You can see it there, right above where the airport sits. The tall rectangle, the glowing blue-yellow window in the blue sleet sky.

The vault.

We are in Longyearbyen. *We are in Longyearbyen.* I keep telling myself that because it's so hard to believe. It looks just like the pictures of it, rows of pointed-roofed buildings painted red and green and blue, bright colors to cheer up the often dreary winters. The late-afternoon lights of the buildings glow yellow against the blue.

The shops on the main street are quirky and cuter than you'd think. On the right, you can see the northernmost co-op shop in the world, with its stuffed polar bear next to the entrance, and on the left there is a red food truck, advertising the northernmost kebab in the world. We leave the bus in front of Mary-Ann's Polarrigg Hotel, where we are staying. After little sleep and all those hours on the plane, it is dream upon dream upon dream. The Polarrigg is a group of wooden barracks where the early miners and trappers of the town used to sleep for the night, now turned to tourist lodging. Inside the main building, it's warm, with a fire going in a coal stove, plank floors, rugs, red leather chairs, and wood beams over-head, mixed with odd trapper paraphernalia—stuffed Arctic foxes and a polar bear head. Singsong accents are everywhere around us. There's a sign in Norwegian with a picture of a shoe.

Dad elbows me and beams. He's thrilled. We read about this—it's local custom to take your shoes off when you enter a building. "It's true!" He's a little loud. It's embarrassing. But then again, this isn't exactly the kind of place where you can fake being a local. If you even watched us trying to get our boots off, you'd know we weren't from around here.

Our room is in one of the buildings that look like the sort you used to make with Lincoln Logs, with wood slats and a low, pointed roof. Our room is small, almost like a train car. It's painted stark white, and there's a pine desk and—

"Stop laughing," I say.

Bunk beds. Yes, bunk beds, and he thinks this is hilarious. "I haven't slept in a bunk bed since I stayed overnight at Tommy Valero's house in the fifth grade," he says. "I get the top."

"Aww," I say in pretend disappointment.

We decide we're completely exhausted, but starving. So we go outside to the now searing cold, Indigo-blue moonlit night (boots on, gear on) and into Koa Restaurant (boots off, gear off), which looks like a saloon in an old movie, except for the bust of an old guy behind the bar, which someone has dressed in a red satin scarf and a pair of glasses.

"Grandfather Leopold," I say, and point. It's how I imagine him, anyway.

"Lenin," my father says.

Our waiter's name is Lars. There is seal steak and whale stir-fry on the menu. I kid you not. Dad orders the Reindeer Wrap "with apologies to Santa," a joke poor Lars has probably heard a hundred times. I order the Arctic Char. A sealskin hangs on the ceiling above us. As we wait for our meal, Lars brings us a snack of polar bear meat and Norwegian berry pickles.

"Dorothy, you're not in Kansas anymore," my father says.

After dinner, we walk in the frigid, bone-crushing cold from one end of town to the other. It is still out, the still and silence of below-freezing temperatures and a mining village readying for sleep. It's a village old enough to be set away from time itself. We go into the single open shop, where the sign reads ALL THE POLAR BEARS IN THIS SHOP ARE ALREADY DEAD. PLEASE LEAVE YOUR WEAPON WITH THE STAFF. I buy a few postcards, and my father gets us each some wool mittens with reindeer on them.

"To remind us of that great dinner I just had," he says.

We hurry, though. The cold is too intense to want anything except warmth. Back in my lower bunk, I spread out my postcards. There are many I need to send, but only one person most on my mind. I choose a beautiful, eerie, blue-tinged photo of Longyearbyen, the one that most looks like what we saw today, and I write this to Henry: *Thoughts. Love.*

There.

But then I change my mind. I think of us poor, old human beings doing the best we can, struggling with being either too much of who we are or too little. I choose a second postcard. I write Henry's address on the back of this one too. The image is of an up-close polar bear face. I write, *My dinner tonight. Love, Sis.*

I smile. So will Henry. And that night, even with my father sleeping in the bunk above me, even with the bite of frigid cold in the air, I sleep better than I have in a long, long time.

Pix's seeds, from the one perfect berry of my mother's carefully tended plant, are in their Mylar pouch, which is in the GORE-TEX bag, which is zipped into the pocket of my nylon pants, under layers of my long wool shirt and fleece jacket and down expedition-wear coat. In the other pocket, I place the compass. We lace up our boots in the lobby of the Polarrigg Hotel.

"I'm nervous," I say.

"Me too," my father says. His hair is tucked inside his hat, and so it is only his own familiar face I see, outlined in gray wool. The balaclava will go over the top, and the hood of his jacket over that.

Outside, our rides arrive. Students from Polar University, Lars Bruun (another Lars—this is the Land of Larses) and Gunther Fjerstad, will drive us up the mountain. Two snow-mobiles, "skooters," wait out front, looking like landed insects with long, folded black legs. Lars and Gunther are both blond and blue-eyed. Gunther is a bit older with a beard; he hands us helmets and another "skooter suit" to wear over what we already have on. They show us how to secure our helmets, their accents rising and falling in a way that sounds perpetually cheery.

What is hard to describe is the light and color of this planet Svalbard, pastel pink and purple everywhere today, this monumental day. And the cold, too, how it drives directly to your bones, no matter how many layers. The visors on our helmets come down, and we sit on the backseat of our scooters, more low-to-the-ground motorcycle than anything, a rounded nose on skis, with a curved windshield. Then Lars looks over his shoulder and gives me the thumbs-up, and we accelerate.

I hold tight to the back of Lars's seat, my boot pressing hard against the running board, shoving an imaginary brake, but then it is clear I am in good hands with Lars, and I put my fear to the side and take in what's real but can't be real. The cold pierces even under all those layers; it slices right to the center of me. My father is off to the side of us in his own black insect capsule, speeding crazily, a neon-orange flag screaming behind him, the flag our point of visibility should a blizzard begin.

But there is no blizzard, no snow even, just wind so loud it's a driving blast around my head, and I've never been so cold in my life, nor in such a dreamlike place. We drive along a flat plane of ice, and there are more of us, more of these black insect scooters with their single glowing headlights, so many black speeding insects that it looks like we are being chased in a spy movie, surrounded by bad guys.

The speeding scooters thin out in the great space. There are only a few now, and off to our side, we see a long line of sled dogs. It is actually many sleds, four dogs per sled, maybe eight sleds in all. The dogs are shaking off the cold, ready to be on the move again, with their packed crews behind them. We see reindeer, four of them together. We see a red sailing ship frozen in ice, an eerie double-masted ship with many lines rising in the pink-purple sky, and I would be sure I was imagining it, but there is the name of the frozen boat, the *Noorderlicht*, painted on its side. It is the *Dawn Treader* caught by the White Witch and frozen until spring.

We are climbing high up the switchbacks now, and there is only mountain and more mountain and we are going slower, moving forward in bursts and starts, and it feels precarious. I don't stop to imagine the film version of this moment because this is the film version. I don't stop to imagine home and the people in it, because this is so far from home, I am another person entirely.

We are at the top of this road now, and it seems we've reached our destination, because Lars and Gunther slide us to a stop, and there is a man in a red and black polar suit waiting for us. We unfold ourselves, numb from cold, and lift up our visors. Then we take off our helmets and we meet Anders Thorstad from NordGen, the organization that operates and maintains the vault. Anders tells us that they've spent the

morning chiseling ice off the door after it had warmed up yes-
terday, causing water to drip and then freeze after temperatures dropped in the evening.

From where we are, I can't see the vault; we leave Lars and
Gunther behind, and we walk, making conversation impossible. My father and Anders Thorstad are in front of me. I am
concentrating on the slick ground, and when they stop, I do
too, and then there it is. My God, it's so much larger than I
thought, so much more oddly magnificent, this rising triangle
of iron and concrete set in this pink-purple land of ice; from
the front, a narrow rectangle with prisms and mirrors reflects
a beam of blue-purple.

It's our destination, and I feel choked up, and I just stop for
a moment to feel this: an arrival, an ending.

Anders is able to open the door quickly after all that previous chipping, and we hurry inside, into the first section of the
vault. The door clangs shut behind us. This area isn't sealed
off completely from the outside, and you can tell. The floor is
sloped concrete, and there is a fluorescent light above us, and
there is frost on the walls, and Anders, a to-the-point man
with a thin red face and burst of yellow bangs under his hat,
tells us to watch our step because the floor itself is icy.

I look around at the concrete walls, while trying to watch
my boots on the slippery floor. Soon there is another door,
another mighty, echoey clang as it closes behind us, and now
we are in a tunnel made of ridged metal, and the floor is no

longer treacherous. Anders and my father are talking, but their words turn to muddled reverberations, and I can't make them out. And now here is another chamber, and we are in a hallway with rough rock walls and silver pipes overhead. We are inside a mountain. It is a rock cave, Batman's lair.

The hallway ends at a large concrete wall with a door to a rock-walled room, with a table and a guest book and some shelves with seeds. Anders gestures to the guest book, indicating I should sign, and as I write my name, I see what they have done for me. I see how large this is. Because there is a president's name, and the British prime minister's. And now there is mine, and now there is my father's.

I think we're finished. I'm sure this is as far as we'll go. But then Anders Thorstad says, "Ready?" His voice echoes.

"Ready."

"Every packet that arrives is scanned through x-ray. We'll assume yours is free of terrorist devices." I am glad my father only chuckles. He is keeping his mouth mostly shut. This is a good thing. He is the sort of person who needs the reminder not to joke about guns or explosives in the airport security line.

We follow Anders into another rock hallway, deeper inside the mountain, where there are frost-covered walls again, and then Anders stands before a single ice-covered door. Of course, this is *the* door. You can feel it. It is the way he stops with import and reverence, but it is also the way that

chapter twenty-five

Anastatica hierochuntica: rose of Jericho. This is the most famous of the plants known as Resurrection Plants. After the rainy season, this plant dries up and curls into a tight ball. It looks dead. Within the ball, though, the fruits remain attached and closed, protecting the seeds within. With a little rain, even months or years and years later, the ball uncurls and the plant wakes up. The fruits open, the seeds drop to the ground near the parent, and the plant appears to come back to life. The seeds can begin to grow within hours.

Back home in San Bernardino, February turns to March and March to April. I stand at our kitchen counter, looking out the window where Pix used to sit. The lemon tree is flowering again. Still.

"I feel like this life is over," I say to my father. He is leaning in the doorway. It hurts me to say it. It feels like something is ripping when I do. But all through these months, we keep bumping into the truth of it.

"I know. Me too."

"We should just—"

We've had this conversation a few times already. "You know that's not an option. You're graduating in a few months. We can't just pick up and leave."

"We can't?"

"No."

"Why?"

He sets his own face in a frame using his index fingers and thumbs. "Thomas Was Finally Tired of Fucked-Up Choices."

Jenny sends me a package with an application for the University of Washington. Sasha calls to tell me that the Parrish Island Library expects a photo-filled talk about our trip to the vault and that Larry has already started the sign-up sheet. And Henry sends me another postcard. It's got a picture of some old composer on it, a guy with wavy white hair and a hooked nose. On the back, Henry has written, *Hope you'll be Bach soon. Your LLS* (*Long-Lost Sibling)*. I send him a postcard with a different old composer on it. *Making a Liszt of all the reasons to return. Love, Sis. PS, Mom likes me best.*

April turns to May. May turns to June. Finally, I take the seed from Pix that I saved and I plant it. I follow the germination directions in Chapter One: "Prevention Is a Good Start" in *How to Keep Almost Any Plant Alive* by Dr. Lester Frank. I use the best soil. I give only the right amount of water after I tap it into the dirt. It means something to me to have this new plant begin its life here, where we will end our old one. The pot, Grandfather Leopold's pot, my mother's pot, mine, sits on our old windowsill where there is plenty of light. A new green shoot rises from the ground.

My father packs my mother's clothes into boxes. We pack our dishes and the contents of our cupboards and closets. I toss out my old project, Fort San Bernardino, where three feet equals one and a quarter inches. Dad and I don't have long conversations about any of this. We just put on old *I Dream of Jeannie* shows and wrap cups in newspaper, both heading in the same direction.

And then June arrives. It is the day of graduation. There are purple gowns everywhere, and hugs, and tears, and bad band music and sappy speeches. I say good-bye to Caitlin and C.J., and even Dillon, but most especially Meg. We hug and cry a little and I thank her for being there for me, always. The minute I am back home, I toss my mortarboard on the kitchen table, which will head to storage with the rest of our furniture. There are roots, and then there are all the new directions they grow.

I look at my father. He barely has his dress-up jacket off. This is the moment we've been waiting for. "Want to do it? Want to just fucking do it?" I say.

He smiles.

I imagine it: the drive across two states, the trip onto the ferry, the arrival on Parrish Island, our new home. Jenny will open the door wearing her paint-stained tennis shoes, holding out her old arms to greet us, as Vito jumps and jumps and barks so happily, you'd think we were made of bacon.

The first chance I get, I will set *How to Keep Almost Any Plant Alive* by Dr. Lester Frank in the basket of Jenny's bike and return it to the Parrish Island Library. I will have the compass in my pocket, the compass that has made the trip to Svalbard. I will hold it out to Henry in my palm, because I love Henry Lark. Oh, I do, and I always will.

True love, the good, beautiful, one-and-only kind, the kind between loving friends and family and partners who are mostly just trying hard to do their best, it manages to overlook some pieces of its story. It overlooks what he can't give you or how she failed you or what mistakes he made when he was struggling. It stays steady at its center. It evolves, through drought and storm. It grows. It *survives*. There *are* things that last. Seeds in vaults in frozen mountains at the edge of the earth, but love, too. Real love does. It lasts beyond death, and it lasts beyond disappointment and misguided expectations and mutual shame and mistakes.

I will hold out the compass and Henry will take it, and then we will begin a friendship where he is there for me and I am there for him through joy and pain, and fullness and emptiness, and highs and lows, tide in, tide out, for years and years to come.

But we are not at that part of the story yet. We are at the part where my father has the map in his teeth, even though the trip we are taking now is too large and long to ever measure the distance of. We are at the part where my father is now wearing his lucky Grateful Dead shirt as he puts the last of the boxes into the pickup and where I take my mother's shoe from the empty closet and tie the new pixiebell plant into it snugly.

In a few moments, I'm in the passenger side of Dad's truck, and just like that, we're heading out of the gravel driveway, away from our house and everything around it, our scratchy tan lawn, the neighbor's dog, Bob, who always stands at the corner and watches traffic.

"Adios, Bob," I say out the open window.

"Bob, may this good life bring you everything you deserve," my father says.

There are many ways to be lost. . . .

Meet Billy and Mads, in Deb Caletti's
Essential Maps for the Lost.

Here's the biggest truth right up front: The way Mads and Billy Youngwolf Floyd met was horrible, hideous. Anyone will agree. You will, too. You'll think it's awful. And then maybe beautiful, which is precisely the point. When the story gets sad and terrible, when there are too many mistakes to count, hang on for the beautiful parts. Wait for them. Have some faith they'll arrive. This is also precisely the point: the hanging on. The waiting, the faith.

Now.

This story starts the same way every morning does, during the spring when Mads meets Billy Youngwolf Floyd. She gets into her swimsuit. She rolls her towel into her bag, sneaks downstairs, careful not to wake up Aunt Claire or Uncle Thomas or Harrison. She edges out the front door, making sure Jinx, their cat, doesn't slip past her on the way out. She starts up Thomas's old truck and heads to the reedy bank of the park by Lake Union.

It is early. So early, only weary insomniacs and people catching airplanes are up. Mads was on the swim team at Apple Valley High; for four years they had practice in the steamy old community pool from five thirty to six thirty a.m., and so this is the routine her body still follows. She loved that hour—it had the peace only habits and rituals can give. There was the snap of goggles and the clean burn of chlorine in the air and toes bent over the edge before the plunge. But now the steamy old community pool is gone from her life for good, and so are all the disciplines that keep you from thinking too much. Swim team, orchestra, AP calculus study group—every one of them is finished since she's graduated, a quarter early, too. Her poor cello seems like the high school boyfriend she was supposed to outgrow but who she still kind of likes.

Look. Here she is, already at the end of the dock, trying to get her courage up. The waters of the lake are much colder than the community pool. The spring Seattle morning is all hues of gray. The sky needs to figure out whether it's in the mood to turn blue or not, like some people Mads knows who will remain nameless. It smells good by the water, that deep kind of murky, and she inhales a few delicious hits of *beneath*.

A row of ducks paddle by. "Good morning, ladies," she says to them. They appear to have serious business. She waits for them to pass because she's a nice person. Then she kneels on the dock, tests the water with her hand. Brr. The waves are choppy and industrious, but not too crazy to swim in. In spite of the gray and the chop, the water is inviting. But it's keeping secrets, for sure.

She dives in.

The cold takes her breath away. Now comes the payoff, though. Not the dramatic rush of water past her head and body, not the shock of immersion, but the thing she swims for, the thing that arrives after the drama and the shock—the calm. The blissful burble of being underwater, being *away*, the moment of otherworldly quiet just before her head rises for air, before the slash of her own strong arms and scissoring legs. Under there, the needs of other people do not press, and the sorrow that's been her most constant companion floats away. Back home, in the water of the community pool, even on the days Coach King's whistle shrieked and her friends shouted above the surface, her own liquid element was like a sweet dream. She could forget those college applications she'd filled out but never sent, and the face of her mother, Catherine Murray, on all those real estate signs, and, too, the way her mother always wept after Mads's father would call from Amsterdam, or else, became furious enough to hide from, like the time she took the kitchen scissors to the family photographs. Swimming is sort of like running away, and Madison Murray has wanted to run away since the first real chance she had, when she was three and got lost on purpose in the Wenatchee Safeway.

And here, in a lake in Seattle, five hours from home, where there is only a kayaker off in the distance and a seaplane taking off against the sky, she is exquisitely elsewhere. She is a fish; she is a mermaid. She lives in a coral castle and wears a seaweed crown. The ticking clock bringing that awful deadline is gone,

gone, carried off on a ripple. Somewhere up there is Harrison's spying, and her own deep sadness, and her profound desire to kidnap baby Ivy. Down here is some centered soul-version of the real her, the one she's not in real life.

Of course, Madison Murray won't feel the same way about any of it, even the water—especially the water—after that day. In some ways, it's a shame. It's a shame, the way you always have to lose stuff to get other stuff.

She swims out until she is parallel with the tall, abandoned smokestacks of Gas Works Park at the other end of the lake. She treads water for a while, floats around on her back and watches the sky, nothing she could ever do when Coach King paced poolside in his blue tracksuit. She has plenty of time. She's in no real hurry. She has come to Seattle to take Otto Hermann's real estate licensing course at the community college, which doesn't start until nine. It goes until noon, and then comes babysitting for the Bellaroses until seven. Back home, she's missing all the end-of-high-school rituals that feel far from her life: the prom and the parties and the ordering of caps and gowns, the group of parents taking photos in her friend Sarah's backyard. But she's not missing other things. She's not missing hauling those open house signs out of the back of her mother's Subaru, setting them up on street corners. Or, even worse: *I can't believe you're going to leave me home alone all weekend. What am I going to do by myself? Fine. Just go.* Or *You better not have some fabulous time in Seattle and not come back like your father.* The flip side of too much guilt is murderous rage, who knew?

She's having fun out here. Houseboats line the perimeter of this lake, and she sees them upside down. They're cheerful and shingled and they rock and sway. There's also a huge upside-down bridge, with tiny upside-down cars. She flips to her stomach. A woman drinks from a cup while standing at the end of a dock as a dog swims laps in front of her. For a second, Madison wishes she were that woman, or maybe even that dog. He looks like he's having the time of his life.

Okay, that's it. She's had enough. She decides to head back. Pancakes sound good. Swimming makes her so hungry.

Now. Think of this—what if she'd stayed out there just a few minutes more? Or what if she'd gone in just a bit sooner? It can make you believe in the Big Guy Upstairs, even if he seems coldhearted a good lot of the time.

She kicks hard, strokes with a power that would've made Coach King cross his arms and smile. She slows when she nears the bank. It's still deep there, but she begins to feel the slip of reeds by her legs. Mads is used to that feeling, the surprising slide of a slick cordy something past her calves, the quick what-was-that of plant or fish. It isn't anything that makes her uneasy. But after this day, even a long time later, *years*, whenever she thinks of this moment, she will shiver.

She ducks her head again. Her eyes are closed. It's best that way near the shore. Sometimes it's safer not to see.

She feels—well, it isn't a thud exactly, more of a bump, a wrong bump. She knows that—the wrongness—straight off. Her head has knocked against something, something that gives and then knocks again, and what comes to mind, oddly enough, is a life raft. A tight, inflated life raft. Is she at the dock already? Is this a float, or a buoy? She has an irrational image—that dog from the dock. She and he are colliding. This is his thick, giving side.

But she knows it isn't a float or a buoy. Certainly, it isn't that dog. Nothing she says to herself is true, of course. You always know when you're lying to yourself. Already she can feel the hair twined around her fingers.

Madison rises to the surface, opens her eyes, and sees her. She is so white she almost glows, and her face is vacant and still as the moon in a night sky, and when Mads shouts and flails, she drags the woman's head under. It feels awful to do that, and so sorry, the details are terrible, but it's the truth of this story. Mads's fingers are caught in the woman's hair, and her face dunks and dunks again until Mads untangles them.

A different person, not Madison but Madison, is making sense of this. She is crying out and flailing, but her brave and functioning self (*who is* she? Mads wonders) is putting the pieces together: the lake, the bridge, despair. Mads's terrified self tries to get away from this horrible, sickening body, while her strong self, hidden before now, has seen a woman. An actual human being. This is the self that understands things about the water—the way it can swallow you, keep you concealed, maybe forever.

This rational one, she is the person who reaches under the woman's arms and grasps her shoulders, while the other

Madison grimaces and pretends not to feel the cold flesh. Mads is now the lifeguard she was from age fourteen on, at the Apple Valley Estates neighborhood pool. She strokes and tows, strokes and tows that body, the way she never had to in the sparkling cement crater filled with shrieking toddlers in water wings and teenagers showing off.

The woman needs help, the terrified Madison thinks, while the other Madison knows this: She is beyond help. Mads hears a strong, clear voice. She realizes it's coming from inside her: *Bring this woman to shore. Bring her and bring yourself to shore.*

She will. She has to, because the woman, the body, will disappear if they don't make this horrifying swim together.

Madison kicks past the waves with her strong legs. The woman's own legs float and bob against her. Soon the two of them are near the bank, where Mads can stand. There are rocks underfoot; slimy, slippery rocks, and Mads is out of breath. The reeds are waist high, and the body skirts along their surface like a sled on ice. The woman has gotten so, so much heavier now. Mads sees that her body is bruised, splotchy, banged-up purple. She faces the woman's eyes, which she's been avoiding. They stare up toward the clouds as if they can look past them. Whatever has brought the woman to this morning's fate—it disgusts Mads. The woman herself does. Mads is angry with her, for causing this. But Mads's heart is sick and heavy with grief, too.

She hauls the top half of the body onto the bank, as far as she can.

And then she screams.

She screams and screams, the way you do in bad dreams, the way she always feared she might have to someday for a different reason, a desperate-mother reason.

Things happen fast after that. Suddenly, there is a man wearing a tie, and a young woman in jogging shorts, and then the spinning lights of a police car, and then an ambulance. A heavy blanket gets tossed onto her shoulders, and in spite of the sun now showing through the clouds, she needs that blanket, because she is freezing. Her own body is doing tricks—shaking out of control, her knee a strange entity that's clacking up and down like drumsticks on a cymbal.

"Maddie! Mads!" It's Aunt Claire, running to where Mads sits on the ground. Somewhere in there Mads called Claire, but she barely remembers that. It feels like she has been there for a week and for a second. There's the *thwack thwack thwack* of a helicopter overhead, announcing tragedy.

Two men carry a stretcher. The body is on it, covered in a deep-green plastic. There's the *slam-slam* of doors.

That's it, Madison thinks. *This nightmare, my relationship with that woman, is over.*

Of course, she is wrong. She is so wrong. Because traumatic events like this, acts like *that*, spread far and go deep. The water soaks delicate layers; the waves crash and crash again. So many people will break and change and stay changed.

Awful, yes?

Yes.

But don't misunderstand. While, true, this is a story about the horrible things people do (the way hurt people hurt people, if you want to get self-helpy about it), it is more importantly about what happens next.

This is what happens next as she rises from that grass with Claire's arm around her: Madison sees that dog. He is back up on the dock now. He shakes himself off on the woman with the coffee cup, who is watching all the commotion. He sits right down, as if hoping for a treat.

See? Life goes forward. More, much more, will happen after this. Things involving maps and books and true love and tragedy, tragedy like you wouldn't believe. But fine things, too. The best ones.

Even if it might not seem so at the time, even if there is something as horrible as a body and police and cold, life has some beautiful surprises up its sleeve, and don't you forget it.

Sometimes, Billy Youngwolf Floyd plays real life like it's the video game Night Worlds. For example, right then as he's leaving to go to work, Gran gives him a Gaze Attack, which can curse, charm, or even kill. His options? He can avert his eyes from the creature's face, watch her shadow, or track her in a reflective surface. The glass of the coffee table works. It's better than meeting Gran's breaking-and-entering eyes, which are searching around, rifling through his head, hunting for the sign that he'll be the next one to jump off a bridge.

"You okay?" Gran asks.

"Sure."

In the reflection, he sees the old woman staring at him, but he also sees his own face. It surprises him, because it looks young. It *is* young—nineteen. After everything that's happened, though, he feels thirty at least, and some days, fifty-sixty.

"I don't have to send you to a bunch of doctors, too, now do I?" Gran says.

Billy shakes his head. That's one kind of magic he's lost belief in over the years. Doctors or no doctors, medicine or no medicine, his mom was sad and then okay, sad, okay, always coming back to sad. *Sad* sounds almost soft, but it wasn't soft. It was aggressive and mean. It was a gas leak that felt suffocating, when usually they were fine, great, making their way together. He feels bad thinking that: *suffocating.* He shoves the word away, imagines them watching the Hobbit movies together instead. He was still little, so she'd hide his eyes at the gory parts, but he'd peek through her fingers.

"Just as well, because look at all the good those shrinks did." Gran gestures toward the urn on the fireplace.

"Jesus, Gran!"

"What? Do you know how much money I paid those people? She had to have the last word. She always did."

"Gran, come on." She's lucky she's old, or she'd be on her ass! He used to think his mom was too sensitive about things Gran said, and he didn't get why Mom just couldn't move past the stuff from her childhood, stuff she told him about, like how Gran would yank her head backward by her ponytail when she didn't listen, or practically rip her arm from her socket when she asked for something in a store, or how when she was six, she waited for Gran for hours after school, crying and scared, because Gran wanted to teach her a lesson about being late. But shit, his mom was right. Gran won't even give her a break now that she's dead.

"'Come on'? Come on, what?"

"*You're* the crazy one. You should go." He makes it sound like a joke, because Gran can't stand being criticized. No one fucks with her. Depression doesn't even fuck with her. *Stop sitting around feeling sorry for yourself*, was what she used to say, like Mom's sadness was some kind of moral failure. Can you imagine being depressed and then being judged for being depressed? Who's crazier, anyway: people who struggle honestly, or the people who act like they never do?

"I worry about you, is all, Buzz."

His nickname plus Gran's small, tired eyes give him a weird stabbing in his heart. You know, a love stab. He instantly regrets his mean thoughts. She's about the only one he has left in the world. Gaze Attacks—they doubly affect ethereal creatures, even if that's a shitty, unfair rule. If Billy is anything lately, he's an ethereal creature. They can exist on the material plane, but everything there is gray and dim and ghostly. Only a magic missile can break through their walls. The most important thing about them, though, is that they do not fall.

"Don't worry. I'm okay."

Of course he's not okay. He's coping better, but the storm system still sits off the coast, waiting for the right temperature or unstable airflow. He watched that in a show about cyclones. It was more interesting than you'd think.

He gives Gran a hug good-bye. He can't stand to be an asshole. When he grabs his keys, Gran's old dog, Ginger, gets excited and hops around. "I gotta go. Sorry, Ging, you've got to stay and babysit the old woman."

"Never mind, smart aleck. See you later."

"See you."

He's taking off a little early, because there's someone he's got to pick up before work. He leaves Gran's houseboat and walks up the ramp that connects the dock to the parking lot, and he gets in his mother's black truck. The SUV has seen better days, but it's still fast. It has *get-up-and-go*, as his mom used to say. She used to love that truck. *A car is your own little capsule of freedom*, she said. He wanted a car of his own, but he didn't want it this way. He'd been saving up, and now he just has a bunch of money. It isn't have-to money anymore. It could be dream-money. If he tells anybody his dream, they'll think he's nuts. They probably think he's nuts anyway, after what his mother did a couple of months ago, but dreams seem extra important when life as you know it can be gone in a second.

Her radio station comes on. That station hurts his stomach. He isn't going to change it, though. He longs for more of anything she loved. He already knows all the lines of the Eagles songs, and the Doobie Brothers and Simon and Garfunkel ones, all the la's and oh's of crazy old nights and bridges and black water. He pictures her singing to the radio with the windows rolled down. He used to pretend it was bad singing, and plug his ears and make a face, but it secretly made him happy, seeing her just being herself like that. She'd say, *I know, it's too beautiful to stand*, and sing louder.

It's a good memory. Still, he gets so mad, driving that car.

Once, he pounded the steering wheel and screamed that one word, the only word, over and over. *Why.* But he feels close to her here. The her that was her real self. He slept in the car one night, but it worried Gran when she woke up and he wasn't in his bed.

Billy pulls out of the lot. He drives past the Fremont troll and goes up the hill, heads to his and his mom's old neighborhood. There's a FOR RENT sign on the house, he sees. Jesus! He barely just got their stuff out of it! His stomach clenches up again. He feels sick. It's a cross between a throw-up feeling and a crushed-soul feeling. God, he hates that! *Focus*, he tells himself. He has a job to do. That asshole Mr. Woods always lets Lulu out right around then. It's going to be easy, as long as Lulu doesn't flinch and hide at his outstretched hand. That's what happens to them after a while.

He parks in his old driveway. If Mr. Woods spies the car, he'll think Billy is just bawling his eyes out inside or something. He spots Lulu cowering in the corner of the garden. No problem.

Billy gets out. And that's when he sees her. Sees her again. That girl, parked on his street in that truck. The truck needs paint, bad. It has big bald spots of primer. Come on, get it fixed up! A truck like that deserves some respect. He knows shit about cars, but he knows that much.

The girl—her hair is shiny. He noticed this before. She has very white teeth; he can see them even from that distance. She's the kind of girl who smells good. She's all scrunched down, pretending she's doing something innocent, like checking her phone. What *is* she doing there? He's seen her before, the day he moved his and his mom's junk out of the house.

Oh, yeah.

Oh, yeah, of course. You know why she's probably there? That guy, a few houses down. It's got to be. Billy forgot all about him. Some senior; goes to one of the private schools. Blanchet? One of those Catholic ones. A real douchebag. Girls like that always have a thing for boys like him. He probably hurt her, just as she always suspected he might, and now, after proving her right about herself, she can't let him go. This is how it plays. He knows that particular story too well.

J.T., he suddenly recalls. J.T. Jones. What is it about assholes with initials instead of names?

The girl is going to be a problem, though. Usually, the idea is, make it natural, do this in the broad daylight, but not when you have a witness. He's going to have to act natural, is all. He'll use an Ability Modifier from Night Worlds, probably Charisma. He'll make her think this is the most regular thing ever. He'll be calm, smooth, decisive.

His heart is beating a hundred miles an hour, but ignore that. He could be in a movie, he thinks, 'cause he's precise as a laser, cool as a blade. Lulu is one of those cute little white dogs, so she's an easy one. He scoops her up in one clean arc. He sprints like a sharp breeze. He doesn't even look at the girl. What girl? Here's hoping she moves on to a better guy and forgets that douchebag once and for all.

Lulu is excellent in the car. She turns a circle on the passenger seat and falls asleep, as if she can finally rest. Here's hoping she moves on to a better guy and forgets that douchebag once and for all.

Billy pulls into work. Heartland Rescue is noisy as hell and stinks a lot less than you'd think. He loves this fucking place with all his heart. He carries Lulu under his arm and then sets her on the counter.

"Billy," Jane Grace says, and runs her hand through her short hair. "Not again."

"I don't know what you're talking about," Billy says.

"Where did you get this dog?"

"Found it. Lost. Walking around lost." Lulu's tags are in the pocket of his jeans.

"Lost."

"Uh-huh."

"Just walking around lost."

"That's right."

"Okay." She sighs. "Fine. What should we call her, do you think?"

Heartland Rescue always names their animals, and never ever puts them to sleep.

"She looks like a Lulu to me," Billy Youngwolf Floyd says, and then Lulu winks at him, the way dogs do sometimes. He swears it wasn't an accident. He knows a real wink when he sees one.

DEBCALETTI

is an award-winning author and National Book Award finalist. Her many books for young adults include *Stay*; *The Nature of Jade*; and *Honey, Baby, Sweetheart*, winner of the Washington State Book Award and the PNBA Best Book Award, and a finalist for the PEN USA Award. Her books for adults include *He's Gone* and her latest release, *The Secrets She Keeps*. She lives with her family in Seattle.

more from bestselling author
DEB CALETTI

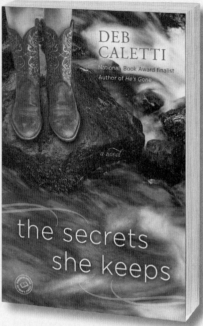

"This is a mesmerizing novel."

—bestselling author Sarah Addison Allen, praise for *He's Gone*

"A thoughtful exploration of love and marriage and the power of family and friendship to help along the way."

—*Booklist*, praise for *The Secrets She Keeps*

Jordan's life is pretty typical . . . until it isn't. Her new boyfriend is turning out to be a major jerk, and her father is seeing a married woman. Both relationships will implode, but only one will go down in a shower of violence.

Ruby's always been The Quiet Girl. Dating gorgeous, rich, thrill-seeking Travis Becker changes all of that. But Ruby is in over her head and will become a stranger to everyone . . . including herself.

Cassie is in love, but she can't let her stepfather know. He's a beloved public figure, but a private nightmare whose manic phases and paranoia are getting worse. Cassie begins to fear for the safety of her boyfriend . . . and herself.

Jade struggles with panic disorder. Her boyfriend is a calming influence . . . until she learns that he's hiding a terrible secret. A secret that will force Jade to decide between what is right and what *feels* right.

When a stranger leaves Indigo a 2.5-million-dollar tip, her life as she knew it is transformed. Indigo's sure the money won't change her . . . until the day she looks around and realizes everything that matters—including her boyfriend—is slipping away, and no amount of money can buy it back.

As if it's not bad enough that Quinn is surrounded by women who have had their hearts broken, she's just been dumped. Tired of being taken for granted, Quinn joins forces with her sisters and sets out to get revenge on the worst heartbreaker of all.

Scarlet spends most of her time worrying about other people. So when her older sister comes home unexpectedly married and pregnant, Scarlet has a new person to worry about. But all of her good intentions are shattered when the unthinkable happens: she falls for her sister's husband.

Clara's relationship with Christian is intense from the start, and like nothing she's ever experienced. But what starts as devotion quickly becomes obsession, and it's almost too late before Clara realizes how far gone Christian is—and what he's willing to do to make her stay.

Cricket's entire family has come together for her mom's wedding. It's supposed to be a celebration, but for Cricket, the timing couldn't be worse: her longtime boyfriend has walked away, maybe for good. Now Cricket must face her fears and decide once and for all what she wants and how she's going to get it.